Tom Clancy's

OP-CENTER

STING OF THE
WASP

TOM CLANCY'S OP-CENTER NOVELS

ALSO BY JEFF ROVIN

Tom Clancy's
OP-CENTER

STING OF THE
WASP

CREATED BY
Tom Clancy and Steve Pieczenik

WRITTEN BY
Jeff Rovin

St. Martin's Griffin ☙ New York

TOM CLANCY'S OP-CENTER: STING OF THE WASP. Copyright © 2019 by Jack Ryan Limited Partnership and S&R Literary, Inc. All rights reserved. Printed in the United States of America. For information, address St. Martin's Press, 175 Fifth Avenue, New York, N.Y. 10010.

www.thomasdunnebooks.com
www.stmartins.com

Designed by Omar Chapa

The Library of Congress Cataloging-in-Publication Data is available upon request.

ISBN 978-1-250-18302-6 (trade paperback)
ISBN 978-1-250-15692-1 (ebook)

Our books may be purchased in bulk for promotional, educational, or business use. Please contact your local bookseller or the Macmillan Corporate and Premium Sales Department at 1-800-221-7945, extension 5442, or by email at MacmillanSpecialMarkets@macmillan.com.

First Edition: May 2019

10 9 8 7 6 5 4 3 2 1

Tom Clancy's

OP-CENTER

STING OF THE
WASP

PROLOGUE

New York, New York
July 22, 9:15 a.m.

It did not feel like 2019.

Eighty-one-year-old Ernie Keene, retired corporal, United States Navy, stood on the misty flight deck of the USS *Intrepid* and looked out at New Jersey. Only it wasn't the Garden State his squinting gray eyes saw in the filtered summer sun. He didn't see the other tourists who had come early to beat the summer crowds.

It felt, to Keene, that the year was once again 1962, and the mid-afternoon sunlight had been sharper, the sky bluer, the sea endless off the coast of Puerto Rico. The smells? They were every American seaman's constant companion, salt and fuel, a mix still present all these decades later, and welcome in Keene's nostrils. Back then, after sixteen months, the sounds of the aircraft carrier had become white noise to Keene, but on that day, May 24, the heavy beat of the rotor of the HS-3 was different from before. That day, the Sikorsky helicopter was riding through a page in history.

Peering into yesterday, Keene's wrinkled, sun-bronzed cheeks framed a proud smile, his eyes moist as he looked, breathed, heard, *was* in the past. His daughter, son-in-law, and granddaughter were elsewhere on the decommissioned vessel, now a stately museum. They had flown him here for his birthday and he had wanted this moment alone with his old vessel . . . with the memory of the day Astronaut Scott Carpenter, the fourth American in space, was recovered from the sea following his orbital flight.

Keene had not spotted the three parachutes of the Aurora 7 bringing the capsule down. The space traveler had been off-target, too distant to see. But the seaman would never forget the black, red-nosed chopper soaring in and settling down among them. The beaming voyager hopping out, as if he hadn't just spent hours in a weightless state, the entire crew applauding him—and the nation. *Our* nation cheering their latest hero. And he would never forget the late Scott Carpenter who, after his career in space, made it his life's mission to explore the sea.

Fifty-seven years later, the vessel was once again under Keene's feet, the shadows were vivid in his mind's eye, and the lump was still thick in his throat.

My God, Keene thought, his chin quaking a little, his breath tremulous as he relived that singular moment. Not just a moment in his life but a moment in the life of America. *What we had, then*, he said to himself. A new frontier. A visionary young president. A prosperous nation, at peace.

He was privileged to have been a part of it, present for the recovery of an American who was just back from *outer space*. Keene was no longer in the Navy three years later when the *Intrepid* recovered Gus Grissom and John Young of Gemini 3, but he saw it on television and knew what every man onboard was experiencing. Keene still felt humbled, as he had then, just to be a cog in that grand effort, standing there with Petty Officer 2nd Class Dick Tallman as Commander Carpenter was deposited on the flight deck, *this* flight deck, right where Keene was standing now. Time, age, life, everything seemed to evaporate. He was youthful again, his wife alive, his daughter just a baby, the future long and deep and rich.

Where had it gone? Keene wondered. Not just a lifetime but that powerful, uplifting sense of unity he had felt with every man onboard this very ship.

Slowly, reluctantly, the Groton, Connecticut, resident returned to the present. The landscape of the intervening years returned. Here and now the choppers he heard were regular traffic along the Hudson River. The voices were not fellow seamen but tourists. The flight deck—well, it was not rolling and pitching and slippery with the sea but anchored emphatically in a river that seemed better-suited to pleasure boats and water taxis than to an 872-foot-long, 27,100-ton juggernaut.

His sagging shirt pocket chirped. Keene fished out his cell phone, held it at arm's length so he could read the message. It was a text from his daughter.

YOU DOING OK?

He thumbed the microphone icon. He spoke in a quiet voice, mindful that there were others around him enjoying their own thoughts and emotions. He said softly:

FINE. BE THERE IN A MINUTE. LOVE POP.

Susan, her husband Jason, and their youngest daughter Lisa were waiting for him in the space shuttle pavilion. He had wanted to rekindle his personal connection with history before enriching it.

Keene poked *send* then, proud of his sudden inspiration, used the phone to take a picture of his feet on the deck. That was something he would want to look at again when he was back in his home, on his terrace overlooking the Long Island Sound. This vessel had taught him discipline, which, added to his inborn love of the sea, served him well in his career as a boatyard worker operating hydraulic trailers, lifts, learning maintenance, and finally managing a marina.

Well, he thought with an inner sigh, *every man onboard that day made his own journey. I thank God for the many joys in mine and—*

Ernie Keene did not get to finish his thought. It was cut short by a very loud and very powerful explosion not far behind him.

The operation had been worked out with military precision by a military officer.

The plan, conceived by Captain Ahmed Salehi and Dr. Hafiz Akif of the Professor Abdus Salam Centre for Physics in Islamabad, Pakistan, had been personally approved by Salehi's sponsor, the powerful prosecutor Ali Younesi of the Special Court in Tehran. The plan had been operational for five days, since they had traveled from Washington, D.C., to New York. Iran shared diplomatic space with the embassy of their fellow nation; under Islamabad's "protecting power," Iran enjoyed the same privileges as any foreign representative in America—despite the fact that formal relations between Washington and Tehran did not exist. A reciprocal arrangement existed between the United States and Iran via the U.S. Interests Section of the Swiss Embassy in Tehran.

With the patience of a veteran seaman, Salehi had waited for exactly the right atmospheric conditions: mist rolling in from the harbor, lingering over the Hudson River, enough to dampen the air but not the plans of tourists. The meteorological records of the Atmospheric Science Department at Cornell University in Ithaca, New York, were most thorough and helpful when it came to pinpointing humidity in specific regions of Manhattan and its environs. Dr. Akif had personally approved the conditions from the foot of 46th Street and 12th Avenue, right on the river.

Salehi was a fearless, sixty-one-year-old former officer with the Navy of the Islamic Revolutionary Guard of Iran. Since "retiring" from active service, he had sailed the Middle Eastern, Asian, and South American seas delivering and acquiring black market weapons for Tehran. Less than a month before, his efforts to obtain nuclear missiles for the state had been thwarted by American commandos off the coast of Russia. Their lawless action had also cost the officer his ship, the cargo vessel *Nardis*. It had cost him his reputation as a man who could be entrusted to carry out the most difficult and dangerous missions. It had steeled him with a hunger for swift, merciless revenge.

Salehi had arrived at the *Intrepid* Sea, Air & Space Museum with the chemist—the scientist wearing a Yankees baseball cap, pulled low—as well as with Akif's daughter and granddaughter, Iram and Amna. The others remained on the street. The young mother had taken the nineteen-month-old from her stroller and was feeding her a bottle in a corner away from the water, against a gunmetal wall overlooking Pier 86 not far from the entrance. Pushing the collapsible pram—which was far from empty, despite being childless—Salehi had walked on like the eternally patient grandfather he was pretending to be.

He did not have to play the part of a man who was simply waiting. That was what he did at sea—waited to leave a port, arrive at a port, cross a sea, go wide around a storm. His life was mostly waiting.

And thinking. Right now he was doing both. He had been to the *Intrepid* a week before, wearing a Sikh turban, looking for the security cameras, picking a spot where he would be seen and where the event would be recorded from as many angles as possible. He had watched to see where tourists went first. Most arrived and took videos of the aircraft lined up side by side by side. Naturally, the security cameras were arrayed to cover those assets as well as the actions of those milling around them. It was a classic attempt at deterrent: a terrorist did not go there if he did not wish to be photographed.

But what if he did? Salehi thought, making sure he did not look at any of the devices. Not yet.

Salehi had padded his belly slightly with the turban, which he would need when he was finished here. There was a stuffed animal in the seat where Amna had been seated. It was a plush saber-toothed tiger he had bought at the American Museum of Natural History. He had taken pains that he and his family should show up on several video feeds so that facial recognition software would not show a known foreign advocate but someone who had a longer beard and a Jew's head covering, someone who would get a pass on future automated profiling systems. To the NYPD, to the FBI, to Homeland Security and anyone else who was watching he was simply a Pakistani diplomat visiting several tourist spots over a period of days. A plastic beverage glass from *Wicked* had not only passed scrutiny, it barely got a first look from security personnel. It was a term he applied loosely since the man and woman he had encountered were openly bored and clearly expected no trouble. Had they opened the big container, they would have been the first to die when the specially fitted interior loaded with murky yellow chlorine trifluoride was exposed to the damp river air.

Salehi was glad it hadn't happened that way. He was prepared to die both as an Iranian officer and as a soldier in the eternal Revolution. He was not a jihadist, just a proud Iranian who honored the proud and ancient history of his nation. But he wanted to survive. He wanted the Americans to know who had done this, and why, and to compound their shame and misery with the inability to prevent future attacks. Dr. Akif, who would be following him onboard within moments, would see to their hasty exit using his diplomatic credentials.

An elderly man was standing just in front of Salehi. He was looking out across the river. The American stood like a seaman: his slightly bowed legs seemed to grow from the deck and his wisps of gray hair blew like they had danced before with the sea breeze. But mostly it was his breathing. He was as a man reborn, inhaling as if he had been removed from life support. Salehi knew because he had felt that way as soon as he set foot on this deck. It did not matter that the ship was American; it was a beast of the sea, a creature without politics, only nautical experiences.

It pained the Iranian to do what he was about to do. And yet,

if he were to ask this man, if he were to commune with the metal
hull below, this is the fate they would desire. As the proverb went,
Choose not for others what you do not choose for yourself.

The fire emerged from the deck so abruptly, so forcefully, it was
as if a rent had opened in the very roof of hell. The souvenir cup
had attracted barely a glance but the self-igniting wall of flame
turned every head on deck.

For many of those observers, it was the last thing they saw.

The fire caused the moisture in the air to transform into a
deadly steam that melted the eyes and destroyed the throats and
nasal passages of everyone it touched. At the same time, the chlorine trifluoride poured over the deck and under shoes and consumed everything and everyone it touched, beginning with Ernie
Keene. One moment he was warmly embraced by the past, the
next he was burning to death in the present. He fell to his knees,
charred black; his flesh falling away in dead lumps. Other tourists
shrieked in the few moments they had left, some, afire, attempted
to hurl themselves into the river. But the burning deck overtook
them, outraced them, the air sizzling incongruously as the chemical was carried toward the river.

Salehi paused to look directly at a security camera before turning and calling for the Pakistanis posing as his wife and daughter.

"Here!" Dr. Akif shouted, motioning him over—as if Salehi
were a victim and not the perpetrator.

The chemical engineer already had his diplomatic identity
card in his hand as he ushered his daughter and granddaughter
through the security checkpoint, just ahead of the mob that had

managed to circle around the massive fire. Standing outside the museum, Dr. Akif actually got one of the guards to help him pull an older Jewish man through to safety. He had left the stroller behind, since it had mostly melted like candle wax in the conflagration; with a handkerchief over his mouth, all he took with him was the pungent smell of death inside his nostrils.

The four made their way down the stairs. As always on their homeland, Americans were reacting to an event, concerned with the victims rather than the perpetrator. They could not afford to seal the area while tourists were trying to escape.

The world of the *Intrepid* was comprised entirely of chaos and sobbing, of shouts and distant sirens, and the choking pall that had settled over the entire flight deck. Just breathing the vapors produced by the chemical was adding to the numbers of dead and their raw, dying screams. Security personnel who had raced in turned around just as quickly, realizing that they had no idea what they were dealing with and that, at the very least, gas masks were required.

Salehi looked around as they hastened from the pier, observed as recreational boats moved from the stricken titan, as air traffic swung wide, as lights and police took up positions on the opposite side of the river to keep onlookers from the deadly cloud. At least getting away from the museum was easy, as no vehicular traffic was moving other than ambulances along with fire and law enforcement vehicles.

The Iranian and the Pakistani scientist did not exchange looks. It was one thing to work in isolation, as he did, as Dr. Akif did at the Pakistan ordnance factories in Wah Cantt, Punjab. It was

another to take a weapon of mass destruction into the field, helping to deploy it, and being forced to witness the results. However,
the good life Akif and his family enjoyed—and Iram's own
future as a well-paid official at the Ministry of Industries &
Production—demanded they cooperate. And they were not
without their own hostility toward the United States. Father and
daughter recalled the decades of abuse Pakistanis had suffered
under American petrochemical companies before they were
bought out by employees and local corporations. The educated
elite in Pakistan resented the United States for violating its regional supremacy in the ongoing war against the Taliban and
other terror groups. While few professional Pakistanis would have
coveted this assignment, the tainted political climate had cor-
rupted the moral environment as well. They would all be out of
the country in a matter of hours. And for the Akifs, life would
continue as before.

In that turbulent region, the price of stability was often high.

CHAPTER ONE

Op-Center Headquarters, Fort Belvoir North,
Springfield, Virginia
July 22, 9:26 a.m.

Every device owned by Chase Williams came active at once—personal cell, office cell, tablet, and all three landlines. He had been reviewing intelligence reports from Asia when the symphony of tones and beeps told him that something terrible had gone down. The only question the director of Op-Center—formally, the National Crisis Management Center—had was who he wanted to hear it from.

Williams chose the secure landline on his desk. The caller ID was Matt Berry, deputy chief of staff to President Wyatt Midkiff. The team of intelligence advisors who worked or visited the White House regularly was known around town as the "party planners"; among those, Berry was a bit of an outlier, a mystery. He did not have the respect of the heavy hitters but the president trusted him. Berry was a close friend of Op-Center's Brian Dawson and he had become the team's unofficial inside man at the White House. If Williams had to get bad news, the former Navy four-star combatant commander wanted it immediately contextualized. But he simultaneously flipped his desktop to CNN to see what he had missed. The crawl and live images gave him a quick, sickening synopsis. Nor was Berry's information as comprehensive as Williams had hoped.

"Matt?" Williams said. "What—"

"Conference call with the president, in the Tank, now," Berry said.

Berry hung up the phone just as Deputy Director Anne Sullivan swung through the door. The sixty-year-old Op-Center director rose, answered her concerned look with a shrug, and told her what Berry had said.

"You know anything?" Williams asked as he grabbed his sports jacket from the hook behind the door.

"I think we're in shit," she replied, nodding toward his desk.

He looked back at the tablet. There was a security camera photograph from the computer of Kathleen Hays, Op-Center's visual analysis specialist. Beneath it was a name in black type.

Williams swore. Anne was correct, as always. He jabbed the name with a finger, waited a moment. The only data that came up was a tab for the file they had closed on July 3.

"Find out why we did not know this," Williams said vaguely as he hurried past Sullivan toward the electronic and scientific brain center of Op-Center.

Williams's voice seldom reflected what he was feeling. Decades of service at Pacific Command and Central Command had taught him, as Kipling had written, that he had to keep his head while all around him were losing theirs. But his quiet order to Anne concealed rage that burned at an uncommon level. Captain

Ahmed Salehi had been their target. His defeat had been their doing. Even though he had disappeared into the shrouded corridors of Iran's Ministry of Intelligence, they should have seen him emerge.

Not just *emerge*, Williams thought. *Emerge quickly and with a plan of counterattack*. His team had underestimated the man and civilians had died, another black day marked on the American calendar.

It was a short walk, and Williams did not consciously avoid the looks of the employees he passed. But his thoughts were scattered, partly on what to do next and partly on what the president would do next. He could not even allow himself to dwell on the horror of what he had glimpsed a minute ago. That would come at night, when he tried to sleep.

The Geek Tank was Op-Center's technological heart, the locus for all raw, incoming data. Williams looked out across the ring of fourteen young tech wizards, all bent toward their multiple screens. Most would be continuing to look for threats. Others would already be investigating his directive to Anne.

"Find out why we did not know this . . ."

His own words played over and over like a dirge. But he could not allow himself to mourn. Most of the twenty- and thirtysomething Op-Center team had never experienced a national disaster. They would have to be motivated, bootstrapped, made more vigilant, not allowed to wallow. Senior management would have to revisit every active individual, cell, warlord, anti-American movement both domestic and global, foreign radical—search for more than just threat analysis algorithms but use intuition and experience to identify potential threats.

Why did we not know about Salehi? Williams asked himself

with anger that was now tinged with shame. The team had failed but, worse, the leader had failed the team. And people died as the world watched.

Williams's index finger was scanned and the Tank door popped open. He pushed the sound-absorbing panel shut behind him, sat at the small conference table, and spoke his name plus a code word—"Nedla," his father's name backwards. That activated the wall-mounted audiovisual system that only a handful of voices could turn on. Not only was that photonic band line secure, the room itself was sheathed in an electronic web that prevented any other signals from getting out. Anne had once described the Tank as a grand jury room where the fate of civilization was on trial. Williams felt that now, though when he saw the face of the president and the others he knew it was not the future of the world being decided. Also present on the split-screen view were National Security Advisor Trevor Harward, who was in the Oval Office with President Midkiff; January Dow, who headed the INR, the State Department Bureau of Intelligence and Research; and FBI Deputy Director Allen Kim. The vice president was in China, planning for a post–Kim Jung-un unification of North and South Korea, and the president saw no reason to terminate that critical mission. The man who had told Williams about the meeting, Matt Berry, was not present. That told the director all he needed to know. Without an ally, and with Dow having actively and openly campaigned against the autonomy Op-Center had enjoyed, this wasn't a meeting. It was an execution.

The African-American woman was speaking as Williams plugged-in.

". . . movements were not known until he wanted them to be known," she was saying. "As far as we can determine, someone matching Salehi's general physical description arrived at the embassy on July 7 just before midnight. If he moved in and out he did so in Pakistani state vehicles."

"The man who seems to have been traveling with him today?" Midkiff asked, consulting his own tablet.

"We do not yet know that," she said. "He was wearing a baseball cap and seemed to take care not to appear on camera."

"Any competent New York mugger knows how to avoid our goddam security cameras," Harward complained.

The president finally looked at the screen. "You have anything to contribute, Director Williams?"

It was "Director Williams," not "Chase." That was the first salvo.

"No, Mr. President," Williams replied.

"Nothing after July 3?" January asked Williams pointedly, referring to the file Op-Center had distributed among its fellow intelligence services. "No red flags?"

"No, Ms. Dow."

Confirming nearly three weeks of inactivity. That was the second salvo.

Williams was watching the president carefully. Midkiff's eyes shifted to the clock on the screen. The president's mind was not, at the moment, on forensics. It was not on the past but on the future. That was the third salvo.

"Director Williams, effective fourteen minutes from now, at ten a.m., the charter for Op-Center will be revoked. The personnel has just been informed that they are to remain on-premises until notified, though all security access has already been terminated and research locked in place. The reassignment of said personnel will be turned over to Mr. Harward. In recognition of your service, Mr. Williams, the delictum organizational status will not require your resignation. You will, I trust, have no difficulty vacating by ten?"

"None whatsoever, Mr. President," Williams replied.

The screen went black. The silence in the Tank was overwhelming. The weight of his negligence, of his failure, of how he let his team—his friends—down was greater still. Every shred of vitality seemed to leave him; like Dorian Gray's portrait, he felt as though he had aged countless years in a moment.

Williams could not lift his big frame from the chair. He looked around the Tank, at the pitchers of water, at the glasses— Anne had written her name on hers—at the ghosts of countless meetings, of crises successfully resolved.

All but one, he thought bitterly. *And that is how a career, how a life, is to be defined*—like George S. Patton slapping a frightened soldier, not helping to win the Second World War. Like George Armstrong Custer massacred at Little Big Horn, not courageously leading attacks at Gettysburg, commandeering a horse when his own was shot from under him. Williams briefly chided himself for not accepting this defeat like a man, but an officer was more than a man: he was an ideal. And this exemplar of leadership had collapsed into ash.

And self-pity, he told himself. That had to stop, since he still had to walk from the Tank to his office to the front door within about ten minutes. Failure to do so could well result in his being escorted out by the security officers at the front door. How Williams made his egress would also mark him in the eyes of those who had served under him. It would stick to him and, perhaps, remind those around him to be more vigilant.

He could do that much, make it to his car as though all was right with him. Pressing his palms to the table and pushing off, he strode to the door, drew back his shoulders, and made his way briskly through faces that were averted but eyes that followed. He acknowledged no one, not even Anne who was waiting outside his office.

"What can I do?" she asked as he moved past.

"Whatever Harward needs," he said, then stopped and looked back at her. "Take care of yourself," he said less stringently. He smiled, his eyes moist. "And thank you."

She nodded, tight-lipped, as Williams grabbed his cell phone from the desk and left. He refused to carry photographs and mementoes from his office; they would be sent. There was a difference between retreat and defeat, and maybe that was it. As MacArthur understood when he left the Philippines, how you left mattered.

CHAPTER TWO

Bradley International Airport, Hartford, Connecticut
July 22, 12:03 p.m.

Were it a direct flight, the trip from Bradley International Airport to Benazir Bhutto Airport in Islamabad was nearly 6,800 miles. From there, the trip to Tehran would have been another 1,200 miles. But it was not a nonstop trip, nor would the schedule have worked for Salehi or his three traveling companions.

They had taken two separate Ubers for the two-hour drive, and would be traveling on different flights. The Akif family—still on tour—would be flying to Montreal and then separate, the chemist taking a train to Toronto for "diplomatic" business and then flying to Vancouver, his daughter and granddaughter waiting a day in a hotel before joining him. From there, they would go to Tokyo and then home. Salehi, traveling as Balvan Prabhu, was headed to Puerto Rico en route to Antigua. Because his face and probably his identity were known, it had been decided that he would not go to a major European or Asian airport but, again, to show a Sikh face and identity at a smaller terminal. None would use their diplomatic credentials since American intelligence services would be watching for that: the connection between the attack on the *Intrepid*, Iran, and Pakistan was too direct, too obvious. Instead, they used false passports that indicated they were Indian citizens, headed home from their respective vacations. Each had the souvenirs to prove it, packed in luggage that held clothes, toiletries, reading material, and little more. The only reason they were departing from the same airport was so that each could keep an eye on the other. If something went wrong, representatives of Pakistan would be informed; they were waiting in a nearby motel room to lend assistance. These agents would insist on taking the Akifs or Salehi into custody, in Pakistan, to await proper extradition procedures. It was unlikely that the request would be denied; Washington would be hard-pressed to explain what they had done to Salehi to merit his radical act. The narrative would quickly turn to an unprovoked attack on an Iranian cargo ship in international waters. The incident would also involve the Russians, who would deny that nuclear missiles had ever been involved.

Salehi never had any use for international politics or diplomatic posturing. In this case, however, he was a useful shield.

Because his command of English was limited to a few nautical terms, Salehi did not understand the news reports on the Uber radio, or the comments of the driver. But there was a tablet on the passenger's seat and Salehi indicated that he should like to see the images. There was video that showed the fires still burning and firefighters in hazmat suits combating them. Rows of aircraft had lost their footing and lay lopsided and damaged, some beyond recognition. There were numbers in an accompanying article. The higher number, seventy-seven, must have been the wounded and hospitalized; the smaller, fifty-two, the number of dead. There was a momentary twinge of sadness when Salehi thought about the man he saw, the old seaman, who was the first to die. The captain apologized inside; a sailor should die in water, not flame.

As for the rest? He felt nothing much one way or the other. He had seen people die before, many times. Soldiers, seamen, civilians, children. This was simply the price of a new ship, the need to prove his worth as an Iranian man and naval officer. Above all, Salehi was grateful for this opportunity to redeem himself. That did not happen often in life, less so in Iran.

Which made the triumph all the more sweet.

Before getting in the Uber, the captain had removed his yarmulke and replaced it with the turban he had concealed under his shirt. He was now Sikh. He did not see the Akif family and, better, saw no other Sikhs—which was one reason he had chosen to depart from a less convenient location. He had only rudimentary training in Sikh customs and might be easily exposed. Anyone going to India or Pakistan from this section of the country would most likely leave by way of New York or Boston. Which was the other reason for leaving from Hartford: it was easier for persons on watch lists or with no-fly tags on their names or faces to lose themselves in one of those airports, or Philadelphia, or Washington, than to hide here. An older Sikh man with a perpetual smile would attract no attention—other than a kind of deferential courtesy. He had been told that Americans like to signal how tolerant and embracing they were by acting pleasantly around those who boldly asserted their cultural, religious, national, or sexual uniqueness.

The wait for his flight was uneventful. Salehi watched the

news on overhead monitors, uninterrupted coverage of what he had done. President Midkiff said something from the White House, other officials looked grave and also spoke. They even showed his picture, the one he had virtually posed for prior to leaving the *Intrepid*. Sitting here with a cup of tea and a roll, he seemed to all the world like a man with nothing on his mind other than going home.

Which was entirely true. That, and presenting himself before the magistrates of Branch 1 of the Iranian Military Court to officially request the cleansing of his record and the assignment of a vessel to replace the *Nardis*.

Shortly after one p.m., the four figures from the *Intrepid* were airborne.

Only one had been noticed and, being noticed, would not be permitted to continue as planned.

CHAPTER THREE

Fort Belvoir North, Springfield, Virginia
July 22, 12:05 p.m.

If the morning had not gone as Chase Williams could have imagined, the afternoon was more unlikely still.

The reason Matt Berry had not been on the call from the White House was because the deputy chief of staff had been waiting in his BMW in the Op-Center parking lot. When he saw Williams leave through the opaque glass doors, Berry left the car and walked toward him. The DCS was a head shorter than Williams, but no one would have known that to look at them. If a man's broken spirit could shrink him by a foot or more, that was Williams.

It took a moment for the former director to recognize his colleague, that's how lost he was inside. He stopped a few feet from Berry.

"Hostile friend or friendly hostile?" Williams asked. It was a question that had been debated in training sessions for combatbound soldiers ever since Desert Storm: which would you rather encounter and who would you be more likely to trust.

"Neither, Chase," Berry said. "I'm the guy with your next assignment."

The statement was as impactful as it was unexpected. "What is this, a mercy fu—"

"No," Berry interrupted, mildly insulted. "I'm here by order of the president." He jerked a thumb behind him. "Get in the car. We'll talk."

Williams eased his large frame into the seat, buckled in, and slipped on his sunglasses. His head felt empty, his breath—if it had not been automatic—shallow and disinclined to greater effort.

Berry drove toward the gate.

"Where are we going?" Williams asked flatly.

"Lunch," Berry replied.

"Thanks. Not hungry."

"I am," the DCS replied. "Didn't get to have breakfast this morning."

"Matt, I'm really not in the mood to chat, eat, or anything else. You got something to tell me, shoot."

"When we're secure," Berry said less affably. If Williams wanted business-only, then that's what he'd get.

They drove from the lot and literally around the corner to the massive home of the Defense Logistics Agency, the McNamara Headquarter Complex, nine five-story structures attached to form a semicircle. The edifice was named for the first director of the DLA, Lieutenant General Andrew T. McNamara, U.S. Army. The façade of the lower two floors were white, the upper floors were rust-colored, and they embraced a large reflecting pool and tennis and basketball courts that gave the facility the feeling of a campus. The DLA is a division of the Department of Defense, charged with providing combat support. Because of its vast budget, rich with unspecified costs, the DLA was also rumored to be a repository of numerous black ops and dark ops groups tasked with secret military and technological operations, respectively. Popular thought at Op-Center and elsewhere was that this was where the dirty work of spying on leaders both foreign and domestic was done. What FBI Director J. Edgar Hoover was to the 1950s and 1960s, a blackmailing, information-hoarding power broker, Director Stephanie Hill was said to be today. It was said quietly, of course, since she would know everyone's secrets.

"You weren't kidding me, were you?" Williams said as they swung into the large parking area behind the complex.

"About a new assignment? No," Berry replied. He touched a button on his cell phone when they stopped. "Show the guard this e-badge when we go in."

Williams's personal phone pinged but he didn't remove it from his jacket pocket. E-badges had a life span of ten seconds once activated. And he'd screwed up enough for one day.

The former director was not entirely present as they made their way to the entrance. He was thinking about the people he'd left behind, the team he'd built, the lives that had revolved around the mission, the sacrifices everyone had made, the death. Without the framework of Op-Center, none of it seemed to have any meaning. They had all worked together to create something vital—

And you failed them. It kept coming back to that. *Not from self-pity*, he told himself, *but as an inescapable conclusion.* What made it worse was something that had barely registered before but was looming larger now: that look from Captain Ahmed Salehi. Dark eyes, set mouth, directed right at the security camera. Fierce resolve made flesh, a defiant statement about the price of interference, a grim reminder that no action occurred without a reaction.

Purely by rote, Williams followed Berry through security into an elevator and up to the fifth floor. The older man realized how suddenly uncomfortable he was recognizing no one, being utterly unaware of where everyone was hurrying, what data and files and memos were being read, where he himself was going. The men and women in uniform seemed a little older than everyone else, which made sense given the military goals upper management would be overseeing. However personally or deeply affected these people were by what had happened just a few hours earlier, it did not seem to weigh heavily on them. That would seem to be a requirement for working here. Whatever the military or intelligence response to the attack might be, it was the job of these people to make sure there were sufficient vehicles, ordnance, personnel, and supply lines for every white paper eventuality. There was simply no time to reflect or mourn.

Williams's own destination was another elevator. This one was going down. Not to the lobby but to a section below. There were no numerals in the elevator, just a scanner that responded to Berry's thumb. They emerged in a long, semicircular corridor that seemed to match the curve of the building. There were people moving about here as well, though no one carried a device, or spoke. If anything, nods were exchanged and nothing more. There were also fewer people in uniform. That did not mean there were no officers, only that they were incognito. He had a clear sense—call it his military-intelligence instincts—that logistics were not what was going on down here.

Black ops. Dark ops. As with most rumors, the stories about this facility were apparently true. He was both impressed and a little disappointed that for all his interaction with Berry, the man had never breathed a word of it.

The DCS took Williams to a small room that opened to the print on the new arrival's index finger—just as the Tank had done at Op-Center. He looked at the door before entering. Inside was a desk, a laptop, and a landline. There was a chair for one guest and the walls were bare.

Berry shut the door behind him. The click of the latch came with the slide of an internal bolt.

"It's not what you think down here, what anyone thinks," Berry said.

Williams sat on the edge of the desk, looked around. "I know. The lock just told me that."

Berry remained by the door. "Oh?"

"Electronic data is protected by tech, not a double elevator system and electronic deadbolts," Williams said. "Four physical assets require that. People, a forgery department with all kinds of documents on-hand for emergency operations, and weapons are three of them. The employees are coming and going, so that's not it. Documents can be bought on the open market, so it's probably not that either. Experimental weapons require structural reinforcing, which you don't have here, so they are not on-site either." He tipped his forehead toward the door. "Wood panel, steel and fiberglass interior for security and mold abatement in a subterranean environment . . . just like Op-Center." He pointed at the overhead vent. "Warehousing biological agents and toxins require an air filtration system that isn't standard issue like this one."

"Impressive," Berry said.

Williams shook his head. "Average. I'm just trying to ease my head back into the game."

"So what's the fourth 'thing' that needs security?"

Williams fixed him with a look that was suddenly wise and confident. "Pallets of ash. Stacks of gold," he said. "This is a logistics facility. Ops aren't conducted from here. They are financed from here."

Berry nodded. "That's right, Chase. Screw bitcoin. Outside of the Fed and Fort Knox, there's more physical money in this place than anywhere in the country. Not just for ops but for every bloody thing you can imagine, from buying journalists with chump change to funding revolutions. Most of the people you saw down here? Accountants."

"More invisible than spies because they live their lives right out in the open," Williams said. "Everyone knows who they are, what they do. Just not for whom." He crossed his arms over his chest. "Whose office was this before the *Intrepid*?"

"Mine," Berry replied. "I needed a larger office anyway."

"I should have guessed it," Williams said. "You handle all the president's black bag operations."

"It's challenging work and a great insurance policy," Berry said. "I know where all the skeletons are. Gives me a lot of freedom in the real world."

"I wondered why Harward never laid a glove on you," Williams said, referring to the president's abrasive national security advisor.

"Even my own boss doesn't know exactly what I do here," Berry told him. "Not that Evelyn Graves is the brightest chief of staff who ever walked those corridors."

"She knows where different skeletons are buried," Williams suggested.

Berry smiled pleasantly.

"So the administration has you laundering money," Williams said. "I'm not a financial guy. Why am I here?"

"For exactly that reason," Berry replied. "It's the last place anyone in D.C. would think to look for you."

Williams frowned. "Am I a target, Matt?"

It took Berry a second to get his meaning. "No, no," the DCS said. "Sorry, it's nothing like that. Yeah, intelligence people are miffed because they got a black eye on your account, but they're not *that* pissed, I don't think."

Williams was relieved. Every agency in town would have to explain how they didn't know about Captain Salehi. And then they would have to do additional damage control as word got around that Iran was no longer just financing terror but actively participating in it. The participation of the ayatollahs in Tehran bumped the global jihad from deserts and mountains to a major world power.

Berry looked down, began to pace in the small room. "Still, Chase, I'm not going to sugarcoat this. Your team blew it and everyone knows that. No one will have anything to do with you and placing a lot of them in other agencies is going to be a bear."

"Yet here I am," Williams said, returning to the topic at hand. He did not want to think about the others. Not now. It frightened him to think that for many of them the nightmare would not end this morning. Many were good and blameless intelligence officers who would be snapped up by other agencies. But some of them would not be offered jobs, even though they had nothing to do with the surveillance on Captain Salehi. Those who were close to Williams, like Anne, like other members of upper management, would be tainted. They would have to seek employment in the private sector. And a few—especially those with second mortgages, single-income families, college-age kids, and credit card debt—would be used as bait to draw out foreign agents. Other nations had deep repositories of gold and cash as well. Not just enemies but allies like Israel, Japan, Saudi Arabia. Money would be offered to the unemployed in exchange for any names, information, tactics, or off-the-grid facilities they could identify. Anyone who took the money—and two or three might be tempted—would then be approached and offered the choice of prison or the opportunity to feed false information to their contacts.

It's a stinking business, Williams thought.

"Did you say something?" Berry asked.

"Here I am," Williams repeated.

"Oh. I thought—never mind," Berry went on. "You are here because no one knows you—and there's something you have to do."

"For who?" Williams asked.

Again, Berry was stopped short. He looked at Williams. "For

yourself, Chase. And for the president. This isn't charity from me to you. I rubber-stamped it because I know you're one of the best intelligence directors we've got. The captain goes down with his ship but you weren't the one who hit the iceberg. That"—he threw a hand in the air, a burst of long-simmering frustration coming to the surface—"that was our government's across-the-board, over bloody reliance on tech and its lower-cost, inexperienced young practitioners. We ask too much of them and their goddamn algorithms." Berry stopped pacing and looked at Williams. "Of course, we older guys have our albatrosses, too. We've been at this long enough to make enemies internally. January Dow, for instance."

"I'm well aware," Williams said. "No intelligence fail there."

"So back to my point, if I can continue without interruption," Berry said. "The president knows you, I know you, and we both had the same reaction when January showed us the security camera image from the deck of the *Intrepid*."

Williams guessed it a moment before Berry spoke.

"You're going to let me go after that bastard," Williams said.

"No one has a better reason," Berry said. "And no one," he added, "is going to have a better team."

CHAPTER FOUR

Fort Bragg, North Carolina
July 22, 12:22 p.m.

"Corporal, I want you to hurt me."

Lieutenant Grace Lee of the U.S. Army Special Operations Command, Airborne, stood five foot two and seemed slighter than that in her loose-fitting sweat clothes. The twenty-six-year-old wore her black hair in a very short military style, tufted on top and buzzed on the sides; her eyes were dark brown but their intensity made them seem almost black.

Lee stood in a circle comprised of seven men and two women, all of them members of the 1st Special Forces Command, Airborne, each of them larger than she was. She had invited the brawniest of the new recruits to stand in the circle with her. He faced her on a patch of dirt that had been raked-free of rocks and spaded to make for softer falls.

The man, Corporal Andy "Behemoth" Evans, stood six-five and weighed more than twice what Lieutenant Lee weighed. Growing up, Behemoth had always wanted to face a trained martial artist. He did not believe, in his gut, that anyone could overcome

his size and muscle—especially someone like the woman standing before him, whatever her rank in the kung fu form she had
announced in her short introduction. Yet she seemed to think she
could take him. No weapons, just her tiny hands. And that gave
him pause. From where he stood, it looked as if he could easily
snap her in two.

"Corporal?" she said when the young man did not move. "I
gave you an order."

"Lieutenant, can we walk through this?" he asked.

There were quiet titters all around and Behemoth realized,
suddenly, the question had created the impression that he was
afraid of being injured.

"You will attack me, now, or—"

Behemoth moved. He came at her like a charging bear, all
arms and torso, and the next thing he knew he had been stopped
hard by those tiny hands pressed to the bottom of his rib cage.
The next thing that happened was her right forearm had traveled
from there straight up his breastbone, introducing her open palm
to his chin and snapping his head back painfully. A heartbeat later,
he felt his right leg buckle as her right heel slammed against the
back side of his knee. That foot then went directly to the ground,
bending her knee behind him. With her hand still pushing up on
his chin, supported by her arm on his sternum, he fell back over
her right knee, hitting the ground with the small of his back and
a loud *oof*.

"Stay down," she instructed Behemoth while she addressed
the others. "My frontal attack incorporated the following tools,"
she said. "First, I employed Tiger Mouth, my outstretched hands

drawing stopping power, energy, *chi* from my core. There was no muscle involved and none was required. Second, Tiger Form Palm Heel Strike—also coming from my core, guided along his own center into one of his most vulnerable spots, the chin. That gave me control of his center and," she added, pointing up, "turned his eyes in a useless direction. Finally, Snake Leg, wrapped around his, allowed me to plant my heel in behind his knee and force the joint to bend, his posture to buckle. Finally, I placed my right leg in a Crescent Step position behind him creating a straight line using my upper leg. Combined with the continued pressure on his chin, pressure that kept his momentum going backward, he had no recourse but to fall over."

She looked down again at Behemoth.

"You want to try again from there?" she asked. "Keep in mind that what you think you know about hand-to-hand combat can work against you."

Without hesitation, the big recruit scrabbled along the ground and threw himself toward the instructor, wrapping his big arms around her legs, just below the knees, and hugging them toward him. Lieutenant Lee permitted herself to fall—straight down, elbow pointed down. She planted the hard bone between his shoulder blades, causing him to cry out . . . and let her go.

"That spot reacts almost like the reflex action of the knee," Lieutenant Lee said, rising. "Pile driver pressure will pop the arms open like a toy action figure. That leaves you free and him vulnerable to having his fingers crushed with your heel, his neck snapped with a knee-drop, or any number of other damaging results. Brute force, however it is applied, will never, *can* never defeat technique."

She offered her hand to Behemoth and helped him up. He was actually wobbly from the strike.

"That is what we will learn here," Lieutenant Lee said as the dusty Behemoth rejoined his comrades—none of whom was tittering now. "*Chi* and form over savagery and muscle. We will do six weeks of hand to hand, followed by two weeks of knife fighting. Over the next two months you will be hurt. You will be cut. You will learn to enjoy the pain as a lesson in where you must improve. You will learn to be alert. You will acquire an acute sensitivity to hostile energy around you. You will not only look out for yourselves and your comrades-in-arms, you will watch out for civilians in your day-to-day life so that monsters like the Iranian terrorist who—"

The young woman was interrupted by a distinctive chime on her smartphone, the deep tone of a Tibetan singing gong. She excused herself and ran to the table outside the circle where she had left her device. The lieutenant picked it up, opened it with facial recognition, and read the single phrase:

BLACK WASP

"Menendez, take over!" she shouted over her shoulder to one of the other women before hurrying off in the direction of the Special Operation Training Facility Building.

CHAPTER FIVE

Camp Pendleton, California
July 22, 9:47 a.m.

Despite the morning's events—indeed, because of them—Captain Pete Talbot of the media office, 15th Marine Expeditionary Unit, felt it was important to keep his appointment with Fox News. The segment about rapid military deployment seemed even more relevant than it had in years, and both Pendleton command and the Department of Defense felt it was important to reassure viewers.

The enthusiastic career officer was walking the crew through a field to where they would watch a display by the unit's top marksmen.

"The Fifteenth provides a sea-based Marine Air Ground Task Force that is able to conduct both crisis response and designated special operations, whatever the theater requirements of geographic combatant commanders," he said in a single-breath, perfectly parsed statement of principles. "In support of that broad military mission, it is essential that fields of operation can be cleaned from a safe distance by our sharpshooter personnel."

The interviewer, Amara Holiday, rolled her eyes a little at that description—"sharpshooter personnel." It was the kind of redundant official-speak that made these military assignments so grating.

When did "sharpshooters" no longer become enough to describe people who could hit a distant target? she wondered. *Why "personnel"?*

She wouldn't be a boor and ask. It was just the way of things, of people wanting to sound more knowledgeable by piling on needless words. Her fellow reporters did it on-air—"afternoon hours," "rain event," "health condition," "multiple people." All added words that added, in fact, nothing. She wondered what the marksman they were out here to video would say if he were told to put two or three bullets in the same place each time he fired. Insurance or overkill?

While Captain Talbot droned on—Amara would listen to him later, when she edited the footage—she glanced at her tablet, at the biography of the man who was already standing in the shooting range. Lance Corporal Jaz Rivette was a Los Angeles native of Cajun descent, twenty-two, who discovered his proficiency with handguns at age ten when he stopped a bodega robbery with the owner's .38; two shots fired, two assailants down with matching shots through the hip. The LAPD enrolled Jaz in a gun safety program where he excelled in the junior marksmanship program. Since joining the Marines at age twenty, the young man had won a Distinguished Marksman Badge, a Distinguished Pistol Shot Badge, numerous other citations and medals, and had a stated goal of breaking the 2.2-mile pickoff record established by a member of Canada's Joint Task Force 2 in 2017 against an ISIS fighter.

"Is he a man or a machine?" Amara wondered aloud, interrupting the captain's narrative.

"Excuse me?" Talbot said.

"Lance Corporal Rivette," she said.

"He is a man, and a remarkable one," Talbot said to the reporter. "Considering the poverty in which he was raised by a single mother, the fact that he found his calling and has been provided with the means to a productive and satisfying career in the Marines is nothing short of—"

"Wait, where is he going?" Amara asked suddenly.

Talbot glanced behind him. "Damned if I know," he said.

The captain texted Rivette's commanding officer to ask where their star was headed. The answer came back quickly and concisely.

"Sorry," Captain Talbot said, shutting the screen of his smartphone. "I'm told it's a personal matter. I believe the squad will be sending over—if you'll scroll down the list, it should be Maria Primera?"

As he spoke, a woman came running toward the shooting range. Talbot continued his discourse on the 15th's preparedness as if there had not been an interruption. Rivette, however, knew the meaning of the two-word message, one that would not be found in any of the code books:

BLACK WASP

CHAPTER SIX

The Judge Advocate General's Legal Center and School,
Charlottesville, Virginia
July 22, 12:50 p.m.

Major Hamilton Breen liked his life. He liked the woman he was dating, Inez Levey, an American history professor with a particular passion for Andrew Jackson. And he liked where he lived and worked, at the University of Virginia campus. The stately campus, with its whispers of the Old South, reminded him of the equally stately old buildings in Philadelphia where he had grown up. As a child, living in a brownstone on Spruce Street, around the corner from Independence Hall, he had first learned about Benjamin Franklin, Thomas Jefferson, and John Adams. When he read that there was an early draft of the Declaration of Independence in the National Archives—a handwritten draft by Jefferson with marginal redactions in Adams's and Franklin's hand—he implored his parents to take him to see it when it was displayed at the National Archives in Washington. It was there, then, that he intuited how to get into the thought processes of other people. He was not just looking over the shoulders of these great men, he *had* learned how they thought. He saw their life and times, their values and ideals, through their eyes. That empathy proved invaluable to him in his later career.

Most importantly, his readings took him to George Washington, whose life and career became an obsession. Upon his shoulders sat the matter of American independence. In his hands lay the decision: what form of office will lead the newly forged nation. He could have been emperor. He chose president. It was a remarkable moment of humility and perception, sacrifice and wisdom.

Not then, not now, did Breen involve himself in the debates over some of the Founding Fathers being slaveholders. They were imperfect people, as was everyone Breen had ever known and respected and loved. But that didn't change the wisdom they possessed, and courage—and vision. They created a nation that, for all its flaws, had been the guiding light of the free world for centuries.

Breen took America very, very seriously. He took its defense very seriously. And he took its laws most seriously, for without them everything else would be subjective, ungovernable chaos. That was why he had become an attorney and a criminologist, it was why he had joined the Judge Advocate General's Corps, which had been founded by George Washington himself, and it was the reason he taught students at the JAG Legal Center. All the branches of law the young minds studied here were important, from military criminal law to international law. Curiosity and a broad-based knowledge was important because trials—and thus lives and careers—often hinged upon attorneys *knowing* things, being able to extemporize about everything from aircraft mechanics to human visual acuity, from the Quran to bitcoin, from global geography to lunar phases. A good attorney had to collect and store data. But above all Breen's desire was to instill in them the same ideals that had guided him.

The only aspect of his work that Breen did not enjoy was the start of the summer, when the pace and intensity of two semesters came to a sudden stop and the next three months were used primarily to work with interns or to spackle educational holes in military personnel who needed specific classes or skills. All were invariably polite and attentive, but there was rarely the passion he found in a handful of regular judge advocates.

One thing the summer did do, however, was give Breen a chance to play a little with his forensic skills. It was rewarding to have a hobby that was a vocation, and Breen liked to spend time with his friend Chief Bob Fender of the UVA Police Department. The men enjoyed walking around the campus, smelling the variety of foliage, and occasionally engaging with students who—more often than not—had issues with police, the military, and members of both professions. Fender, who was forty-two, older than Breen by five years, had just enough patience to listen without engaging; Breen, however, enjoyed a respectful debate.

At the moment, the men were reflecting on the events in Manhattan, lamenting the inability of law enforcement to do a better job of anticipating attacks like these.

"We've both been on the preventative side of things for years," Fender was saying. "We see the data, the analytics, the trends. What are we missing?"

"Human intelligence," Breen replied without hesitation.

"We've surrendered hunches and instincts to satellite imaging and social media intercepts."

"But those have been increasingly successful," Fender said. "That, plus luck, has about eighty-eight percent of the terrorist world covered. Compared to nine/eleven and before, we catch most of the activity that's out there. Certainly most of the major stuff."

"That's true," Breen agreed. "I just don't accept the fact that the rights and objectives laid out in the Declaration of Independence are not being sustained."

"'Life, liberty, and the pursuit of happiness'?"

"That's the list, sweet and simple," Breen replied.

"Speaking of happiness, are you going to be taking one of your regular sabbaticals?"

"I'm sure I will," Breen told him. "There are legal repositories in Missouri with draft writings by our first chief justice, Roger Taney. I want to read them."

"Any reason in particular?" Fender asked.

"He wrote the Dred Scott decision that said the federal government had no constitutional authority to limit the spread of slavery," Breen said. "I want to understand how he came to that conclusion."

"Stripped of contemporary sensibilities," Fender said. "Tough to do."

"Like it or not, that decision is part of who we were and it brought us to where we are," Breen said. "People who only consider current thought gain information at the expense of wisdom."

"You tell that to your students?"

"Every session," he smiled.

Fender shook his head. "That should be the mission of this place, of all universities, to challenge people with unpopular ideas. Instead, we coddle them. You know why I came out today, Major? Because President Oxendine felt my presence would reassure the faculty and student body that everyone is safe, that the top cop has eyes on the campus." He shook his head. "I can do a better job using the security cameras in my situation room."

"Well, there is a psychological value to seeing a physical presence," Breen said. "Like the old beat cop."

"His job was rousting drunks from street corners," Fender said, his voice lowering. "Not looking for improvised explosive devices in a discarded can of energy drink. Do you want to know what Oxendine asked me after the attack? If we could, in fact, look into acquiring the FIT system."

"The liberal lion said that?"

"The selfsame woman who opened the school year with a speech on the need for that great oxymoron, 'public privacy.'"

Fingerprint identification technology was a program created by a private firm that was currently being field-tested at Fort Benning, Georgia. The fingerprints of every soldier were scanned and special readers were installed throughout the base to identify prints on trash, on doors, on handrails that were not on file. Security cameras automatically searched backward for whoever left them to identify outsiders and provide a superficial threat assessment.

"FIT is a great technology with one major drawback," Fender said.

"It only works in warm weather," Breen replied. "But it still fills gaps in your eighty-eight percent, and I'm sure there are mitten-readers in development. Those would certainly be easier, spectro-graphically, though building the database would be a pain."

Fender sighed. "This is not the world I was trained for, Major. And these kids?" he gestured broadly. "They're all going to be afraid of shadows before they even venture into the real world."

Breen was about to remark about the value of baptism by fire when his smartphone chimed. It was a distinctive sound, the bugling of a cavalry charge.

"That's new," Fender remarked, hearing it.

"Yeah, and I'll have to take it," Breen said. "Excuse me, Chief?"

"I'll keep walking," Fender said pleasantly.

The JAG officer turned and walked away. He did not bother to explain that he wouldn't be coming back. He headed directly toward his residence; the major had been half-expecting something like this for the last three hours. His "sabbatical" would be happening sooner than he expected, and he felt the rush of adrenaline as every part of his training came alive at once. Only when he had reached his quarters and snatched his canvas go-bag from the closet did he bother to check the message for confirmation:

BLACK WASP

CHAPTER SEVEN

Jizan, Saudi Arabia
July 22, 9:00 p.m.

The port city on the Red Sea was as ancient as it was dangerous. An agricultural center serving the kingdom by sea, it was also the only seat of lawful civilization in the region. Directly south of the seaside haven, just a short drive along roads favored by refugees, was the dangerous five-hundred-mile border with Yemen. For nearly a decade, since the ascension of the Houthi jihadists, the failed nation had been a haven not only to that Shia-dominated Zaidis sect, but to Al-Qaeda in the Arabian Peninsula and other terrorist groups.

Though Saudi troops are stationed along the border, the mountain foothills are ungovernable, shepherds cross from nation to nation without regard for sovereignty, and trade in the drug qat is the only source of income for many of the locals. The shrub is a widely used narcotic, a stimulant that is chewed or steeped in hot water. Along with hashish, cannabis resin, and opium—most of which was sold in Saudi Arabia—qat was one of the main sources of income for Yemen's terrorists. Another revenue stream was ransom. Foreign nationals were routinely abducted and held, and those who were returned were often gravely ill due to the poor quality of the food, water, medical attention, and shelter.

A third source of revenue was Iran, a Shia nation that was quietly or openly at war with Sunni nations—which were virtually every other power in the region, from Egypt to Saudi Arabia, from the United Arab Emirates to Jordan, from Qatar to Syria. Only Iraq was as heavily Shia as its eastern neighbor. Yemen was somewhat evenly divided, helping to keep it a roiling, sociopolitical crisis zone widely regarded as the most dangerous region on the planet.

It was a nation where few citizens moved beyond familiar paths, and far fewer with confidence. Among the latter, no one moved with greater range or influence than Mohammad Obeid ibn Sadi—referred to simply as Sadi. Officially, the short, fifty-year-old Houthi was the head of Sadi Shipping, which operated widely in the Red Sea, the Bab-el-Mandeb Strait, and the Gulf of Aden. He had an office in Yemen's largest city, Sana'a—an office he never visited for reasons of personal security. American airstrikes in Yemen had been increasingly bold, and many leaders of Al-Qaeda in the Arabian Peninsula had been killed—men that Sadi knew, like external operations facilitator Miqdad al Sana'ani who was martyred in the al-Bayda governorate . . . Habib al-Sana'ani, deputy arms facilitator, who perished in the Marib governorate . . . Abu Umar al-Sana'ani, a Dawah committee member, who was killed in the al-Bayda governorate. With each attack, the greatest loss was experience. That was why it was necessary to constantly recruit veterans from the outside. It was the part of his work Sadi most enjoyed: reaching into the hearts of Muslim men and using his own passion to stimulate ancient tradition. First remotely, by computer or cell phone, and then by personal interview.

Since Sadi knew that his own experience and talents must not be allowed to perish, he lived in a lavish bunker built beneath Saba University, a school he helped to found in 1994. The facility was active with young men year-round, making a missile or drone attack too costly to be of value.

Sadi remained contentedly in hiding because, from his high-tech facility, he was able to command an operation that focused on his own personal passions: the smuggling of arms to Shia fighters throughout the world and the trafficking of young men and women—some for profit, some for a grave point that needed to be made.

As he was doing at this moment.

Sadi was seated on a plain wooden chair in the middle of a small room. There were no windows and just one door, which was locked from the inside. There were hanging electric fixtures in all four corners and a bright overhead in the center of the room; they were ornate lanterns hand-made in the style found in tents of the ancient Saba'ite Bedouins. An ornate rug covered most of the floor and tapestries depicted scenes of Arabic shipping through the ages.

Sadi was dressed in a black robe with a tight white kufi atop his head. He wore his salt-and-pepper beard trimmed just above his collarbone; he fervently believed that anything more than a fistful of hair was *makruh*, not just unlawful but abominable. It was one of many things he found offensive—including women who did not cover their faces in public. When such a woman, especially a rebellious young woman, crossed the path of any of his trusted lieutenants, she was often followed, taken, and brought to him here.

The girl before him was about sixteen, dressed in Western clothes; her simple white hajib did not please him. Neither did the fact that she had been working, selling homegrown lemons in the market. She was on her way home when she was apprehended.

"Do you not agree that it is immodest and deeply disrespectful to dress as you do?" he asked in a voice that was barely above a whisper.

Hands clasped tightly behind her, the spindly young woman was not sobbing, but she was trembling. It was a blend of fear and cold; despite the eighty-seven-degree heat outside, an air conditioner kept the room comfortable. She could hear the hum of the generator somewhere behind her, in another room.

"How shall I answer, sir?" the woman replied helplessly.

"Truthfully," Sadi encouraged.

"If I agree, will it be said that I have sinned? If I do not agree, will it be said that I sin now?"

Sadi's long face showed no emotion. His pale eyes stared from beneath full white eyebrows.

"What is your answer?" the man asked.

"I humbly plead for forgiveness," she replied after brief reflection. "I ask for your help that I may be guided by the Disciplinarian of all mankind, by the noble Quran."

Sadi considered this as he rose. His right hand, which had

been behind him, behind the seat, emerged now with a long switch made of hickory. He slashed the air as he approached.

"You are too clever," Sadi said.

The girl backed away as the switch once again cut through the air. "I . . . I do not mean to be," she said.

"You sin and you lie and you profane my eyes and ears with both," he said, his voice rising now. He held both ends of the stick in his hands as she thumped against the steel door. "You will do penance, on your hands and knees."

Shaking, the girl dropped to the floor, bowed to the man, and sobbed the names of her loved ones in an effort to find courage—

The first lash tore through her white blouse and drove the words from her, transforming them from wept syllables to a single, inarticulate shriek. The second strike collapsed her arms and dropped her face-first onto the rug while the third whip caused hands to shoot out and turn awkwardly back in an effort to protect her ripped flesh. The fourth blow caused her mind to reel into unconsciousness. The fifth caning caused long sprays of blood to coat the door and a wide area of the rug beneath her.

A half hour later, Hanifa al-Fishi was found facedown in the street, unconscious and barely breathing. She was covered with a white sheet that was soaked through with her blood; it had dried and caked, making the shroud impossible to remove without taking a great deal of skin with it.

The next day, more than the usual number of people purchased al-Fishi lemons at the market. They paid a high 14 rial apiece to her father Ali, the money going to pay for the bandages and ointments his daughter would need to survive.

Few spoke to the quiet, solemn man—and those who did asked in the softest possible voice after the girl's health. The answer was a helpless shrug. As one man was bold enough to remark before turning away, "That is the answer to everything, is it not?"

CHAPTER EIGHT

Fort Belvoir North, Virginia
July 22, 2:20 p.m.

Matt Berry took Chase Williams back to the Op-Center parking area to get his car. No one would have left yet; a team of human resources personnel from various intelligence agencies, including Dow's office at State, were coming over to talk to the employees and to give them instructions as to how to submit for new positions. Williams wished he could have been with them; a commander belonged with his people.

He knew he would see some of them again, the people he was closest to like Anne, operations director Brian Dawson, and intelligence director Roger McCord. The others, especially Aaron Bleich and his tech team—it would be awkward and most likely brief. None of them had sufficient experience in government to know that there were no reunions, no movie nights, no baseball games for failed systems.

Just a boot in the ass and you land where you land.

Before leaving to return to the White House, Berry left Williams with three passwords—all of which changed daily and all of which would be texted to his secure personal phone the night before. Berry also left him with the three codes and instructions that were as clear as they were blunt.

The first password Berry furnished was to operate the food and beverage vending machines at either end of the corridor.

"With so much money lying around, everything would come out of petty cash anyway," he had said.

The second was the code to the lavatories. There were four, nongender specific; changing codes prevented any outsider who got this far from recovering any spy devices that might have been placed in the facilities on a different day. Many people continued to work on tablets in the restrooms and key strikes could be read remotely.

The third code was to Williams's own Op-Center files. They were read-only, and access could be revoked at any time.

"Everything you were able to read this morning, you can continue to read," Berry had said. "The code will also connect you to multiagency files pertaining to the *Intrepid*, Captain Salehi, and anything else that is learned about the attack. You will be piggybacking on my own access, Chase. No one in any of these agencies knows that you are still in the business and that you and your new team are all that remain of Op-Center. If anyone should ask—former coworkers or someone you meet at Wegmans or Walmart—you can tell them that you're working at the DLA thanks to my having pulled strings. Which is true."

"I appreciate what you've done, Matt, but that sounds less like guidelines and more like I'm being put in my place," Williams had said.

"I don't think I meant to do that, but maybe you're right," Berry had replied. "Midkiff isn't running for reelection but I still have a career. That's on the line if something goes south here."

"I understand," Williams had said.

"When you input the file code," Berry told him before driving off, "all the data you need to know about your team will come up first. That will include the time and place of your first meeting—which has already been called. Oh," he added, "and speaking about 'called,' I will make every effort to keep you apprised of what other agencies may be doing off the record in pursuit of the target, just so you don't trip each other up. Otherwise, you and the team are on your own."

"You said 'the' team," Williams said. "Not 'my' team? Should I read anything into that?"

"All you should read is the file," Berry said. "But I'll tell you this. You will be working with people who presented the military with a problem: what do you do with individuals who are so good that conformity in a traditional special ops team would set them back?"

"The Department of Defense came up with the answer?"

"You know as well as I do that they do a lot of out-of-the-box thinking there."

"Yes," Williams agreed. "And rarely act on any of it."

"This time they did," Berry told him. "Any other questions, comments?"

Williams shook his head. Berry knew the other man too well to seem surprised or wounded. Part of Williams was grateful for this opportunity, since being locked out of the pursuit would have been torment. But a large part of him also resented how these scraps, the little fish bones that remained of Op-Center, were a minimal, meager, invisible thing . . . the result of a political show of force by January Dow. After Salehi, he wanted the hide of that professional power player. In its own way, using a tragedy for personal gain was nearly as heinous as creating it.

As Williams drove back to his new office, he listened to radio reports from New York and also tried to contextualize the responsibility that had been given to him. It was too early for that. For the first time in his professional life he knew nothing yet about the size, makeup, or nature of the complement he had been given. He did not know if the others had worked together, trained together, or even knew each other. He did not know where they were based or where he would be meeting them.

Even if it feels like a demotion, look at it as a clean slate, he counseled himself. As regrets began to really sink in, he accepted that for taking his eye off Salehi in the first place, he probably didn't deserve even that much.

Williams eased himself into his new office with the coffee and Danish he had not had earlier in the day. Even this felt like penance—a waxy paper cup and vending-machine food wrapped in cellophane. At least no one was looking at him. No one knew who he was or why he was here . . . just another bull at the trough.

Sitting at the desk, Williams almost walked away twice in as many minutes. The feeling he had wasn't about a demotion, he realized; it was about dehumanization. Machines to give him information; transportation up, down, and sideways; and even to serve him food. Once he met his team, they would interact with one another but not with him.

Christ. He was wrong. Years in the military and in government had not prepared him for this. And with the January Dows and Trevor Harwards running things, he would never have the kind of daily personal interaction he had known, for good or bad, for just over forty years.

There were different kinds of purgatory for public servants who failed and dishonored their sacred trust. Being shut out was one. Being shut in was another.

Before opening his files, Williams glanced at his smartphone, saw the messages from his former coworkers. Just the subject heads, all good wishes and thanks. Even from the Geek Tank. He didn't have time to read them now, but they were the right connections at the right time.

He got to work.

CHAPTER NINE

Luis Muñoz Marín International Airport, San Juan,
Puerto Rico
July 22, 6:09 p.m.

Ahmed Salehi was not expecting to be greeted upon his arrival in steamy Puerto Rico. The plan had been for him to wait for the 6:15 p.m. flight to Antigua. The idea was to get away from American territory as soon as possible, stay the night, and leave the next day for home through South Africa, then Egypt, and finally Iran. Salehi had spent part of the flight wondering what it would be like to shed Balvan Prabhu after so many hours. He was beginning to enjoy projecting the serene, silent air he had conceived for his alter ego.

The captain arrived at the gate and was surprised to see the name Prabhu printed on a card. The man holding it looked like he might be a native. He might also be an opportunist, someone who had bribed an official for a look at the manifest in search of a foreigner who was traveling alone and might need assistance.

The man seemed to spark with recognition when he saw Salehi. It could be the disguise—no one else came off the aircraft looking like a Balvan Prabhu—but it could also mean he was a law enforcement agent who had been sent to draw Salehi over for a takedown.

The captain had no weapons and he would not get past the shorter man without being accosted. He did not speak the language but saw no option but to go over to him.

Salehi nodded at the man as if he had been expecting to be met. The man lowered the sign as the captain approached and smiled broadly. The man did not speak to Salehi in Persian or in Urdu, the rudiments of which the captain had learned for his work with Pakistanis. What he spoke, surprising the captain, was Russian. Salehi had learned that, too, for his work in Anadyr.

"Walk with me," the man said.

Salehi complied, though he moved slowly. "Who am I walking with?" he asked.

"Juan Urrutia," he said. "From Havana. The Russians spotted you in the airport in Connecticut. I have been sent to conceal you."

The information was as surprising as it was unwelcome. "Go on."

"Moscow was informed of your operation by Tehran," he said. "It was part of a deal to conceal the involvement of the Ministry of Intelligence in the attempt to acquire nuclear missiles."

"What interest has Moscow with me?" he said, struggling through the Russian.

"A pawn," the man said. "To give to the United States or Tehran, whoever is willing to bargain."

Salehi experienced the kind of rage he had not even felt for the Americans when they attacked the *Nardis*. To be betrayed by his own people was something he had never considered.

"What do you want?" Salehi asked. "Your interest?"

"You have a friend, Captain Yuri Bolshakov of the Main Intelligence Directorate."

Salehi nodded. That was the GRU operative who had arranged the missile sale.

"Bolshakov seeks to strengthen the relationship between his own unit, the Division of Military Technologies, with the Special Clerical Court in Tehran. He cannot be involved directly, but he informed colleagues at the Russian base at Lourdes of your situation."

"What is my situation?"

"The Russians planned to pick you up at V. C. Bird International Airport in Antigua."

The rage grew as Salehi chastised himself for being a trusting fool. Yet in this, there was also the loyalty of Captain Bolshakov. While it was true the Russian had his own self-interest at heart, the GRU officer had earned the respect—a valuable commodity—of the Iranian officer.

But there was also this man, who Salehi did not know and who came with a story he could not verify. The man had information that seemed to have come directly from the GRU. Bolshakov was a man who would certainly have seen the security footage from the *Intrepid* and acted.

"What is your role in this?" Salehi asked.

"I am a liaison at the Lourdes listening facility which the Russians operate," Urrutia replied. "I am simply a messenger."

"Can you verify this?" Salehi asked.

As they walked, the Cuban looked around then showed him a smartphone image of Bolshakov in front of a computer monitor.

The image on the screen was from the burning *Intrepid*. It was a dramatic image . . . but it could have been composed by the Americans. A quick, elaborate scheme—perhaps too complex for the few hours since the attack, but a possibility nonetheless.

"What is your plan?" the cautious Salehi asked as they emerged in the late-afternoon sunlight. There had been no reason to go to the luggage area, since his one bag full of trivia was going through to Antigua.

"I have a private plane to fly us to Havana," Urrutia said. "From there, you will fly to Delhi and then to Yemen."

Salehi stopped. "Why Yemen?"

"Because you have an admirer in Sana'a who will give you sanctuary . . . and a boat."

CHAPTER TEN

Fort Belvoir North, Virginia
July 22, 6:17 p.m.

"And that is that."

Chase Williams had not left the office except to visit the lavatory and get a vended lunch. He could not think of it as "his" office because there was nothing of him in it, physically or emotionally. He felt like a squatter—one who, now, was talking aloud to himself.

He had read everything that was provided on his new team and on the search for Ahmed Salehi and any accomplices. The latter was bare to the point of being no help. They obviously had big state cover: travel plans and false passports, IDs, provided by highly professional forgers. Their new identities would have been known to their sponsors, or else transportation could not have been arranged. At the moment, they appeared to have vanished thoroughly. The only group that had any leads was the NYPD Counterterrorism Bureau. A total of thirty-seven cabs and Ubers had been hailed or summoned to get people away from a multiple-block radius after the attack. Of those, none had an embassy destination and only nine went directly to public transportation: two to Penn Station, two to Grand Central Station, and one each to the local airports, JFK, LaGuardia, and Newark.

"Two went to Bradley in Hartford," wrote Chief of Detectives Stuart Fox. "Driver Mike Alexander of 330 West 45th Street, an actor, age twenty-two, describes a family of possibly Indian origin who seemed extremely agitated. Despite the presence of a young child, they were not traveling with a stroller. The remains of a stroller was discovered on the flight deck of the target. The adult male, age approximately fifty, paid for the ride with cash. He was accompanied by a woman approximately thirty and a child approximately two. They spoke English.

"The second Uber was driven by Eva Scroggins, age forty-one, a wedding photographer residing at 1530 East 14th Street, Brooklyn. She reports 'an Indian gentleman in a turban' who 'smelled of smoke.' He did not speak, though she attempted to engage him about the incident on the *Intrepid*. He, too, paid in cash. When shown the security photograph, Ms. Scroggins said 'I think that could have been the man.'

"The family is suspected to be Dr. Hafiz Akif, daughter Iram Ausaf, and granddaughter Amna Ausaf of Islamabad. Iram Ausaf's husband is Sayed Ausaf, deputy attorney general of Pakistan. He was not present for the trip. The family flew to Montreal, deplaned, passed through customs, and their whereabouts are presently unknown.

"Ms. January Dow of the State Department Bureau of Intelligence and Research has canceled a climbing trip to Everest and assumed co-command-point of the international investigation of the Akif-Ausaf matter along with National Security Advisor Trevor Harward.

"The whereabouts of Ahmed Salehi are not known. A passenger traveling as Balvan Prabhu who generally matches Salehi's description was not captured on security cameras with evidentiary clarity but is known to have traveled to Luis Muñoz Marín International Airport, San Juan, Puerto Rico. He did not collect his single bag and departed the terminal. Local authorities are in possession of the luggage and are returning it to our laboratory. The FBI, through Senior Counselor Carol Smith, has asserted right-of-first-discovery and forensics will await the outcome of that ongoing discussion.

"There is one possibly significant additional person of interest," Fox's report concluded. "Security cameras in Hartford recorded the presence of Nikolai Lagutin, a known operative attached to the Permanent Mission of the Russian Federation to the United Nations. He is identified as a spotter for the assassin Georgi Glazkov, who has operated internationally for many years. Glazkov's whereabouts are not known. Security camera time stamps indicate that Lagutin arrived at the Bradley terminal forty-seven minutes before the arrival of the Uber carrying Balvan Prabhu. Mission Security Director Lev Blinnikov categorically denies having heard of either individual, let alone knowing their whereabouts. His denial is not to be relied upon."

An update from January Dow's chief of staff said the investigation of the INR was ongoing. Williams was not surprised by her absence from that file; she would never put her name to a document that added nothing—the kind of report that Roger

McCord had once called "a career-stalling declaration of ig-
norance."

Having finished the status reports and sat back, Williams was
now left to consider how the team he had been given could ma-
neuver around, through, or under the brick walls in this case. There
was a big, meaty gap between what was known and the creation
of a road map forward. In the past, in the military and at Op-
Center, Williams would have bounced ideas off a team, delegated
specific areas of research, quickly formed a consensus plan of
action.

"Now," he said aloud, "you've got you and . . ."

His voice trailed off. He had a team that was "skilled clay."
That was how Mike Volner had once described promising new
recruits. Volner was the leader of the Joint Special Operations
Command team attached to Op-Center for military field operations. They had served him well on mission after mission and he
felt their absence now most acutely. He wanted to pick up the
phone and get Volner's thoughts. McCord's, too. Input from Brian
Dawson, International Crisis Manager Paul Bankole, former
Op-Center director Paul Hood.

Someone. That was how he had always worked. And Berry
knew that. Williams was coming more and more to believe that
this was not salvation but punishment. He wouldn't put it past the
president, whose ear would be poisoned by Harward. But Berry
was a better man than that.

"No, he's more than 'better,'" Williams murmured. "He knows
how to push and who to push."

So stop navel gazing, Williams thought and went back to the personnel dossier. He had time for one last, quick read before he had to go meet these three elite volunteers who had regularly trained together for a year—just a year—like army reservists and had never been deployed off base.

The three members of the newly formed Black-ops Wartime Accelerated Strike Placement.

CHAPTER ELEVEN

Fort Belvoir North, Virginia
July 22, 6:45 p.m.

The Officer's Club was located at 5500 Schulz Circle, Building 20, and it was closed on Mondays. Except for orderlies who maintained the club services, the three-story, antebellum-style structure was usually unoccupied during off-hours.

That was not the case this evening.

Three people awaited the arrival of Chase Williams, about whom all they were told by DCS Matt Berry is that he was "a retired Navy four-star commander." Since none of them was Navy, Major Hamilton Breen wondered if the commander was a nod to service diversity.

"You gotta think that they wouldn't risk our lives on being militarily correct," said the last team member to arrive, Lance Corporal Jaz Rivette. His voice still had the slightest lilt of his mother's Louisiana heritage. "I mean, we're the best and he should be, too."

"He may well be," Breen said. "My question is whether he was also a volunteer. And whether he'll be going into the field."

"I hope not," Rivette said. "Didn't train with us."

Lieutenant Grace Lee shrugged. "They say the best parachute jump you make is the one you didn't train for, because you don't know the things that can go wrong."

"I wonder," said Breen, "if the statistics bear out that common wisdom."

The three were sitting at a circular oak table in the dining area, their gear plopped on the floor behind them. They had piggybacked in on departing aircraft, were met on the field by a corporal who was accustomed to not knowing anything about who he was escorting to the base, and let in by an orderly who was equally in the dark—save for orders from the White House to do exactly what had been done: put the three anonymous arrivals together to await their supervisor. Except for their final destination, it was a situation identical to the training the three had undergone since the establishing of the experimental multiservice program.

Two of the three had eaten an early dinner of soup and sandwiches. Rivette had had B-rations on the C-130 that brought him here, a meal-sized prepackaged, microwavable hamburger, fries, and small slice of apple pie. Food was not on their minds; the mission was. They agreed it had to have something to do with the attack on the *Intrepid*, but were divided as to whether it would be a quid pro quo counterattack, which was Breen's belief; a hunt-and-destroy mission against whatever group had sent "the son-of-a-bitch," as Rivette put it; or a takedown against the perpetrator who had caused it. That was Grace's wish.

"I want his throat," she said—not with vengeance but as a blunt statement of fact. She formed an open claw with her hand.

"Death grip," Rivette said knowingly. "I hear ya."

Grace nodded. It was a Southern Dragon hold. You practiced as if you were holding a sponge and imagined water being poured into it. You squeezed the water out without closing your grip but by tightening the fingers. Before long the imaginary sponge was hard as rock. The area between the thumb and index finger was the opening that went around the opponent's throat. The tightness of those and the remaining fingers was what immediately and thoroughly choked the windpipe and cut off blood flow. Unconsciousness resulted in just over five seconds.

Rivette turned to Major Breen. "What about you, counselor sir? You want to put him on trial?"

Breen nodded. "I want to know everyone and everything he knows. I want him judged by ordinary Americans instead of a military tribunal—so I can be reminded minute by minute who we are serving. And then," Breen said, "I want to watch him die."

"At least we're on the same page there," Rivette said. "Though I'd wanna interrogate the prick with a cold silencer pressed to his temple. It's kinda like a lie detector there, y'know? You feel his pulse. Until you pull the trigger and don't."

Chase Williams arrived promptly at seven as Rivette had his right hand extended like a gun. The lance corporal lowered it to the table and folded both hands as if a teacher had just walked into class back in Los Angeles. The three soldiers looked from one to the other with alert eyes and what seemed to be sudden understanding. Then Breen and Grace both stood, as Rivette did after he saw them do it. Though it was not required for a retired officer, all three snapped out a sharp salute.

Williams returned it, pleased to know, at least, that though he was not in uniform these three knew he had served. He had read that they knew little else about him, other than his name and former rank. That was not surprising: until a few hours ago, he was not their commander. And for all Williams knew, he would not be again.

But you do not think that far ahead, he told himself. There was a target on the dartboard and his job—his only job—was to hit it.

"Please be seated," Williams said, walking over, turning around a chair in the last open slot, and sitting. He looked around.

"No one's here, sir," Grace said. "Surveillance is off."

Williams saw the camera in a far corner and grinned. The camera was not off, exactly; a chair had been pulled beneath it and the lens had been covered with a slice of white bread crushed to the glass.

"I like it," he said.

Williams looked around the table once, lingering a moment on each of the team members. Their expressions had a rugged independence but their relaxed body language suggested familiarity. That was a good start.

"Our objective," he said directly, "is to find and kill the man who attacked the *Intrepid*, Iranian captain Ahmed Salehi."

Williams waited a moment to let the three process that statement. They reacted according to age: Rivette smiled, Grace seemed satisfied, and Breen's expression did not change.

"Other than that," Williams continued, "there are no specific directives or orders. I have, at my disposal, the combined reports of all of our intelligence services and the authority to put the team anywhere it needs to be. Beyond that, troops—we are entirely on our own."

"We are plausibly deniable," Breen said.

"That is an understatement," Williams replied. "I *will* tell you that we work for the White House. So whether we succeed or fail, disavowal is a given." He thought back to what he had just said. "You're going to have to help me here. I've read your files, your biographies, your citations, your achievements—it's all damned impressive. What I don't know is about your training as a team. Who organized it, what kind of drilling you have done. Was it all in the field or were there psy-ops, interrogation techniques?"

"We trained to stay out of each other's way, sir," Rivette said. He looked at the others. "I mean, I think that's fair to say?"

"Let me back that up," Williams said. "Who did you report to?"

"No one," Breen told him. "We were each solicited for black ops training. We were brought here, taken to the gym or the firing range or some random room, and told to work together."

"On?"

"Nothing in particular," Breen said. "It was pretty clear from the start we were put together because we had so little overlap."

"We thought it was a kind of social experiment," Grace said. "Until we were informed about the involvement of a retired four-star, we weren't sure we were really a team—as such."

"Informed by whom?" Williams asked.

"Whoever sent us the call to arms," Breen replied. "One line, en route, who we were to meet."

The idea returned to Williams that this was either a supreme vote of confidence or a nothing-to-lose Hail Mary. It suddenly didn't matter. He wanted to take these floaters, this experiment, and use it to bludgeon Captain Ahmed Salehi to death. It might not be enough to buy redemption, but he suddenly wanted very much to try. The question was where and how, and there was still no hint of an answer.

Williams was about to ask about the team's accommodations when they trained. He was delayed by a text. It was from his former intelligence director, Roger McCord.

Must talk at once. Pls call.

CHAPTER TWLEVE

Fort Belvoir North, Virginia
July 22, 7:17 p.m.

"Chase, how are you? Everyone's worried."

Williams had stepped outside to place the call. He had ignored the other messages and emails from former coworkers until now; McCord was obsessed with intelligence work and was the least likely to be calling about something personal. Though his personal phone was still secure, he had to remind himself that he was no longer working with any of those who had been so close to him for these past few years.

"I'm okay," Williams replied.

"Are you in or out of the cold?"

"Not free to say," Williams told him. Which was, of course, an answer. If he were out of the intelligence game he would have said so.

"That's fine," McCord said. "I am being interviewed tomorrow and unaffiliated until then. To which point, feel free to use this. You know where I was a few weeks ago. You know who I met with. He is there, Chase."

"Eyes on?" Williams asked.

"Don't know," McCord replied. "Her email, to my personal account, was vague."

Williams mentally replayed everything McCord had said. The former intelligence officer had been to Cuba where he met with a physicist, Dr. Adoncia Bermejo, who helped him uncover the nuclear missiles being turned over to the Iranians and then helped him escape from the island. Salehi was last seen in San Juan. Dr. Bermejo had obviously seen or heard of him and knew what he had done.

That tied into the Russian connection mentioned by the NYPD chief of detectives, he thought. It was in no way clear how that piece fit, but with the strong Russian role in Salehi's last mission, a connection was certainly possible.

"Roger, thank you," Williams said. "Please tell the others I will be in touch when I can."

"They know that," McCord told him. "Everyone is wishing you the best."

Williams thanked his colleague again and hung up. This was not information he could act on—there was no telling how long Salehi might be staying in Cuba—but it was also too important not to pass along.

He called Matt Berry.

"Go ahead," the DCS said.

"I just heard that the solo target is in Cuba."

"Reliable?"

"Highly."

Berry was silent. "You want me to put that in play?"

"Yes. See what it triggers."

"I can't source it to you," Berry said, thinking aloud.

"I don't care."

"They'll want to know. One of your people was just down there."

"That's right."

"His informant?"

Williams hesitated. "*An* informant," he said. "This can't blow back on anyone."

"All right, I'll finesse it," Berry said. "Watch the files and let me know when Black Wasp needs to move."

"I will," Williams told him and clicked off.

He stood outside a moment longer, watching the last of the sun set over the base. The energies were flowing again, along with something he hadn't felt since the earliest days of his thirty-five-year active duty career. As a lieutenant fresh from the Naval Academy, a champion lacrosse player with a love of team and action, he had relished every assignment, embraced each mission—the more dangerous the better because it challenged both of those qualities: camaraderie and physicality. Op-Center had not needed the latter even though Williams had.

There was one thing Williams did not tell Berry. One thing that the men had not discussed—perhaps because Berry was leaving it up to him. Or maybe he had simply made an assumption that wasn't correct.

In either case, Williams understood how stale he had become in a field where stagnation resulted in death. He returned to the officers' club invigorated and with a much clearer sense of what Black Wasp was going to be.

CHAPTER THIRTEEN

The White House, Washington, D.C.
July 22, 7:49 p.m.

When the transfer of power occurred in just under six months, President Midkiff would miss the perks of office. He would miss being hand-carried from place to place, locally and around the globe. Deciding to vacation at his mountain cabin in the Pacific Northwest, he was whisked there. Feeling the need for spiritual uplift, he could decide to see the Israeli prime minister and fly to the Sea of Galilee, or pay a state visit to the Vatican . . . and privately view the ceiling of the Sistine Chapel while he was there. Selfies with God and Adam. He could see any championship sporting event, any film, any sold-out concert. He could have the performers brought to the White House for a private party. Midkiff would also miss having people do things for him, from food shopping to taxes to simply remembering everything that had to be done.

He would miss convenience but he would not miss power. He would not miss having to decide when people must die to make a point or assert a principle. Or, like now, to pay for the sins of others.

The proposal on the table in the Oval Office was a military strike against Iran.

"A deterrent," Chief of Staff Evelyn Graves had just called it. National Security Advisor Trevor Harward had seconded that. Chairman of the Joint Chiefs of Staff General Paul Broad had agreed; he was the one who had initially proposed a military response to the attack on the *Intrepid*. Of course, there was more than tactics behind that. Captain Salehi had directly bloodied the nose of the military.

Only January Dow had argued against the idea.

"We fired first in two interconnected events," she said in her quiet but focused way. "We took in a top-ranking asylum-seeker, Brigadier General Amir Ghasemi. And then we attacked and sank Salehi's ship *Nardis* in open, international waters."

The voices of the other three rose at once, like a chorus in Gilbert and Sullivan.

"They were trafficking in nuclear weapons!" Broad said, seemingly as outraged by January as by the Iranians.

"We should aggressively sanction the Russians economically for their part in this," Graves said. "The Chinese would back us!"

"We ought to quit the U.N. for being the useless money siphons they've been," Harward suggested.

The president raised a hand to silence the others and preempt an aggressive response from January. Like migrating birds in the Coast Mountains, each had gone to their own default agendas in response to the crisis. He needed a moment to think and lowered his hand only after everyone had settled back.

"Trevor, where's the intelligence community on the terrorists?" Midkiff asked.

Harward checked his tablet for any updates. He took longer than the president had expected.

"This is interesting," the national security advisor reported. "Update from Matt Berry—we have word that Salehi went to Cuba."

General Broad was visibly discomfited by the speaking of the terrorist's name. The others were too busy trying to make sense of that.

"Why would Havana be involved?" Graves said.

"They wouldn't do anything without a push from Moscow or their sugar-for-oil buddies in Caracas," Harward said.

"Where did Berry get his information?" Dow asked.

"Confidential source at the SIGINT station in Lourdes," Harward read.

"Op-Center was there a few weeks ago," Dow said, suspicion in her voice. "Is this from someone trying to put a piton in a new job?"

"That would be a stupid risk to take if the intel weren't one hundred percent," Graves pointed out.

"If these people were sharp to begin with, if they weren't all buddy-buddy at Fourth of July cookouts, they would not have taken their eye off Salehi," Dow shot back.

"We don't have to go there," Midkiff said. "Trevor? Anything else?"

"All of the investigating officials have checked in, are looking into the lead," Harward told him.

"So we wait on that," the president said.

He looked across his desk at the others, seated on sofas on either side of a coffee table—one that had been gifted to President Woodrow Wilson shortly before the United States entered the First World War. The devastation of that century-ago conflict, the cost in life, limb, and psyche was suddenly very present in the room.

Midkiff sighed. "I share the same anger and frustration as everyone in this room. Nearly twenty years ago, we felt the same helplessness after the attacks of nine/eleven. But we are not now dealing with bandits, warlords, and nominally trained agents from the mountains of Afghanistan. I agree that this attack cannot go unanswered. The question is not 'why' but how, where, and when." He pointed at Harward's tablet. "The answer may lie somewhere other than in Tehran."

"Do you believe, Mr. President, that the Iranians had no part in this?" General Broad asked.

"They may very well have," Midkiff said. "Pakistan's hands may also be dirty if, as some of you believe, this was worked with the assistance of their embassy here. Russia was behind the nuclear weapons deal—"

"We do not know that the Kremlin was involved or even had knowledge of the action in Anadyr," January pointed out. "It appears to have been worked by a faction of the GRU."

"In which case do we confront Russian intelligence?" Midkiff asked. "We were still putting all of that together before this morning and we cannot afford to create a patchwork alliance of our enemies by overreacting or striking the wrong target." He shook his head. "I want to hit someone, General Broad. I want that very much. But we have to be sure of who."

"The Iranian government is a corruption," the general said.

"We saw that when they stomped, again, on their own protesting people."

"You can't go wrong targeting the ayatollahs," Harward suggested.

"Unless by so doing you give every jihadist from Yemen to the Philippines another radical martyr to rally around," January said with open disgust.

"Then we go after them next," Harward replied. "Bring them out in the open and destroy them."

"That is how wars are won," Broad noted.

"That is how wars are begun," January fired back.

"This one started with the Crusades—" Harward began.

"All right," Midkiff cut him off, firmly enough to also end the debate. "Whoever was involved peripherally or even directly, the roots of this attack are in Tehran. Salehi is Iranian. That's proof enough."

"We do not know who he was working with there, whether it was officially sanctioned," January said.

"That's too fine a distinction for the public to give a damn," Midkiff said. "The nation has to answer for the act of its representative. I want options for a limited response against the Iranian military. Not the nuclear program—we don't want to conflate old issues with new, or shine a light on the covert ops that took down the *Nardis*."

"How do we avoid that?" January asked. "Tehran will bring it up."

"Let them," Harward said. "We'll deny any involvement, work up some story that it was a row between the Russians and their arms dealers and Iran."

"It will look like Tehran is pulling that scenario out of its ass," Evelyn agreed.

"Again, except for fringe bloggers, the public won't care," the president said. "And if the media bothers to investigate, they'll come up against speculation instead of evidence—and a much juicier story about how the nukes got buried in permafrost."

The Oval Office was silent as the president considered the matter. "General, let's look at a state-run chemical facility somewhere outside of Tehran. We don't want many civilian casualties. Even if it wasn't involved, people will believe it was. And it will send a strong message to whoever did provide the chemicals."

"Why not wait until we find out who that actually was, Mr. President?" January asked.

"We will give that some time," Midkiff agreed, rising. "But the public won't give us as much time as we may need. And you know as well as any of us, no one in Iran just makes disinfectant and brass polish. Mr. Harward was not wrong. Some targets get you a free pass."

The president dismissed the others so he could take a late dinner in the residence, though before he left he texted Matt Berry on his DOTO smartphone, a dedicated one-to-one presidential "burner."

Was Cuba connection from CW?

Berry replied that it was.

From colleague?

Berry answered in the affirmative.

The president signed off. He smiled at the one bright spot in the day. He was not wrong, he thought, giving Chase Williams this chance. But the smile was more than that.

He envied any man who merited that kind of selfless loyalty.

CHAPTER FOURTEEN

Havana, Cuba
July 22, 8:21 p.m.

Other than during storms, haste was anathema to a man accustomed to the rolling majesty of sea travel. But storms occurred—rarely, but they happened. And they kept a seaman constantly vigilant, feeling a change in the swells, observing the color and humor of the skies, sensing the slightest rise or fall in the intensity, direction, even the smell of the wind, the humidity, the temperature.

The past few weeks had been a series of small storms for Salehi, and had culminated in a big one. The difference was that he knew this one was coming and he knew how long it would last. Mentally, emotionally, and physically he had prepared for that—for a recovery from the burden of guilt and rage and for unburdened sailing on the other side. Perhaps, he had fantasized, in a nation still tossed by its own storms, by political and domestic unrest between religious and secular forces, he could be a source of unification. Not as a public person but as a reminder that the world was at war with Iran and its sovereignty.

Juan Urrutia sat beside Salehi in the rear two seats of the Lancair IV-P. During the two-and-a-half-hour flight the men had not spoken very much. The Cuban had offered his companion food and drink but that was all. After the prop aircraft had plopped to a landing, the door was opened, the pilot departed—he had not spoken at all, save for communication with the towers and with a contact at Lourdes—and humid heat, sea tinged but oppressive nonetheless, poured through the open door. Salehi had removed his turban upon takeoff and used it now to dab at the perspiration around his neck. He unbuckled his belt in preparation for deplaning but Urrutia remained and requested that Salehi do the same.

"Why?" the Iranian asked, instantly suspicious and with a sudden, sickening sense that he had been told a lie.

The Cuban held up his smartphone. "I am awaiting information."

"Why not wait inside?" Salehi asked, indicating the low, aging terminal of José Martí International Airport, which was just a short walk away. Rooftop apparatus suggested air-conditioning.

"Because this is as far as my instructions take me—take *us*," Urrutia clarified.

"Then how did you know about my trip to Delhi?"

"That is information, not directions, *si*?" Urrutia said.

Salehi was liking this less and less. He half-expected American commandos from Guantánamo to storm the tiny aircraft. He looked across the airfield. He saw jets with a variety of international names splashed across the sides. Any one of them could be Delhi-bound. Or it could be that none of them was. He had not even been told if he was to leave today or the next day, by public or private transportation. There were a great many questions he realized he should have asked before allowing himself to be hustled from a threat he had not even verified.

The men sat for over an hour. With each minute, Salehi was more convinced that this was a trap. He had already looked out at the field and what he could see of the countryside beyond. He saw a direction in which he might be able to run if necessary. The aircraft and terminal would afford him some protection from gunfire. He had watched the pilot during the flight, had a rudimentary idea of how to work the controls—which was the only reason he had not left the aircraft despite Urrutia's admonitions. He did not think he could take off but he had an idea about how to use the small plane on land.

The men had finished the water they had, and the Iranian's turban was soaked along with the rest of his clothing, when the Cuban's phone finally beeped. It was a text message.

"There is a private jet coming for you in a quarter hour," the Cuban told him.

"I am gratified," Salehi replied. "Who is sending it?"

"I do not have that information," Urrutia replied. "I only know, for the purpose of identification, that it is a Falcon 8X out of Trinidad."

Again, that could be true . . . or it could be a cover story. Salehi knew that the jihadists worked in this region. There was a possible Yemen connection there.

Possible. Maybe. Once he was on that jet, he was helpless.

"I do not believe I can board without more information, more proof," Salehi said.

"I see," Urrutia replied. "Shall I pass that along?"

"Yes," Salehi replied, convinced that—if necessary—he could overpower the Cuban and make a break along the eastern edge of the tarmac and over a low chain-link fence. He was already imagining making his way to the port and finding passage on some freighter, paying his way with manual labor.

"The proof you request will be forthcoming," the Cuban replied.

"How soon?" Salehi asked.

"That I do not know," Urrutia told him, letting his hand and the phone flop on his knee. "Before, I hope, we are entirely dehydrated. And my phone battery dies."

The expected jet landed, taxied to a spot some fifty meters from the prop plane, and sat there. The white aircraft seemed, to Salehi, like an albatross—powerful and unknowable, save as an omen.

Urrutia's phone signaled. It was a text.

"I cannot read this," he said, showing it to Salehi.

"It is Persian," Salehi said, then read, "'My war requires leaders and men of courage, not dabblers.'"

The men waited. After a few moments the video function took over the phone. The image was murky, the sound full of extraneous scrapes and bumps. It seemed to show the interior of a van. Suddenly, a man was thrust into the picture.

"Do you know him?" Urrutia asked.

Salehi said nothing; he was too experienced to answer or to incriminate himself. This might still be a ploy of some kind, something to get him to confess—though it was seeming less and less like that by the moment. The man in the picture was Dr. Hafiz Akif and he looked frightened. He was breathing quite heavily; his neat black hair was disheveled and his tie was askew. It looked as though there were cuts on his cheek, perhaps from a blow, but it was too dark to be sure. The chemist was only visible from the chest up, though it seemed as if his arms were behind him—his hands bound, it appeared.

No words were spoken until the barrel of a .45 appeared in the image. The chemist's eyes broadened unnaturally, his mouth opened as if to speak, but he did not have time to say anything before his forehead erupted in a spray of red. What remained of his head jerked back, taking the rest of his body with him.

"*Madre de dios!*" Urrutia cried, swallowing hard.

Salehi had seen executions before, and he was more numb than revolted. After another moment the text function returned and a new message appeared on the screen.

"'He will be found, with evidence, by the Canadian authorities,'" Salehi read. "'Working backwards, you will be found. The aircraft will wait just five minutes.'"

The Cuban looked at him. "*Amigo,*" he said before remembering to speak Russian. "I suggest you board." Urrutia was perspiring from more than the heat now. He nodded anxiously toward the jet. "I think some of those guns may be there, too."

"No," the Iranian officer replied. "If I don't go, they will let the Americans know where I am. Death would be preferable."

In less than a minute, Ahmed Salehi had left his traveling companion behind him and was on his way across the tarmac to the private jet. He did not know who had betrayed the chemist—

but, clearly, this was no longer an operation over which any one man in Tehran had control. As he neared the jet, Salehi thought back to his last mission, the one that had gone so wrong.

There was a stray thread, he realized—one that was openly hostile to his sponsor, Prosecutor Ali Younesi of the Special Court, Sazman-E Ettela'at Va Amniyat-E Mellie, Iran.

The powerful Majlis-e Khobregān-e Rahbari in Iran—the Assembly of Experts.

CHAPTER FIFTEEN

The Assembly of Experts, Tehran, Iran
July 23, 6:00 a.m.

Ayatollah Ali Asqar Alami, senior Iranian cleric of the Khorasan Province, First Deputy Chairman of the Assembly of Experts, completed the *Fajr*, the morning prayer, with a heartfelt petition that Allah grant him His forgiveness and His mercy. With a grateful heart, he stepped from the prayer rug in the corner of his office.

Dressed modestly in a clean, loose white tunic that reached below his knees, and a large white kufi, the seventy-seven-year-old cleric went to the laptop on his desk. He had arrived, as was his habit, just before sunrise to read emails from the previous evening. Today, however, he had another reason for being here: to follow the news from Montreal.

He had not expected to read anything on the website of IRNA, the Islamic Republic News Agency. But judging from the photographs and video he had looked at before his prayer, the death of the Pakistani chemist was all over European and North American news services.

As he clicked through the news updates on Western sites, the cleric received the personal message he had been waiting for. It was from Dawoud, in Montreal, the sleeper who had been sent to the train station to collect the Pakistani chemist and then to the Hotel rue Stanley.

Second and third targets silent.

The gaunt, bearded figure switched back to Canada's CTV website to await that report and to watch for any indication that Dawoud and his young brother Fazlur had escaped identification. From all he had heard, the two émigrés who worked as food deliverymen were valuable assets in Canada.

Yet valuable, too, he reflected, *are those who would die in the war against infidels.*

The news site erupted with an update about the strangulation death of the Pakistani mother and daughter in their hotel room.

An unfortunate necessity, the ayatollah thought. Learning of the chemist's death, his daughter would have sought protection for herself and her child. She would have been compelled to reveal what she knew of those who had been involved in this enterprise. His own role in transferring information from Prosecutor Younesi to Yemen might be uncovered. Despite his failure to obtain nuclear weapons from the Russians, Younesi remained a powerful and vindictive figure and a personally ambitious one. He was also the kind of moderate who, achieving even greater power, might bow to the will of the secular public and seek regime change from within. The supreme leader did not see that but Alami and other members of the Assembly did. It was necessary to stop Younesi and replace him. To do that, however, his trusted puppet, Captain Ahmed Salehi, must be persuaded to help.

Though Akif and his family were Pakistani, they were also Muslim. The cleric was permitted to offer a prayer for the dead, which he did . . . while also thanking Allah that they had been silenced.

CHAPTER SIXTEEN

Fort Belvoir North, Virginia
July 22, 9:49 p.m.

Chase Williams had sent the three Black Wasps to the rooms in the Officer's Club that had been assigned them on the second floor. Though everyone was keen to know what was next, Williams had no idea how long they would be here—or where they would be going. It was best to rest while they could.

He remained in the club's dining area. He knew he should be resting, too, but it was his job—just as it had been at Op-Center—to keep track of incoming intelligence during a crisis. Now, as then, unless he had a team in the field, information was sporadic and fragmented; the glue was usually guesswork, provided by a team of professionals who had been in similar situations. In that respect, Williams felt uniquely helpless at this moment. Ideas sparked ideas. Thoughts took him on tangents that had nothing to do with the mission.

The *Intrepid*. The old team. The new team, no member of which had ever been in the field. January Dow, who was jockeying for bigger things. He had to focus on the task at hand and, to do that, he needed something to focus on. The silence from the other services was deadly.

The news was on in the corner of his screen. CNN was reporting that a dead body had just been recovered in a van by the Montreal Police Department.

"Unconfirmed reports say that he was apparently murdered execution style, while diplomatic documents found on the body indicate that he was attached to—"

The phone chimed. It was Berry from a scrambled White House line. Williams punched in a code on his Bluetooth to give him access.

"Here, Matt."

"Someone just killed a Pakistani chemist," the DCS said.

"The homicide in Montreal?"

"That's the one, and it's too damn neat," Berry said. "The Canadian Security Intelligence Service is checking the guy's ID and also the plane ticket he used to fly from New York. Name's Dr. Hafiz Akif. He's a chemist."

"Tortured?"

"No injuries reported . . . other than the top half of his head being gone. Assuming the dead man was involved, who would have known about it, known where he'd fled—and why did they serve him up?"

"Either it's a ringer so we'll chase our tails, or someone wants us to follow this guy backwards to whoever sponsored him or to Salehi."

"Then why not turn the guy in for interrogation?" Berry asked. "Why shut him up?"

"Was he headed to see someone there?"

"We don't know. And he was traveling with a young woman and a child, though they haven't been found yet."

"You don't think we should go to Montreal, do you?"

"No," Berry told him. "We've got an army of investigators already en route. And that's not what the president wants you for, which brings me to another thing. Salehi didn't travel with this guy."

"That's standard operating procedure, Matt."

"Yeah, but we're checking to see if they might have left from the same airport. You know, watch-your-back scenario."

"Right. Assuming the plane ticket is legit and the dead man was involved in the attack."

"Yeah. Dammit, this is all balled up."

Berry covered the phone and talked to someone—Harward, it sounded like. Williams took a moment to step back and let everything percolate. Nothing obvious jumped out, nothing that suggested a motive. If this was legitimate, someone knew where the chemist was headed and met him there.

Berry got back on. "The van was leased just three hours ago to someone from Tobago. Security camera shows a young black man, clerk said he had a Jamaican-like accent—but the ID was false."

"So there's another player," Williams said. "Someone who knew—or just found out—where this Akif was going."

"I'd bet on the latter," Berry said. "He had to hustle to get that van and pick Akif off—outside the Montréal Central train station, I've just been informed."

"Headed where?"

"Don't know yet."

"You know what this feels like?" Williams said. "The same thing we had in Ukraine, with government forces versus rogue operators versus Russians."

"Factions who were not on the same page."

"Right," Williams said. "Salehi had a reason for going after us. That's why he posed for a picture with his handiwork, debt paid. But we don't know that Iran sent him. Hell, we don't know who there actually sponsored his nuke operation and whether that was a deep-cover mission."

"Could be a pro- or antigovernment element," Berry said. "Someone wants the theocracy hit, by us, so they sponsor Salehi in order to pin this on the ayatollahs. Could be."

"Exactly."

Berry laughed humorously. "We had that debate two hours ago."

"And?"

"President's leaning toward a wrist slap within their borders," Berry said.

"You know," Williams went on, "we also don't know if Pakistan simply harbored Salehi or had an active hand—sanctuary at the embassy, a chemist, a lab."

"Risky," Berry said. "Especially if the hit on this guy proves that."

"Risky, yes, but Islamabad's in a corner," Williams said. "Since we cut back our financial aid to Islamabad—you read the report from our consul general in Karachi? About how they were intercepting transfers from Tehran."

"Honestly, no."

"We're talking so-called loans worth billions of rupees," Williams said. "Tehran has to be getting more than embassy space for that. And there's something else. Even if Iran and Pakistan did everything we said, none of them may have been involved in killing the chemist."

"Because it was an execution," Berry said.

"Yes."

"Harward and I had the same reaction," Berry said. "Over the top for anyone you mentioned. I suggested we look for someone who's gonna be deaf for a few days, pulling the trigger in a closed van."

Williams shook his head. "We're not seeing something, Matt."

"Something hiding in plain sight or something we haven't found yet?"

Williams replied, "Neither. Give me a half hour. There's a file I want to read."

CHAPTER SEVENTEEN

Fort Belvoir North, Virginia
July 22, 10:06 p.m.

No sooner had Williams hung up with Matt Berry than CNN reported on the discovery of two more bodies in a hotel.

"They were found strangled in the hallway outside their room," the reporter said. "Access is believed to have been through a stairwell, but that report is unconfirmed and now security footage has been released."

The sense of something unfolding with many moving parts was now stronger than ever. It reminded Williams of the assassination of John F. Kennedy, when Lee Harvey Oswald was in the book depository shooting a president, then in a theater shooting a police officer, then being shot himself by Jack Ruby—

"But we don't have decades to puzzle over this one," he thought aloud.

What he was thinking earlier, about using outside experience to help map a current situation, was also stronger. He typed in a code to access a particular transcript.

"This whole thing is related to the sinking of the *Nardis*, which attaches it to everything around that operation in Anadyr, Russia," he murmured. That left one avenue still unexplored.

He clicked on the file labeled **Brigadier General Amir Ghasemi: Interview.**

"Of course it says 'Interview,' not 'interrogation,'" he said unhappily. The file belonged to January Dow and everything his self-appointed nemesis did had to skew toward nonaggressive language.

Williams had been present for the questioning, and he remembered the Iranian asylum-seeker ranging all over the geopolitical map. After the session had ended, no one in the room—which included January and Allen Kim, whose FBI facility was holding Ghasemi—could agree whether their guest was simply frightened and unfocused or whether he was being intentionally imprecise. A consensus still had not been reached.

January had moved Ghasemi to a safe residence somewhere in Virginia while the question of sanctuary was decided. There was no point interviewing him again, since these latest events had occurred after his defection. But often, during these sessions, people dropped truth among the lies to create a sense of verisimilitude; he knew he was not dealing with amateurs and that his every statement would be thoroughly investigated.

Scrolling through the transcript, looking for names and factions, Williams came to an exchange between himself and the Iranian officer:

> AG: I, of all people, was sent to assess the faith of a
> small force of Houthi who had come up from Aden
> to fight Kurds.

CW: That would be an extension of the tactical and
    financial support your government has been providing
    the Houthi throughout Yemen.
AG: That is correct.

That did not seem to connect directly with today's attack. But Williams couldn't dismiss it.

The phone sounded.

"Yes, Matt?"

"The Canadians are looking into a connection between the two hits and the terror group Jamaat al-Muslimeen."

"In Trinidad," Williams said.

"They're based there, but they're all over the Caribbean," Berry said. "The president thinks we should get you down there. If there is a Canadian cell, and if they were directed from that region, it's possible Salehi is being leapfrogged from Havana to the Caribbean Basin and then to parts unknown."

"Possibly," Williams agreed.

"It's a five-hour flight," Berry said. "If your team leaves within the hour, you can drop in under cover of darkness."

"I'll let them know," Williams said. "One thing, Matt. I'm going with them."

The phone was silent for a moment.

"Matt?"

"You know, I told the president you'd say that."

"What was the president's reaction?"

"He said he didn't care as long as you caught Salehi."

"Tell him I appreciate the support," Williams said.

"Consider it more leeway than actual support," Berry told him.

"I know," Williams replied. "I'll let you know when we're in-country."

"I'll arrange with the Fourth fleet to have sea extraction to be standing by—until then, watch yourself," Berry said before hanging up.

That, too, was a little soft—but understandable. If Williams or any team members were caught, attention would be drawn to whoever sent them there. To protect the president, it was likely that Berry would have to fall on his sword. In its own way, it spoke to the man's patriotism and trust that he put the apprehension of Salehi above his own career security.

The only team member actually asleep was Major Breen. He had learned, in his years of crisscrossing the country on JAG business, to grab snatches of rest when it was at all possible.

Assembling in the dining area, in civilian clothes and with only their equipment vests, the team was met by Sergeant Major Stewart Siena of the Army Air Operations Group. Williams did not have a vest but he improvised in the kitchen, taking food implements—including a butcher knife—he felt he could use. He put them in a white apron and used the strings to make a bundle of it. They piled into a camouflaged Humvee for the short ride to the 12th Aviation Battalion's Lakota Hangar.

"Your chutes are aboard the UH-60 and I'm informed you've all jumped," the sergeant major said.

"We're prepared," Williams assured him from the passenger's seat.

"Very good, sir," Siena said. "We're going to ferry you to Elgin in Florida and they'll fly you the rest of the way on an F27 Friendship. The plane's turboprops sound the same as a lot of the local aircraft so it won't attract attention. The '60 would have to make one refueling stop and, even with the top airspeed, that would not put you on target in darkness."

"Understood and thanks for pulling this together."

"It's what we do, sir." The young man smiled. He received a text as he drove. "The atmospheric dynamics chief down there says . . . you're good. Sunrise is at 06:51 so you've got about a thirty-minute buffer, given that they're an hour ahead plus air speed variations due to possible headwinds and a storm system west of Saint Vincent and the Grenadines."

Williams loved this, the efficiency of the military. They got knocked around a lot by politicians and the press for their high expenditures, pork, and boondoggles. And that was fair. But the people in the system, their professionalism, had never failed to inspire. It felt good to be back. It also felt good to be appreciated. At the end of the drive, the sergeant major complimented him on his grip.

"Old school field improv, sir," he said with a salute. "I like it."

The Black Hawk was waiting and the team was airborne just over a half hour after Williams and Berry had spoken. The parachute check went quickly; the riggers had done an impeccable job with the T-11 Personal Parachute Systems. The main canopy had a larger inflated diameter and an increase in the surface area than the T-10, which minimized the yank of opening and also descent sway. Injuries upon landing were reduced by the reduction in the rate of descent from twenty-four feet per second to nineteen feet per second. The reserve canopy had a faster discharge in the event of malfunctions.

Williams had jumped several times with the T-10 and was confident he could handle this.

As long as you factor in the nearly twenty-year gap between jumps, he reminded himself.

The trip to Elgin passed quickly as the team reviewed data on their target area and both regional, English-language newspaper files and intelligence reports on the terror group. It had been sent to Williams by Berry and forwarded to each member's secure smartphone. On-file data about the Caribbean terror group had been assembled for the Department of Defense with rapid-deployment attack strategies and special ops scenarios worked out by the U.S. Southern Command Response Group for Transregional Threat Networks. Berry had earmarked as "operational" Special Ops Insertion Plan D for the Black Wasps. That plan called for a drop north of the Navet River on Trinidad, just west of where it met the Nariva Swamp preserve.

"That's a lot of water if you miss your spot," Major Breen noted.

"White paper says the terrorists use the river to move supplies and personnel to Cocos Bay," Williams said, "and from there to the Atlantic. Good place to gather intel. And also to get away—" he said as he checked a text from Berry. "Guided Missile Cruiser USS *Jacinto* is in the region along with other intelligence ships shadowing the Russians in the Atlantic."

"A lot more activity down there than I'd've guessed," Lance Corporal Rivette said as they were landing.

Rivette was right about that, Williams thought, but what

grabbed his attention and wouldn't let go—again—was what he had been considering back at Fort Belvoir: there was a diverse cast of players interacting here, any one of which could move the target in a different and unpredictable direction.

CHAPTER EIGHTEEN

Port of Spain, Trinidad
July 23, 12:34 a.m.

The air-conditioning had been reason enough to have boarded the jet.

Ahmed Salehi was welcomed by a copilot who did not speak any language Salehi could understand, and the Iranian was left alone in the plush cabin. The flight from Havana to Piarco Airport, Trinidad, had taken an hour. During the trip, Salehi had used his smartphone to read about his destination. That was something he always did when he sailed; even en route to Havana, he had looked the nation up on his phone.

The islands of Trinidad and Tobago had been separate European fiefdoms since the arrival of Christopher Columbus, uniting in 1889 and finally becoming an independent republic in 1976. The republic thrived on tourism, and he could see why it was an ideal staging area for Jamaat al-Muslimeen. Travelers came here from around the world, and departed from here for countless global destinations. It would be easy for anyone with the proper document to come and go without having their background checked.

Not that the terrorists were able to function openly, as they once tried, as a political party. In July 1990, the Jamaat al-Muslimeen attempted a coup d'état that had failed—though it lasted for six days, during which the prime minister and members of his government were held hostage in Port of Spain. When it became clear that the effort had failed, the group arranged an amnesty in exchange for ending the crisis. Working underground, the group was responsible for bombings and at least one assassination, though the rise of other extremist groups had forced them to turn their attention on their rivals more than on their enemies. It wasn't just a territorial battle but a fight for funding that motivated them.

Provincial and poorly managed, Salehi thought. *Yet someone with resources believes in them. I have been recovered at some expense.*

Salehi used the rest of the time to do Krav Maga forms. Hand-to-hand combat was not only a necessary skill in his line of work, it also forced his brain to cede control to his body. Not thinking was a good thing, especially now. He was met by a lone driver in a nondescript black Toyota minivan. He felt a jolt when he deplaned and saw the car on the tarmac; he immediately thought of Akif in his van.

But if these people wanted you dead, they could have shoved you *from the aircraft*, he told himself.

The capital city was brightly lit and there was more traffic than he would have expected. There were large buildings here, as one would see in any substantial port city around the globe, and an active nightlife. That was left behind as they headed north from the dock area to the Diego Martin section. They pulled into the circular court in front of a modern, seven-story white apartment complex.

From there, Salehi was driven to the side of the building, down a ramp to an underground parking area where he was met by a pair of locals who were dressed in black T-shirts and black shorts. They were both tall, lightly bearded, at least six foot three, wearing sandals and dour expressions. The two appeared to be in their late twenties. They spoke to the driver, who departed. Eyes watchful and constantly moving—not nervously but methodically—one of the men got in front of Salehi, another behind, and they entered an elevator. During the short ride, the men introduced themselves as Nik and Vincent. Reaching the top floor, the Iranian found himself on a clean, quiet floor that brought them to a spacious, airy modern residence. Vincent lit a cigarette, offered one to Salehi. The Iranian shook his head. There was no fatwa about Islam and smoking, though without that legal opinion most of the people the captain knew erred on the side of abstinence. This man was probably less jihadist than angry, poor, and rebellious.

The apartment had a variety of weapons casually distributed about the living room: on a coffee table, on the kitchen counter, on the floor beside armchairs and the sofa. The ones he recognized were a CZ-75 self-loading pistol, a pump-action 12-bore shotgun, and a MAC-10 submachine gun. He also noticed the hilt of a machete sticking out from beneath the cushion of the sofa.

By the armrest, ready for a right-handed grab if needed, Salehi realized.

He briefly considered picking up one of the guns. He did not know if he might need it.

Salehi was directed to an arched doorway that lead to a terrace. En route, he passed two bedrooms, each with foldable cots stacked in a corner. Evidently, these two men were the gatekeepers of a transit hub. Members of the organization or its affiliates were no doubt housed here, briefed here, armed here, paid here, and then sent on their missions.

Vincent followed Salehi into the night. It was dark here, and quiet. There was a small, round, granite-topped table and a single iron chair. A laptop was open and facing the chair. The back of the computer faced outward; there was no angle from which the monitor would be visible other than the seat. It was obviously no secret who operated from this apartment.

Vincent bade the Iranian to sit. When he had done so, the other man left. He returned shortly with a bottle of water and a tray of fruit. Salehi selected an apple and looked out as he ate. He hadn't realized how hungry he was until now.

The captain's head was swimming with disorientation. He could not believe it was just a little more than fifteen hours since the attack; the event seemed remote, as though it had been the work of someone else simply borrowing his body. The past few weeks had felt like that. And now, rather than being home, he was once again whiplashed to someplace new. At least, with sea voyages, there was time to adjust.

Thinking of the sea, any sea, gave him focus and helped to steady him. He looked across the table. There was an identical tower across the way, a few hundred meters distant, and beyond it, in the distance, the unruffled Bay of Paria; the lights of the boats upon it barely rippled. He had sailed to the Atlantic, to Venezuela and Suriname, but never to the Caribbean.

" *'You have an admirer in Sana'a who will give you sanctuary . . .*

and a boat,'" Juan Urrutia had told him. When Salehi pictured this region, saw the Boca de Serpiente, the Serpent's Mouth, he suddenly wanted nothing more than to feel the motion of the mighty sea beneath his feet. The wild ocean, the unpredictable strait, the tranquil bay.

If for no other reason, that ship needed to burn, he thought back to the *Intrepid. You do not put a warship in a zoo. You give it a fitting funeral, fire or water.*

The laptop snapped on. Salehi put the apple core on the tray and turned his eyes toward the screen. A face filled the center.

It was a face he did not know and yet . . . did. It was a long, pale face, modestly bearded. There were black-rimmed eyeglasses, thick brows, and intense eyes. A white kufi sat on what seemed to be a bald head; the paleness of the skin seemed almost to blend into the headwear. The look was benign, apart from the eyes. The man looked similar to almost every senior cleric Salehi had ever met. He wondered if it were the learned serenity that made these faces seem alike.

"Welcome to Trinidad, Captain Salehi," the man said.

The words were a pronouncement and the soothing effect of the sea had met its match: it was a gift to hear his own language spoken to him after so many weeks. Salehi did not doubt that was what the speaker had intended.

"Thank you, eminence," Salehi replied—defaulting to a general honorific since he did not possess additional information.

The man on the monitor nodded slightly at the courtesy. "Call me Sadi," he said quietly. "And it should be I who thanks you for your brave and important work today."

"I feel I should tell you that it was a mission of honor, not ideology," Salehi said. "And for my colleague, the late Dr. Akif, it was not even that. It was simply a task he had agreed to do."

"I had a task for him as well," Sadi said. "He would have been wise to accept, if not for himself than for his daughter and grand-daughter."

The comment caused Salehi to stiffen.

"Yes, Captain," Sadi said, as casually as if he were accepting an offer for tea. "The mother and child were stopped as they attempted to reach the Canadian authorities."

"Dead?" Salehi said. It wasn't so much a question as an accusation.

"Sadly, yes. In my world, there are two kinds of people," Sadi went on. "Those who are with me and those who are dead. The Pakistanis no longer matter. You do. Which will you be?"

"You ask this with an arsenal at my back," Salehi said.

"A necessary precaution," Sadi said. "In order to remain secure, the safe house you are in, as well as the people and methods that brought you there, must remain secret. But remember, too, I am also the one who saved you from becoming a pawn of the Assembly of Experts and the Russians. You would have been abandoned by your own people, turned over to the Americans, tried and publicly humiliated. I offer you life, service to Allah, and the sea."

Salehi did not like this man or his methods. There was no honor, only fanaticism. There was no room for dissent. The captain had his disagreements with the ayatollahs in Iran, but like so many of his countrymen he had learned to live a largely secular life.

Though he would be out of reach of Sadi himself, would he ever be free of his operatives?

The ages-old condition of every Persian, he reflected. *Death or servitude. And death in this instance is measured in less than a few dozen heartbeats if Sadi is denied.*

Salehi said, "You have a boat, I was informed."

Sadi smiled for the first time. "I own a considerable fleet," he said. "What I have for you is a bulk carrier, 203,000 deadweight tonnage, yours to command around the globe—along with an ongoing mission."

"Which is?"

"To carry arms, persons, drugs, currency, and other commodities along with the stated cargo," Sadi said. "All of this will be in furtherance of the cause of jihad. And you will be paid, as well. Everything quite legitimate."

"On the surface," Salehi said.

Sadi's smile faded into his beard. "You say, Captain, that you are not an ideologue. But you are a Muslim."

"Of course."

"By that very acknowledgment, you accept that it is our mission to terrorize the unbelievers. 'Therefore smite them,'" Sadi said, reciting from the Quran. "To accomplish this we require men of courage." Sadi leaned slightly toward the camera. "Whether you embrace my offer with conviction or from necessity, the alternative is death. Death at the hands of my jihadists or by the corrupt will of the Americans."

"You would accept a man who has been coerced?"

Sadi sat back. "I would accept and trust a man who became,

today, a hero of the cause. Muhammad, peace be upon him, reveals that our success is only by Allah. To disavow you would be to disavow the Prophet and God Himself."

The speaker did not strike Salehi as a flatterer or a manipulator. Sadi clearly believed in his self-appointed mission and, without sentiment or emotion, he would do whatever it took to fulfill that goal—including swift execution.

Salehi was faced with two entirely unsatisfactory options and a third that was far removed from the patriotic life he had lived. He would be an Iranian in name only and a naval officer not-at-all. Those thoughts were difficult to absorb.

But you would always know where you stood, he told himself, *and given your newfound notoriety, at least you would have people watching your back. Plus you would be at sea.*

And you would also be alive.

"I accept your offer, Sadi," Salehi said. "What is the next move?"

"You will sleep tonight and fly to Yemen late tomorrow morning to see me," Sadi replied. "I was . . . *hopeful* . . . of your acceptance; another of my private jets is already en route. I would shake your hand before you take command of your vessel. God's peace be upon you."

"And God's peace be upon you," Salehi replied.

Sadi terminated the conversation and Salehi reflected on the commitment he had made. There was one aspect of the talk that stayed with the captain as he closed the laptop and looked back at the sea. Sadi had not been wrong. Whatever Salehi's profound differences and disagreements with this man and his methods, just those few words of farewell had pushed all of that aside. They had been an almost magical homecoming—not the one Salehi had been anticipating, to Iran, with its politics and double-dealing, but to something more profound, something deeper.

An invitation to a brotherhood of pure and incorruptible faith.

CHAPTER NINETEEN

F27 Friendship, 2,400 Feet Above the Lesser Antilles
July 23, 4:43 a.m.

The Friendship turboprop was anything but; cold, rattling, and Major Breen could swear that air was whistling in around the windows. That didn't stop him from catching a short nap, after which he thought about the mission. Not the details; that was the province of Chase Williams. He was thinking about the team itself.

"A new breed," their Department of Defense liaison, U.S. Army General Buddy Lovett had called them. The army being the army, of course the team was named after a feared, fleet creature: the black wasp.

That's what happens when you're born in a think tank, Breen thought. In this case, the hatchery was the U.S. Army Training and Doctrine Command. *The command*, Breen mused, *is that whatever is "new" is invariably saddled with the conservative "old," like anything designed by committee.*

Still, the heart of the idea had emerged relatively unscathed. That was the reason Breen had volunteered to serve. The core idea was not just to have a quick-deploy unit with diverse skills, but one that was actually undertrained. Breen could just imagine how that had gone over when Lovett had first proposed it.

The view was that each skill set would complement another, making the team adaptable, fluid, and run by what Lovett described as a "situational command." That meant the ranking officer was in charge until something happened that required the skill of a sniper or hand-to-hand combat expert or forensics analyst.

"I think you could have come up with a better acronym than SITCOM," Breen had told Lovett. But the general replied it was something that no one had even considered.

Breen believed that someone at TRADOC had to have realized it but chose not to say anything.

No one could be sure how the covert attack team would actually function in the field or under fire. Breen had suggested that maybe "progressive infiltration group" would be a more fitting nom de guerre—as in Guinea Pig. Lovett had chuckled at that during their first training session. Or maybe it was just the general's anxiety talking. There were downtimes when the team members and their trainers openly wondered if the idea was brilliant . . . or insane.

Breen still wasn't sure, but they were about to find out. He wished he could tell Lovett that they were undertaking their first mission, but part of the Black Wasp charter was that once Lovett sent them the "call" message, he would have no further communication. The general took very seriously the idea that this was a covert team, on its own. Any breach of protocol would corrupt the experiment.

Then there was Chase Williams, whose career over the last four or five years was a complete mystery. The thirty-five years of military service showed up in the searches Breen had done, in archived articles, photographs, and interviews from the Pacific Command and Central Command websites. Then . . . nothing. It could be that he had retired, but even former officers go on social media. There was none for Williams.

There was also nothing in his prior record to suggest what the hell could have transitioned him from a command desk to Black Wasp. But there was a conclusion to be drawn. Williams's command of intelligence and fluency with the language of security suggested that he had been involved in the field for those missing years. Being involved with Central Intelligence or the National Security Agency would not have been something to conceal.

He had been hidden somewhere, Breen decided. *Something off the radar but important enough for* someone *to trust him, now, with our untested hides.*

Breen could throw a dart at the U.S. government and hit more dark or black ops intelligence operations than public ones, so going any further with his investigation was problematic. Though a few things did stand out.

No one who was as important as Chase Williams appeared to be was not typically, suddenly, free to leave his day job and join a field operation. No one who had not trained with the team, and who had apparently not been out from behind a desk for nearly two score years, would be attached to them without good reason.

What kind of reason? Breen wondered.

It likely had something to do with the *Intrepid*. Otherwise, none of them would be going anywhere. Since Williams was not active Navy, the *Intrepid* connection was probably with whoever had been behind the attack, most likely someone Williams knew or knew of. And if he knew or knew of them, one would have expected him to know where the bastard was.

And there was something else about Williams that had jumped out. Breen had been in enough depositions and military courts to recognize the body language of guilt when he saw it. Chase Williams looked like he was carrying something on his soul the size of a house. That suggested something Breen had also seen, show trials in which men and women were prosecuted not for wrongdoing but for ineptitude.

Williams may have been point man on a major, major intelligence failure. If so, it would be interesting, exciting, and possibly dangerous to see how that all played out.

The vivid images from the morning, and the events that followed, had prevented Chase Williams from sleeping. There was already an iconic image on the news, one that was seared into his eyeballs: the blackened tail fin of the space shuttle *Enterprise*, which had been housed on the *Intrepid*, poking from the charred remains of the roof of its specially constructed pavilion.

In the past, Williams's work was fluid. People and events, meetings and conference calls, information and questions flowed one into the other. Hours passed without boundary. Most times, a day seemed to end not long after it had begun. It was new for Williams not to be thinking beyond benchmarks. The Black Hawk ride. Boarding the Friendship. Checking the parachutes. Rest—no, review maps. Equipment. Intelligence updates. Life by checklist.

An astronaut buddy once told him that his life depended on just such minutiae and structure. Williams did not think he would like it, and he was right. Yet it was the only way to slog through the emotional and psychological morass. The proverbial left foot, right foot, onward of his boot camp days. Because, in a very real sense, that was where Williams was. Starting over, learning over. He had experience but it was mostly managerial fabric with threads of tactics. A lot of that had to be ripped away for what was ahead.

He had been looking at a map on his smartphone. It had struck him, in the dark of the cabin, that one of the things that he had to shuck was protocol. Black Wasp was an antitraditional unit. It was liberated from rules of engagement . . . and, at least in this case, the burdens of morality. Salehi must be found and either taken or killed. That was the only "rule."

The others were awake and Williams squatted in the aisle between them. As ranking officer—albeit retired—he felt he could press a mission outline on the group.

"I'm setting out a very simple profile," he said, "and your input is welcome."

Lieutenant Lee was sitting on the aisle, Rivette at the window. Williams noticed the whites of her eyes shift as she snatched a look across his shoulders, across the aisle, at Major Breen. The glow of the phone revealed an expression that was stoic and unchanged.

"Our drop zone was selected because Jamaat al-Muslimeen— JAM—uses the Navet River to move personnel and matériel," Williams said, scrolling and tracing the route with his finger.

"They are active around the clock to tax law enforcement and use a variety of vessels to move inland from the Atlantic. I suggest we take one of the vessels and rip it, and its people. Either they or whoever they send as backup will be plugged into the local terror ecosystem." He turned the phone to illuminate the team and looked from face to face. "Thoughts?"

"You just described my dream mission." Lance Corporal Rivette smiled.

Williams looked at the lieutenant.

"I like it," Grace said without expression.

"Major Breen?" Williams asked.

"If Black Wasp had a charter, that would be it, short and direct," he admitted. The straight mouth twisted into a smile. "Let's do it."

CHAPTER TWENTY

Before the Friendship copilot, Captain Leanne Howard, emerged from the cockpit, she shut the lights in the cabin. This was to allow the jumpers' eyes to adjust to the dark. Then she came back to help with the black jumpsuits that had been provided for the passengers, and then with the gear and the jump itself. She paid particular attention to the access of each jumper to the operational handles. It was dark, and she wanted them to make sure they could find them by feel.

When they had first met on boarding, Grace Lee put the woman in her late thirties, a little older than the pilot. Grace was immediately outraged. From age four, growing up on Mott Street in New York's Chinatown, Lee had been forced to claw her way upward in the male-dominated world of martial arts. It made her strong . . . and it also made her a reactionary. She had to remind herself that not every dynamic was discrimination—male above female, European above Asian, youth above age.

But, being Grace Lee, the only daughter of a father who published the *Mulberry Community* newspaper and a mother who was his fact-checker, she had to know the true story.

"May I ask a personal question?" Lee asked as the copilot-turned-mother-hen checked her harness.

"Why am I number two?" she asked.

Lee, caught off-guard, said nothing.

"I saw it in the look you gave us when you boarded," Captain Howard told her. "I've seen it before among young recruits when men got picked first. The answer is, I came to piloting late, after I stopped jumping, and the Commander has flown this route before, in this aircraft, on surveillance runs. *I* would have picked him over me."

"I'm sorry," Grace said, slightly embarrassed but defiantly intact.

"Don't be," the captain replied, giving the chute an "all set" pat and Grace a wink. "I wondered the same thing about you."

The remark physically and spiritually inflated the younger woman swifter than anything she had ever heard. As she made her way to the lineup behind Rivette, she felt as though she could walk on air.

Lance Corporal Jaz Rivette shook out his hands the way Lieutenant Lee had once showed him. *Chigong*, she called the quick turns at the wrist, his fingers flopping. Moving internal energy. The young man had even started chigonging before going out to the range. It made his fingertips more sensitive, made the fingers seem directly connected to his will, bypassing the brain, in a way they hadn't before.

"That is exactly what you've done," she had told him the next time they met. "Thought is the enemy of action."

That was not what Rivette had heard growing up. His single mother always used to tell him, "Think before you do something stupid!" Those were the first words he heard after she learned that he'd stepped up to stop the bodega robbery, and they were the last words she told him when he enlisted.

The advice made sense where they lived in San Pedro, a community in the southern part of Los Angeles. The low-income housing near the port was rife with temptation from drifters, grifters, and local gangs who sought a fast buck stealing from ships or sailors. Rivette was lucky: his only interest in the sea was as a means out of San Pedro, a means of relieving his mother's burden of having to support him and his two younger sisters. He would skip rocks or shoot at seabirds with a slingshot he made from driftwood, a waterlogged shoe, and rubber bands he took from school.

Then came the bodega. He did not think then and hadn't since. That was one of the reasons he suspected General Lovett tapped him to be a Black Wasp. Everything Jaz Rivette did was by instinct—instincts honed in the street, ingenuity and survival skills he developed helping his mother by catching fish, by taking out-of-date buns from a fast-food trash bin, by watching EMTs to learn first aid in case anyone in the family was injured. Rivette wasn't chest-thumping proud of those things; they came naturally, all of them. Though he never admitted it to others, he actually felt that those around him were dull . . . not that he was particularly sharp. That belief was reinforced by the sharp, sharp people he had met in the Marines and then in the Black Wasp SAEs—skill assessment exercises that were held at Fort Bragg. In addition to the candidates, seasoned special forces personnel participated to provide a performance baseline. In whatever algorithm they had used, Rivette topped all the recruits and most of the veterans. He did not understand how that had happened since many of the warriors he saw radiated power and confidence.

Me? Rivette thought as Captain Howard checked and then okayed his parachute. *I was just a quiet kid who could shoot.*

Major Breen had stopped wondering about Chase Williams after the shortest mission overview in military history. The JAG officer had no particular liking for enhanced interrogation, either as a human being or as an attorney. But he also believed that nothing must stop them from apprehending the monster who had attacked his nation. If that meant causing some discomfort among terrorists who shared that vision, he could live with that. Certainly the enemies of America and American law, from the Taliban to the drug cartels, had never hesitated to do worse.

Whoever Williams was, wherever he had come from, he understood Black Wasp and he knew what he wanted to achieve. Breen had no problem stepping back from rank command and letting this man lead the mission until SITCOM procedures took over.

A pat on the back from the copilot and he was ready to jump. He did not know about the others, but he was eager to put this operation into motion. He had always wondered what he would have done during the Revolution, when the acts of the Founding

Fathers and anyone who supported them were treason punishable by hanging. He felt he would have risked everything for a cause.

It was good to know he had not been wrong.

Captain Howard stood by the closed starboard door of the plane waiting for the "blast" signal from the cockpit—the okay to jump. They were going out the rear of the aircraft so that any backwash would carry them away from the plane. She knew nothing about the four passengers who were arrayed in the aisle—according to age, it seemed, with the youngest going out first. But she did know, by the casual and dissimilar way they stood, by the uncertainty about which door they'd be using, at the way they actually paid attention to her prejump review of procedures, that they had not had much training. She doubted, in fact, that any of them had a signed clearance to jump. Even before they had queued up, just moving to the aisle from the equipment check in the bulkhead, there had been no sense of the person in front or behind, or of the seat backs; they were like consumers with backpacks at a Starbucks, oblivious to their turn radius.

Not that it mattered much, the captain had to admit. At this low altitude, with those advanced chutes, landing with too much kinetic energy wasn't the danger. It would take hitting a tree or lake for any of them to be seriously hurt. Even experienced jumpers had trouble with those kinds of off-ground touchdowns.

There were no signal lights over the door, no line for the parachutists. The Friendship was not typically used for jumps and there hadn't been time to rig anything. Communication from the cockpit was simple: the pilot signaled once with his flashlight when they were one minute from the drop zone. Captain Howard donned her goggles—a signal for the others to do the same and also to don their black helmets. Then she latched her leather waist harness to a hook forward the door. It was rigging of her own design, adapted from the bellyband of her own jump gear before a broken leg ended that aspect of her military life. When the door was secure, she motioned them forward.

She had been mentally counting down and was dead-on when the flashlight shined again. Since the team was looking at the open door, they did not know it was time to go until the captain pushed Rivette into the darkness.

Chase Williams was the last man out the door. Just before going out, he had been thinking how strange it was to be, effectively, a guest on his own mission; a dependent, rather than a leader. He had been the one determining the nominal policy of Black Wasp to this point, and the team had been respectful about that. He hadn't expected otherwise; for all they knew he was active duty and outranked them. But once they touched down the SITCOM conventions kicked in. When he had first read about it in the Officer's Club, the concept seemed to owe more to tag-team wrestling than to military polity.

But maybe that was the point, he had thought. *To fight savages, you needed to lose the regulations and a lot of tradition.*

Williams's penultimate thought, before he was shoved from the plane, was wondering how much the president and Matt Berry knew about Black Wasp's operational mandate. His last thought was whether they had given him this assignment because he was command-qualified and suddenly toxic—though the military had a more polite black ops phrase for it: very highly expendable.

The wind did not whistle; it drummed like a typhoon against his high-impact, lightweight carbon helmet. He could not see the others as he dropped; all he knew was where, on the map, they were supposed to land. Williams had transferred his gear to a canvas grip that Captain Howard had rustled up for him; it was the same compact size as those carried by the other team members and attached to either thigh during the jump. Williams transferred his phone, printed maps, and his personal Sig Sauer 9mm XM17. It had been gifted to him by Op-Center's JSOC team in 2015, after the unit was attached to Williams's operation. The polymer striker-fired handgun could be customized by the user, with interchangeable grip modules and adjustable frame size and caliber. Rivette was the only Black Wasp who carried multiple weapons; Grace Lee carried none, only a selection of knives, which were sheathed on her legs and hips—four in all.

If any of them landed far afield or became disoriented, they had palm-sized MicroTalkies, battery-powered with a range of three hundred feet and a light that could be seen from twice that distance away. Williams was not a religious Catholic, but right after praying for a safe touchdown, he prayed he did not need to use the beacon. The last twenty hours had already taken enough of a toll on his confidence as a leader.

The decades evaporated as Williams dropped. He remembered how surprised he was, when he first jumped, that there was no sensation of falling. The air seemed as solid as the sea, with very similar currents and eddies. The under-canopy behavior had been reviewed by Captain Howard, but it came back to him just the same; it was easy to remain steady in the box man position—

facing down, his arms at right angles to the torso, legs out forty-five degrees with a forty-five-degree bend at the knees.

There was a digital altimeter attached to the chest-high adjuster fitting of his harness. When it ticked off two thousand feet, Williams pulled the ripcord. The chute ruffled noisily as it deployed, briefly overpowering the sound of the air rushing by. Williams did not exactly ease to a slower rate of descent but he wasn't jolted either. He swung like a pendulum for a few moments, blood surging back into his legs, before is body became its own plumb and his feet were pointed straight down. Then he slipped his gloved fingers into the two toggles he would use to steer.

The sound of a thick, tumultuous atmosphere was no longer in his ears. Magnified slightly by the helmet he heard the creaks and groans of the harness, the lines, the gentle flutter of the canopy, his heart throbbing rapidly in his ears. His eyes were turned downward, the high-performance lenses of his goggles—with antifog coating—giving him a wide view of the terrain that seemed to climb toward him. He did not see the rest of the team nor did he look for them. Captain Howard had sent them out with enough of a gap between jumps to avoid a dangerous canopy collision.

"Better to be a little spread out than die air-dancing," she explained.

As he descended, Williams was focused on what he could see of the opaque black tree canopies spread below, and the ribbon of slightly less dark charcoal gray that would be the Navet River. He looked for a nearby patch that was neither tree nor water but shore. Williams maneuvered toward it; whether he found the dry, flat stretch or it found him, he tucked in his chin as Captain Howard had reminded them to do and hit the ground with a thump that forced his knees to bend. He felt the bump in the small of his back, dropped to his left side to relieve the sudden muscle-tension there, and flipped the plastic lid on the parachute release button that was on the opposite side from the altimeter. Because of the trees on either side there was no wind on the ground. The canopy had already collapsed and popped free without blowing away.

Swinging onto his knees—a strained muscle in his side complained but did not stop him—Williams crawled over the fabric and bundled it toward him.

Lance Corporal Rivette emerged from the darkness, holding his chute. There were weapons strapped to hip holsters on either side. Major Breen followed him, holding an M9 service pistol.

"Bury them?" Rivette whispered, indicating the parachutes when the three men were together.

"Quicker to sink them in the river," Williams said, remembering his training. He stood, looked past the others. "Where's the lieutenant?"

"We haven't seen her," Breen said.

"Or heard her," Rivette said, holding up his radio.

The woman couldn't be far—if they knew which direction to search.

"We looked at the spot where she was supposed to land," Breen said. "Also checked the trees, as far as we could see."

Williams swore but the oath was lost in a gunshot. It was followed by a flurry of bursts. The men looked at one another, then dropped the parachutes and ran toward the sound.

Grace did not carry a gun.

CHAPTER TWENTY-ONE

Rio Claro–Mayaro Region, Trinidad
July 23, 6:19 a.m.

Situated between dense stretches of trees, and flowing into the Atlantic Ocean, the Navet River provided easy access to the Nariva Windbelt Reserve—which was comprised significantly of swamp—the Bush Bush Forest Reserve, Macaw Island, and Omega Island. It was a short but convenient route for smugglers and sightseers alike and, without exception, the gun and drug runners and the tour guides let one another be. At times, the latter provided cover by steering occasional law enforcement efforts in a wrong direction. It was, lamented one politician, a perfect sociopolitical ecosystem.

The eastern end of the waterway was just beginning to reflect the first red of dawn when the twin 250hp Yamaha 4 strokes chugged to silence and the thirty-two-foot sports fishing boat settled in twelve meters from shore. The shallow waters there would not accommodate the vessel, so the cargo would have to be offloaded by hand. Two men stood under the rigid central canopy with three bales of opium; a third man was crouched in the bow, a Czech VZ-58 assault rifle in his hands. The men had been traveling without lights, the engines throttled down to make their approach as silent as possible.

From two hundred feet up, Lieutenant Grace Lee had seen a slight shine from the chrome fittings that surrounded the boat. And if she could see them, chances were good, if they looked up, they would see her canopy blotting an increasing circle of sky. The boat was practically on silent running. She assumed the silence was tactical and, as such, suggested something illegal.

As she saw it, there were two options. Before spotting the silver rim, she had picked out an open spot on the shore, one she could easily hit. But if the boat had not seen her by then, it would certainly hear her come down. If these people were smugglers, they would assume she was not simply a skydiving enthusiast and would cut her down. Even if she had a gun, saddled by the canopy, she would be an open target.

It would be better, she felt, to land on the boat. The question was where. It was still too dark to see anything but the outline. All she could assume, from the size, was that it did not hold more than four or five crewmembers.

She guessed there would be a standing shelter in the center and headed for that. The rising sun finally showed her more detail and she made a last-second adjustment to land square in the center of the covering. There was an armed man up front; she would need some protection as quickly as possible.

Popping the release right before she touched down, Grace sure-footedly planted the landing and hunkered into it, crouching to keep her balance and also to let the canopy drift backward, away from her. The thump of her feet and the ghostly shroud drew the immediate attention of the crew—voices below her and one from the bow.

Whoever was on point would have a weapon, probably an automatic or semiautomatic. She pivoted and went to the back of the roofing, watching her footing on a surface slick from sea mist. Drawing an eight-inch blade with each hand, she jumped to the deck and turned toward the wheelhouse.

There were two men at the controls, with a stack of bales between them. The man on the right, at the controls, was not her immediate concern; the man on the left, who was drawing a gun, was.

Grace ducked behind the bales as the man fired a single shot. Birds screeched and took to the air up and down the shore. Crouching again, hugging the side of the cargo, Grace cut the tendon of the pilot's left knee and he went down with a shriek. The man on the left turned and fired at the empty air. When the empty chamber clicked, she rose and, with a powerful underhand toss, flung the unbloodied blade into his sunlit chest. She ducked just in time to avoid a blasting discharge from the assault rifle. The windshield exploded, covering her with glass, but not before she had spotted what she hoped was the throttle. Still low, she jumped forward and rammed it up. The boat surged ahead, the gunman was thrown onto his back and, using the injured pilot as a stepping-stone, Grace ducked and leaped through the shattered window. She half-ran, half-skid on the slippery surface, reaching the gunman before he could recover. She stabbed his left shoulder to the deck and wrapped her right fingers around the hand holding the gun. She snapped his wrist back and easily wrenched the weapon from his grip.

The rest of the team arrived then, Williams and Breen splashing through the riverbank, Rivette covering them from the shore. While Grace searched both men for small arms, the two older men pulled themselves aboard. After looking up and down the shore, Rivette joined them. As he came on deck he saw Grace's canopy spiral slowly toward the bay.

"No point going back to sink our chutes," the young man remarked.

Williams wasn't immediately concerned about the chutes. The gunfire would have been heard for a considerable distance. Anyone else on the river might come to investigate.

"I'm going to turn back to sea," Williams told Breen. "We're less likely to run into hostiles out in the open."

Breen nodded. "I'll see to the crew."

Breen followed Williams to the control area and, with Rivette's help, pulled the injured man toward the stern. He was trembling uncontrollably, his nerves in revolt, and each breath was a tiny scream. He reminded Rivette of a gull he'd once seen fly into a window and half-snap its neck. The lance corporal found a tool kit with bandages, scissors, antiseptic, and aspirin and brought it to the major. He cut away the man's pants leg and did his best to patch the wound Grace had inflicted. Williams was still wearing his helmet and goggles and left them on. He would need the eyewear to protect him from the wind coming through the broken window. He throttled up slightly and as he put the boat in a tight circle, the lance corporal recovered the knife from the chest of the dead man, wiped the blood on the man's shirt, and slipped the point into one of the bales. He withdrew the blade and angled it in the rising sun.

"Looks like opium," he said.

"These three were smugglers for sure," Williams said, "but not necessarily tied to terror."

"I know Caribbeans back in L.A.," Rivette said. "If they're dirty, they're dirty top to bottom. Only way you compete with the Vietnamese, the Russians, the gangs. These guys? Human trafficking yesterday, cocaine today, terrorists tomorrow."

Williams nodded as Rivette left to take lookout at the stern.

The kid was probably right about these three. That notwithstanding, Williams was angry. Maybe Grace did not have a choice; this was certainly not a good spot to have come down. Or maybe she thought, like Rivette, that three criminals in a boat were worth interrogating. That, too, might be true. But the encounter could just as easily have cost the woman her life. It had certainly cost them the option of reconnoitering and choosing their target. Slash and burn was not the way Williams had ever conducted intelligence work.

But Black Wasp is not about "your" way, he reminded himself. As yesterday morning had vividly demonstrated, his way, the old way, might no longer be enough.

Grace Lee was with the gunman in the bow. The man was awake, writhing and moaning. The lieutenant was crouched over him, having ripped of his T-shirt and using her stiff left arm to apply pressure to his wound.

"What's your name?" she asked.

The man shook his head, as if to say he didn't understand. With her free hand, Grace turned on the smartphone she'd found in his pocket while searching for weapons. The device was locked.

Grace switched her left palm for her left foot to push down on the makeshift compress. She grabbed his right wrist and pressed his thumb to the outline on the phone. The screen opened.

"Your emails are in English," she said, putting the phone in a vest pocket. "What's your name or do you bleed to death?"

"Chandak," he said.

"Chandak what?"

"Maharaj."

"Indian. Were you born here?"

He shook his head.

"Tell me, Chandak. Do you have a local doctor here?"

He hesitated.

"You're bleeding out all over the deck," she said. "You need medical care."

"Cocos Bay . . . Medical Outlet . . . Dr. Newallo."

"Good. We'll take you to Dr. Newallo. Meantime, tell me how to contact a leader of Jamaat al-Muslimeen. You transport drugs—you must have transported terrorists."

The man shook his head vigorously. Grace twisted her foot on his shoulder, as if she were crushing a cigarette. The man screamed.

"I . . . just . . . delivery . . . man!"

"All right. Who do you deliver to?"

Major Breen walked up behind her then. The man was shaking his head again. Whatever he thought of what was playing out, he said nothing. Those were the SITCOM rules.

"My partner will bandage your wound and give you whatever painkiller he has," Grace said.

"Opium, as it turns out," Breen said.

"You hear?" Grace said. "You will live long enough to see

Dr. Newallo or you can bleed out here," Grace said. "Your choice. We've got one of your partners in the wheelhouse—it'll be a waste if you die and he talks."

"*They* kill me," the man said vaguely.

"Your fear is a possibility. Death under my foot is a certainty."

"We can give him asylum," Breen remarked.

"How about that?" Grace said. "A ticket out of this place, this life."

"Movement up river!" Rivette shouted.

Breen set down the first-aid tool kit and picked up the assault rifle Chandak had been carrying. Grace thrust the crook of her right thumb and index finger around the throat of the injured man and squeezed. Her Dragon grip cut off the flow of oxygen and blood to his brain and, in five seconds, the young man was unconscious. Moving fast and low, she gathered up and sheathed her knives then joined Major Breen in the back of the boat.

A pair of camouflage-painted speedboats was rapidly approaching along both shorelines, bobbing up and down. They looked like Russian Navy; long prow and a high windshield reflecting the morning light, making it impossible to see how many people were aboard. It did not surprise Williams that either confederates of these three or fellow smugglers would come to investigate. Whether the gunshots signaled a turf war or law enforcement, it would impact the livelihood of every criminal element on the river.

There was an equipment locker to Williams's left. It wasn't locked; either there were boat tools inside or the crew did not expect unwanted guests. He used the toe of his boot to lift it.

"Grace!" he shouted above the roar of his own twin engines.

The lieutenant had been en route to join the others. She turned and ran to the control area. Williams pointed with his forehead. She looked into the locker.

There were boxes of ammunition and two belts with a half-dozen hand grenade pouches bulging on each.

"They're likely to come in shooting," Williams said.

"Won't they want to investigate first?" Grace asked.

Williams cocked his head portside. Grace saw what looked like bobbing white jellyfish. The fishing boat had snagged her parachute, which had blistered with air pockets.

"Understood," she said, shouldering the belts and turning to join the others.

"Hold on!" Williams said suddenly. "Don't go back there."

"Sir?"

"I have an idea."

It wasn't so much an idea as the result of a desperate process of elimination. Ahead, to the south, was the first of two narrow tributaries that he thought they could reach before the boats were beside them. But he had no idea where they led or how soon either of them might narrow even more, and there was no time to check a map. The last thing he wanted was to box them in. He also wasn't sure what advantage he gained by reaching the bay, assuming they could even outrun those sleek, high-performance boats. They were obviously intended to outrun police vessels; this chamber pot was even less seaworthy.

They were going to have to fight—and not a fair fight.

Williams said, "I'm going to make a run at them. What I need from you is one live grenade in each belt, one belt in each boat."

Grace looked at the sharply pointed bow. Then she hefted the belts, one in each hand. "I'd have to stand to reach them both—they'd pick me off for sure." She pointed. "Up there in the nook behind the tow ring—if I squat I can get you one. Then you spin around and then I'll get the other."

"I'll go starboard, to the one on the left," he said.

"Got it," she told him, then ran toward the right side of the bow.

Williams turned to the stern and yelled, "Hold on!"

The men were too close to the growling engines to make out what Williams had yelled, but when they'd turned they saw the lieutenant running to the other end of the ship with the grenade belts.

"He's doing a Barney Oldfield!" Breen said and braced himself on the rail. Rivette did the same.

When the men were secure and Grace was in position, Williams spun the boat around hard. The boat did a sluggish, wobbling one-eighty, coughed twice, then finally gained some traction in the new direction. The turn had come none too soon: the pursuit vessels were less than one hundred yards away.

Gunfire erupted from both speedboats. It peppered the hull and wheelhouse, Williams dropped to his knees, exposing only the top of his head as he held the bottom of the wheel and looked out the shattered windshield. He steered the boat to the south as if he were making for shore. He did not want to appear to be playing chicken; if the target changed course, Grace would not be in position to deliver the belt.

The speedboat was slapping the water, bouncing as it approached. Williams slowed as the boats neared. The greater the vertical separation between the vessels, the tougher it would be for Grace to time the throw. With the amount of gunfire the target vessel was spraying at them, Williams began considering an abort scenario: instead of swinging toward the speedboat he would swing toward shore, abandon ship, and return fire from behind it. The target was fifty feet and closing. He had seconds to decide—

Gunfire erupted to Williams's left, from the port side of the fishing boat. Major Breen was bent low and moving forward, firing the Czech assault rifle at the speedboat. Breen had figured out enough of the plan to realize that Grace could use some cover fire. The men on the speedboat ducked just as the vessels were about to pass. Grace was crouched like a leopard, peeking above the tow ring, ready—

She pulled one pin, swung the belt over her head, and rose. Directly opposite her, one of the men in the speedboat did likewise, his semiautomatic pointed at her head. A single shot popped on the port side of the fishing boat, to Williams's right. Rivette watched as the man in the speedboat flew backward, his chest spraying red. The grenade belt cut through the air like a bolo, Williams tugged the wheel to the left, and the boat swung past the target. Rivette dropped flat to avoid the return gunfire, which only lasted for a moment; the speedboat was suddenly rocked by a close succession of loud bangs, each of which spewed clouds of charcoal-gray smoke over the deck. There were shouts and cries of pain but no further gunfire.

Williams rose while there was a break in the shooting. "I'm going for the other one!" he shouted to the team as he swung the boat around.

The fishing boat took another tortured U-turn. The stricken speedboat had swung off to the south, idling. The other had tracked the enemy vessel, making its own tight turn so the two boats were facing each other. The speedboat charged in a serpentine pattern, making it difficult to pull up beside them—while the fishing boat was a big, slower target.

Rivette and Breen both ran to Grace's side.

"Hull's probably resin-coated fiberglass," the major told the lance corporal. "Kill it."

Squatting behind the rail, in the blood of the smuggler, both men opened fire. Big, black holes appeared near the waterline; every turn, every dip of the speedboat caused it to take on water and veer, slowing it and preventing the crew from returning fire. The passengers were thrown as the speedboat turned sideways and the pilot tried to right the course; Rivette simultaneously set down his Heckler & Koch MP and unholstered his Beretta M9. A moment later the man at the wheel crumpled. The other three passengers jumped into the water and swam for shore. With leisurely precision, Williams was able to pull along the starboard side of the speedboat. Grace did not bother wasting the grenade belt on the empty, twisting vessel.

"Let 'em go," Breen said.

"Why?" Grace asked as Williams sped downriver.

"They're unarmed," Breen replied.

"They tried to kill us!" Grace said as the three men flailed toward a sandbar.

"And failed," Breen said. "Let's take the victory and get back on-mission."

"Jaz?" Grace said urgently to the lance corporal.

Rivette was still for a moment. Then he shook his head once. "Not in the back. Can't."

"They'll spread the alarm," she said. "They know our boat!"

"Anyone within a mile in any direction heard what happened here," Breen said. "The boat can be an asset."

"How?" Rivette asked.

"We abandon it on the coast, move inland. Draws them in, buys us time."

"How much time?" Grace asked. "Minutes?"

"It will take them longer than that to off-load the drugs and hide them," Breen said. "Someone's going to pay a lot to get them back."

The lieutenant shook her head. "We'll see them again," she said as the men reached the shore, out of range, and scattered. She kept any further thoughts to herself as she turned to their wounded passengers. Rivette followed. Breen headed toward the badly splintered wheelhouse.

Williams had spread the paper map on the console, got his bearings, then looked out at the river. Rich with the smell of moss and mud, he would not say this was a particularly attractive region, but it definitely had local character. It struck him that for the first time since they landed he was not on a combat footing.

Williams watched the major as he approached. Williams had just witnessed something he had never seen during his military career: a fully improvised assault. There had always been impulsive, necessary, individual acts of heroism under fire. But never anything free-form, on this scale. And never anything this effective.

"Good call back there," Williams said when the major arrived.

"I don't know," Breen said. "She may have been right."

"Sometimes you have to err on the side of charity," Williams told him. "Ever think you were assigned to this group as the conscience in the room?"

"Not as such," Breen admitted. "Maturity, maybe."

"Not a huge difference," Williams said. "I worked on a policy paper years ago with the ambitious title of 'Prevention Over Reparation: Training in Personal Restraint and Limitations.' Warriors by nature have little devils on their shoulders. They need the angels whispering in their ears."

Breen considered that. "Maybe. General Lovett sold me on being a biometrics and battlefield analyst."

"That's a new one to me."

"Basically, crime scene investigator on the go," the major said. "That was my SITCOM. It was between me with crime scene training and someone in the Fourth Combat Camera Squadron who found all sixty-five differences between two digital photographs. I didn't win because of my moral compass. I won because I'm an analog operator in a digital world."

Williams chuckled at that.

"Before I agreed to join the Wasps, I talked with General Lovett about my own experiences with select troops," Breen said, cocking his head toward Rivette and Grace. "We train our warriors to fight but not how to dial it down. Then we put them on trial for any excesses of zeal or cracking under the strain."

"I was just thinking that about myself," Williams admitted.

"Then again, this is not a business where you can afford to be sloppy."

"You have a personal reason for going after Salehi," Breen said.

"I do," Williams said. But that was all he said. With every minute that passed he felt a familiar old Chase Williams emerging—the man who did not react to events but ordered them. He did not want to revisit that interim bureaucrat. Not now. "By the way, you were also right about the boat," Williams said as the mouth of the river came into view. "We're going to have to abandon it. We're almost out of fuel."

Breen looked at the bales. "These guys were likely going to off-load the cargo and fuel up. That's where the others probably were—local depot."

"Makes sense. Map shows the clinic just within range of the fuel we've got left."

Breen turned his mind back on the operation. "So we're going to see the doctor?"

"Seems like the best bet for one-stop shopping about the terrorist infrastructure," Williams said.

Breen nodded and looked toward the stern. "I'll let the others know."

The major left and Williams steered back toward the bay. As innovative as Black Wasp was, the commander could not help but reflect on the fundamental rules of engagement that guided every division of the United States military. Though it benefited the enemy not to be murdered in retreat or after surrender, there was a saying Anne Sullivan had quoted more than once in emotionally charged crises—most recently after the death of Op-Center's international crisis manager, Hector Rodriquez, in Mosul.

"'Become what you behold at the peril of your soul.'"

Mercy was not about sparing the life of a foe. It was about avoiding an act, a moment, that could turn your own life into a godless nightmare.

CHAPTER TWENTY-TWO

Diego Martin, Trinidad
July 23, 6:49 a.m.

Having slept well for the first time in weeks, Captain Salehi was taking breakfast on the terrace. There was a well-stocked kitchen and a bathroom with a full and sophisticated selection of drugs, surgical supplies, and bandages. Added to the arms, these people were equipped for a siege.

As he sat there, Salehi was suddenly aware of his hosts talking agitatedly in the living room. He had no idea what they were saying, though they were talking over one another and gesturing with more animation than he had seen since his arrival.

It was still several hours until his scheduled departure and Salehi was suddenly concerned that something had gone wrong. He got up and went to see what the commotion was about.

Nik started to explain, then stopped. He grabbed a tablet, brought up a map of Trinidad, zoomed in on the river and then on a spot close to the bay. He dropped it on the sofa, held up both hands in the shape of guns, and made repeated firing motions.

There was a shootout. Salehi pointed to himself and looked at the men questioningly. They both shrugged.

Uncertainty was not good enough. He went to an end table where there was a Kalashnikov pistol. He picked it up, tucked it in his belt before either of the men could stop him. He raised his hands as they came toward him.

"To protect me," he said, then pointed at himself. He pointed at the others in turn, shook his head. "I won't hurt anyone."

They seemed to understand and backed down.

The two started talking among themselves again, and one looked at his watch. They were obviously trying to figure out what they were going to do to secure Salehi for the next four or so hours. More men seemed to be the answer, since one of them started scrolling through numbers on his smartphone and preparing a group text.

Once again, the captain questioned the wisdom of having come here. It wasn't that he did not trust Sadi. The captain was accustomed to dealing with individuals who operated well outside international law. He found them more trustworthy, as a rule, than people who worked for armies and governments. If they were not as good as their word, they did not survive in business; often, they did not survive at all. The problem, for Salehi, a man accustomed to the open sea, was that he had gone from being mobile to being sequestered. On the *Nardis*, if he did not like the speed or direction of something on radar, if he had a feeling that there was danger on the horizon—he changed course. He could not do that here.

The other men had continued texting. There were answers; some drew snarls of displeasure, a few nods. Salehi tapped one of them on the arm and made a walking gesture with two fingers.

"Stairs?" he asked, then jabbed his finger repeatedly over his head. "Roof?"

Vincent nodded and motioned him to the front door. He obviously trusted their guest now that he had spoken to Sadi. The man held up a hand for the captain to wait, then checked a series of security monitors on the wall of a hallway that led to the kitchen. Salehi had not noticed them before now. He wondered what the neighbors, if any, must think of what went on up here.

The man ran his eyes along the screens, then picked up a shoulder bag that concealed a semiautomatic and cracked the door. He looked out, then stepped into the corridor and indicated for Salehi to follow him. As they did, a door ahead of them opened and a statuesque young Caribbean stepped into the hall. She was wearing a terrycloth robe and greeted the two men as they passed. The room behind her was dark but Salehi could see a man standing inside. That answered his question about the other residents. This floor, if not the entire building, was replete with illicit activity. This woman was probably the mistress of one or more government officials or businessmen. It distressed Salehi that men like this had nothing better to do. It made him think that patriotism was only a part of the equation, that perhaps Sharia law was something he should support with greater enthusiasm. The captain did not allow his own urges and needs to interfere with his work. He had seen, in others, how relationships sapped time and energy, how secrets were seduced from careless men, how focus was lost and never fully recovered. He could not live like that. His vision, his ambition, his sense of dignity transcended petty moments of relief or distraction.

Salehi was happily distracted when they reached a stairwell. *This* was his life. Finding active solutions to problems.

He looked down, counted eight flights of concrete stairs.

Since the building was only seven stories, the steps probably led to the parking garage. That was good to know. He was more interested, however, in the half-flight above him. If someone were going to come at him, it might be from above—not necessarily down the staircase but onto the terrace.

Easing around his companion—who was either guardian, jailor, or both—Salehi trotted up. There was a landing and a square, cinderblock cupola with an aluminum-plated door. In all likelihood that was not for security but to prevent flooding during storms. The impression was reinforced when he tried the door and it opened easily.

The man behind him said something softly—probably "be careful." Salehi cracked the door and looked out. Hearing nothing except the wind he stepped out and looked around. The roof was covered with flat concrete squares, save for six areas where there were metal drains roughly eight inches in diameter. Except for the building across the way, there was no roof access from adjoining structures. Any approach would have to come from the air, and that would be heard.

Up the stairs or by elevator, he concluded, going back inside. *And enemy operatives would be spotted by the security camera.*

Which left only one possibility. Anyone who tried to take him would have to do so between the garage and the airport.

Going back inside, Salehi communicated to his hosts that he wanted a map of the area and they brought one up on the tablet. He checked the most direct route, the most heavily trafficked. The trip would take just over an hour. But with the volume of traffic, the opportunities for ambush were greater.

He looked at alternative roads. If someone followed him from the building, there were numerous lights and stops where he could be shot or taken.

The Trinidadian sought, by gestures, to assure him that everything would be all right. That did little to assuage one of the most hunted men on the planet, with a face that was on every news site.

And then, looking around, it occurred to him that he might not have to risk the worst-case scenarios he had been considering. With hand motions, he told his companion what he was thinking.

Vincent smiled broadly and flashed an OK sign.

Now, all I have to do is survive until then, he thought.

CHAPTER TWENTY-THREE

Cocos Bay, Trinidad
July 23, 7:08 a.m.

"Good call on the hull, sir," Rivette said as Breen walked over. "And you weren't even the guy raised in a marina."

"Once had to investigate Combatant Craft Assault stealth boats," he said affably. "You pick things up."

"Oh yeah, like who the hell is Barney Oldfield?"

Breen smiled. "An old-time race car driver. Real daredevil."

"I gotta look him up," the lance corporal said.

The major walked over to Grace, who was squatting beside the man whose leg she'd cut. The other crewman was unconscious.

"We're headed to the clinic," Breen said. "Anything here?"

"He's pleading with me to leave him *and* the cargo on the boat," she said. "He said they'd all be killed if it's lost." She squinted up into the sunlight at Breen. "What's your take on that?"

"He'll be safer with us," Breen said, more to the injured man than to Grace. "Word gets around about salvage, the pirates out here will descend like ants on sugar."

"No!" the man said, nearly weeping. "Please, no. Please."

Breen squatted beside Grace. "What's your name?" he asked the crewman.

"King," he said. "Kingston."

"King, if you work with us, I promise to get you safely away from here. If you want, you can have a new life somewhere else."

The man shook his head. "I have my mother—she is alone."

"You can send for her," the major said. "We'll help get her out."

"No, I . . . I can still work with one leg. Please!"

Grace was glaring down at the man. The tension in her face suggested that she was losing patience.

"King, that's a bad call," Breen said. "Please . . . work with us."

The man shook his head. "They kill us both."

Grace drew one of her knives and put it hard against the man's throat, drawing blood. "*I'll* kill you right now," she said. "One last time, King. Where do we find Jamaat al-Muslimeen?"

"I do not know them!" he cried.

"I don't believe you," she said. "Maybe *you* are one? Maybe I should just kill you and move on?"

"*No, no!* I tell you truthfully! People come in on boats, we take them to docks upstream—back and forth, back and forth. I pilot! That's all I do!"

The boat, which had been traveling east, made a graceful turn to the south. The air no longer smelled rank and the boat picked up a little speed thanks to the currents.

"Grace, I've heard scared gang members interrogated on the docks," Rivette said. "I believe him. Look—he's wettin' himself."

The lieutenant looked. Rivette was right. With a huff of disgust, she sheathed her weapon, stood, and walked to the bow. She drew deeply of the cleaner air, felt the sunlight enrich her.

If I had not followed my instincts, we would be trudging through a swamp, she thought. Now, her instincts were apparently no longer reliable.

Her training taught her to be like air or water, constantly moving. One of her *sifus*, Master Pai, had once told her, "*Nature doesn't struggle. If you are struggling, something has already gone wrong.*" Something was definitely wrong here; this was not what she had signed on for. The two older men were effectively running the mission. She had made her call during the drop, had aggressively interrogated the one crewmember. Then, as soon as Williams and Breen arrived, her views were marginalized.

But that's not all if it, she told herself.

In the kung fu schools she had attended, Grace had been taught to respect absolutely her elders, their experience, their seniority. All of them had been men, albeit Chinese men, but it wasn't that. She had carried that deference into her military career—again, most of her superiors were men—and they had been a perfect fit. Now that she was in the field, her skills as a fighter and her submission to Williams and Breen were in conflict. She felt that her instincts were perfectly suited to the free-form nature of the Black Wasps, of this mission.

These two men keep jerking back into traditional special ops procedure, she thought. And Rivette was caught somewhere in the middle. That didn't surprise her; Major Breen had been a father figure since the day they all met. The result was that she felt marginalized, not being true to her own nature or to the nature of Black Wasp.

It is an experiment, she reminded herself. When you get home you can say all of this in the debrief.

There were a series of structures ahead and, calmer now, she returned to the others.

The clinic was a small, two-story structure that sat partially on pilings on the south side of the bay. It looked like it had been built from a home design adapted to this other use. From the shine on the siding, it appeared to be new construction that had not yet endured extended exposure to the elements. The facility was accessible by a winding secondary road or by the sea—something Williams felt made it ideal for the kind of illicit trade this crew had represented.

It was still early and there was no obvious activity as yet.

"Second floor looks residential," Breen said. He was standing beside Williams and looking through a pair of collapsible binoculars. The other team members were with the prisoners. "Drapes not opaque like downstairs . . . shell collection on one sill. Hanging plant in one window. No movement anywhere inside."

"I see an ambulance in the driveway," Williams said.

"Probably to take emergency cases to local hospitals," Breen said. "This place doesn't look like it's equipped for major surgery—don't see where they'd fit an OR or recovery room."

"Strictly local, emergency trade, I'm guessing," Williams said. That, too, fit the profile of smugglers and possible human trafficking. People who had been stuffed in ships or sealed vans would certainly need at least superficial medical care.

There was a new and efficient wharf that lead to the back door. It was difficult to see because it sat under a patio that extended outward from the pilings and looked out on the sea. He suspected that was part of the intention of the design. Williams steered toward the floating wooden dock.

"We just going to knock?" Breen said.

"Probably the best approach."

"Whoever answers will probably know the boat. They may have heard the shots."

"I'm counting on both," Williams said and turned toward Grace Lee. "Lieutenant?"

The young woman rose and jogged forward. Whatever frustration she felt earlier seemed to have dissipated. She stopped beside Breen, facing Williams.

"Commander?"

"What do you think about ringing the doorbell and telling whoever answers that we have a patient?" Williams asked. "We go in, ask questions."

"I'm fine with that," she said, but added, "You do realize these jumpsuits are not standard local wear."

"I know. That's why we'll have Rivette go-with. Threat analysis all his. If everything's good, we'll bring the men up."

"If they don't let us in?"

Williams said, "Then it's your move."

Grace did not have to think about it. She nodded.

The lance corporal was at the stern, watching for any sign of pursuit. Breen ran back and replaced him, sent him forward, and Williams told him what they were planning. Rivette did not have to be asked to go ashore and watch her back.

It was a bumpy mooring, but then Williams had not been to sea for years. The irony was not lost on him that the man they sought shared his former vocation. He hadn't thought of the Iranian since they'd jumped. The events of the day before came back with a wave of rage.

Not now, he told himself. *You have people in the field.*

Rivette tossed a rope over the mooring and followed Grace over the rail. Though Williams had hit the wharf loud enough to have drawn someone's attention, he did not detect any movement in the windows.

It had been a very long time since his heart beat as rapidly as it did now.

Grace and Rivette crossed the dock. Right before they vanished under the patio, the lance corporal unholstered his Beretta and held it in the small of his back. He did not look around, he listened around: except for a few seabirds and a dog well in the distance, there were no sounds.

The lieutenant pressed the buzzer. They heard a scraping sound and exchanged puzzled looks. Rivette touched Grace's arm, moved her slightly to one side so he'd have a clear shot if he needed one. The door opened wide and a young woman looked out. The scraping sound had been the wheelchair in which she was seated.

"Dr. Newallo?" Grace asked.

"I am she," the woman said pleasantly. She looked to be in her late twenties, with a narrow, high-cheekboned face and her black hair drawn into a low bun. She was pulling on a waist-length lab coat and did not seem surprised by the attire of the callers.

"We . . . we have injured crewmen," she said. "Stab wound to the chest, cut tendon in the leg."

"No bullet wounds?"

"No," Grace said.

"Bring them in," Dr. Newallo told her with a trace of surprise but without hesitation. "Do you require a stretcher?"

"I don't think so."

The woman wheeled away but left the door open.

Grace turned toward the boat and motioned to Williams and Breen. The crewman Grace had stabbed in the chest was tightly wrapped with bandages and they brought him first, placing him on a low table in an examination room. The doctor wheeled over, slipped on a pair of gloves, adjusted an overhead light, and began cutting away the bandages.

Rivette, Breen, and Williams remained in the waiting room. Grace followed the doctor.

"Doctor, while you do that, I'd like to talk to you," Grace said.

"Go ahead," Dr. Newallo said without looking up from her work.

"I want to know if you treat members of Jamaat al-Muslimeen."

"Who is asking?" the doctor replied.

"I'm looking for the man responsible for the terror attack in New York yesterday," Grace said. "We believe he may be here."

The doctor tossed the bloody bandages in the trash. She wet a cloth with a sterile solution and dabbed at the wound, wiping away the blood. She moved the light again and peered into the cut.

"I do not ask the political affiliation of my patients," she replied, "or inquire as to their livelihoods. Those few who pay for care—and, yes, pay well—support the free medical treatment

I am able to give the rest of this poor community. Such was not available to me when I was a child and run over by an automobile."

"I understand," Grace said. "The man I seek killed seventeen people and injured many more. He had JAM accomplices who murdered a man and his family in Montreal."

"I have heard these reports and have seen a photograph on the computer. I do not know this man." She stole a look at Grace—at Grace's hips. "You did this to my patient?"

The lieutenant nodded.

"So you have injured people as well," Dr. Newallo said. She turned back to her patient. "He has lost a good deal of blood but you missed his lung."

"I know," Grace replied.

The doctor wheeled to her medicine cabinet and removed a squat bottle and a hypodermic. She administered a local anesthetic. "I cannot help you," the doctor said.

Despite a vent blowing cool air, Grace felt warm. "All I'm asking is an address."

"You should try the newspaper office," the doctor replied.

Grace felt helpless and did not like it. "Is your computer locked?"

"It is."

She did not ask for the password, nor did she consider trying to force the woman to give it to her. Grace was about to find the doctor's office, see if there were any paper files, when Williams stepped up behind her.

"Let's go," he said. "We don't need to trouble Dr. Newallo any further."

"Meaning what?" the lieutenant asked.

"We found another way."

Grace exhaled loudly and walked around him. The other two men were not in the waiting room.

"What's going on?" she asked Williams.

"Come with me," he replied as they headed toward the front door.

CHAPTER TWENTY-FOUR

McMark Residence, Washington, D.C.
July 23, 6:33 a.m.

Four months ago, Matt Berry had purchased the row house con-
dominium on P Street NW for cash. It wasn't his cash; it belonged
to the Defense Logistics Agency and, technically, so did the residence. But it would have taken a DLA–White House insider to
trace the funds; apart from President Midkiff, Berry was the only
one of those. The purchase had not been illegal. It had simply been
a lend-lease element of Berry's compensation package that no one
would ever find out about.

Berry slept well when it came to what he called "sleights of
funding" like this. In fact, he slept well most days. Tonight, however, had been an exception.

He woke shortly after five to check the latest report from
Elgin AFB, and he followed the copilot's updates until Williams
and the Black Wasp team went out the door of the F27. There was
nothing after that; no calls or texts from Williams. None of the
others would have contacted anyone; except for recruiting and
training, neither General Lovett nor anyone else at the DoD was

to receive reports from the independent team. That was as much cover-your-ass as security: if something went wrong, no one wanted this on the welcome mat. There was also no danger of the messages being intercepted. They would come directly to Berry's secure international device from Williams's own SID, which, unless he tried transmitting from a seabed or deep valley, were the most reliable communications technologies to come out of the Defense Advanced Research Projects Agency since the internet.

But there was, over his morning double espresso, an alert from January Dow's office at State:

6:57 a.m., Atlantic Standard Time, Rio Claro-Mayaro Region, Trinidad:

Special Anticrime Unit of Trinidad and Tobago (SAUTT) of the Ministry of National Security has received confirmed reports of extended criminal action at the mouth of the Navet River, Cocos Bay. Seaark Dauntless 40 Class WPB, CG 121, dispatched 6:55. No stated link to JAM activity. Satellite report at 7:11.

Katie Stahl, Deputy Director of Open Source Intelligence

INR Office of Analysis for Terrorism, Narcotics and Crime

Berry touched the screen of his tablet to check the map of the Black Wasp drop zone, just to make sure.

"Yep," he said, with a sudden chill that a second double

espresso could not chase. That was where the team was supposed to land.

He checked his SID; saw nothing from Williams. Berry considered texting him but did not want him distracted.

If he was still at large and alive.

The DCS began to wonder if pouncing on Williams's guilt had been fair to the man, if a hastily conceived, hastily executed mash-up like this had not only been reckless but exploitative. It wasn't as if Washington didn't use people countless times a day, every day. Everyone who accepted an assignment like this, Williams included, understood that while success was rewarded, mistakes and the people who committed them got buried. Sometimes figuratively, often literally.

You sent an emotionally wounded sixty-year-old man on a covert operation, and you made it sound like you were doing him a favor, Berry told himself as he looked out the window of the spacious kitchen, watched the rising sunlight bouncing off town houses and signage.

"Ah shit," he said, getting up to shower. "He could have declined."

Berry shambled off to the bathroom feeling, if not clean inside, clean enough to live with this however it went.

CHAPTER TWENTY-FIVE

Cocos Bay, Trinidad
July 23, 7:37 a.m.

Avinash Scoon opened the bedroom door to find a young black man standing just outside holding a Beretta hip high . . . and pointed at his waist.

The twenty-three-year-old man raised his hands face-high and backed away. He was not unaccustomed to seeing weapons in the clinic, and unsavory men with unhappy expressions. But the man in the hall was different. He seemed, somehow—and perhaps it was just the morning light—in an odd way almost saintly.

An older man stepped from behind the man in the corridor. Even though he wasn't armed, and positioned himself between Avinash and the gun, he did not seem so kindly.

Hamilton Breen looked around the second-floor room he had seen from the boat. The draperies had suggested that Dr. Newallo did not live here alone and that proved to be the case. An English-language newspaper on the man's nightstand suggested that communication would not be a problem.

"I have very little time," Breen told the man. "We are looking for members of Jamaat al-Muslimeen here on the island. Where are they?"

The man shook his head. "I don't know. Americans? I like Americans very much!"

Breen dismissed the remark with a wave of his hand and pointed to a dresser where there were car keys. "You drive the ambulance, yes?"

"I . . . I drive Dr. Newallo," he said—apparently hoping to appeal to the man's sense of charity. He did only good and charitable deeds.

Breen considered this. "Of course. That makes sense. Even better. You make regular runs to different places?"

The man nodded.

"The ambulance has a GPS?"

The man nodded again.

"With cached routes?"

The man hesitated.

"With cached routes?" Breen repeated more forcefully, stepping from between the driver and Rivette.

"Yes, yes," the man said.

"Password?"

The man shook his head.

Breen collected the keys, held the ring in front of the man. Avinash did not have to ask what to do. He pointed out the ignition key. Breen removed it from the ring and threw the rest on the bed.

"I am leaving one of my people behind, on the boat outside," Breen lied. "If you alert the authorities, you will die. Understood?"

The man nodded vigorously. "I have no . . . no . . ."

"Favorites, other than the doctor," Breen said as they turned to go. "Behave and she lives, too."

The man gave an even more enthusiastic, even grateful nod. "I . . . I filled the tank last night, sirs!" he said.

Breen thanked him and shut the door.

Williams had been waiting at the foot of the stairs. Upon getting a thumbs-up from Breen, he hurried to collect Lieutenant Lee.

"Where are we going?" she asked as they hurried out the front door.

Williams did not answer until he was sure they were out of earshot of the operating room.

"Inland," he said. "We'll know more when we're moving."

"What about the other crewman?" she asked as they hustled to the ambulance.

"We left him with his drugs," Williams told her. "We don't want to have these people pursuing a vendetta against us."

Grace shot a look at Breen who was coming up behind them. His expression was as neutral as ever, though the phrase "moral ambiguity" popped into Grace's head.

Okay to kill users, not sellers, she thought bitterly.

The team went to the ambulance, Grace and Rivette in back on high alert, Williams driving. The major did not have a lot of experience with technology, but it was more than Williams possessed.

Williams used his own smartphone GPS to plot a course while Breen investigated the device fixed to the dashboard. He scrolled through the archives, comparing it to the paper map of Trinidad.

The swamp was to the south, stretching well inland; the coastline stretched north, where police or smugglers' boats might be watching for anything out of the ordinary; so Williams headed northwest, toward the cities of Sangre Grande—the largest town in this region—Arouca, and Port of Spain. The entire run was just under twenty-eight miles. It actually helped to be driving on the left side of the ride, opposite what Williams was accustomed to; it forced him to be present every moment.

"There are a lot of random trips in here," Breen said, "and only one with repeat visits."

"Where?"

"Port of Spain," he said. "Diego Martin section . . . cul-de-sac called Ajax off Wrightson."

"Street number?"

"Seven," Breen said. "If we engage, it'll take us there."

"Do it," Williams said, closing his own GPS and accelerating as a pair of police cars passed them, racing in the direction from which they'd come. "The clinic?" Williams asked.

Breen watched them from the side mirror to make sure they did not turn. "No," he said. "Nearest police station is eight-point-three miles northeast," he said, checking the GPS. "Even if Avinash called, the timing would be tight. My guess is they picked up chatter about the opium. I hope they're going to seize it."

Williams said nothing. Based on his airplane reading, Trinidad was a major hub for narcotics bound for West Africa and the United States. Political corruption was widespread and that mindset—and profit—trickled down to law enforcement. One of January's own releases stopped short of calling Trinidad a narco-state, but drugs—and murder—helped to drive the local economy.

"Did we screw up leaving those crewmen alive?" Williams asked.

"They'll have found the chutes by now and will tell the same story," Breen said. "Four commandos in their midst. There's no additional damage there."

Williams was not consoled by that and, feeling somewhat shielded by the rush for the big-money cargo, flipped on the siren and hurried toward Diego Martin.

CHAPTER TWENTY-SIX

Diego Martin, Port of Spain, Trinidad
July 23, 8:20 a.m.

The two men in white T-shirts and green running shorts were listening to the police radio and receiving texts from JAM personnel embedded in the smugglers' operations. It was a synergistic relationship, Salehi knew; the terrorists received cover in officially "tolerated" trade and the traffickers were well paid for that cover and for information.

There had been no JAM personnel in the skirmish that morning, but agents were heavily involved now. No one knew who was hidden at the condo but they knew, from the news, that their people had been involved with the hits in Montreal. It didn't take a large, imaginative leap to figure out who the parachutists were after.

Sitting in an armchair facing the door, the gun in his lap, Salehi followed the events by watching his companions and the numbers of additional men who arrived since they sent out the call. The new arrivals were respectful nearly to the point of obsequiousness to have news-making royalty in their midst. Salehi found it embarrassing and dangerous. All it would take was one overzealous idiot to snap a photo of him and text it to a girlfriend to show how important he was. That had obviously occurred to his hosts as well, as they belatedly collected smartphones and put them in a chest beside the coffee table—a chest with sufficient ammunition clips to fight a small army.

Still, Salehi wanted to get out, to make his own moves and choices. That was how he had lived his life. This was a prison. He looked at his watch. Sadi had told him he would depart late-morning. Just ten minutes before he had managed to inquire about timing, he was informed that the jet was due in about two hours.

Inshallah, he thought as he paced the increasingly confined space. There were now seven other men in the apartment, all of them having selected weapons from the cache. Most of them were dressed in what looked like current, casual fashion including loud T-shirts, new footwear, bracelets, and earrings. Here, terror apparently paid well.

That was when Vincent received a text that caused him to say an English word Salehi was beginning to recognize: "Shit."

The others had not been talking loudly but now everyone fell silent. The message was from someone they apparently knew. Someone named Avinash. And there was suddenly a great deal of agitation.

Vincent and Nik sent two men, in pairs, out the door. He pointed up to one group, down to another. Roof and lobby, Salehi surmised. The three remaining men took up positions inside: Nik on the terrace, Vincent with Salehi, the last man by the door.

By movement and sound, Vincent indicated that a vehicle with a siren was coming. And then, making a gun with his thumb and index finger, said one word that even Salehi understood:

"Americans."

CHAPTER TWENTY-SEVEN

Diego Martin, Port of Spain, Trinidad
July 23, 8:43 a.m.

The Black Wasp team reached Diego Martin unmolested. Williams extended a gloved hand and found the switch for the siren under the dashboard. He killed it and slowed. He followed the instructions of the GPS to Ajax but stopped before making the turn. He looked up 7 Ajax on the street-view map; it was the only large structure on the street.

"An apartment," he said.

"Almost certainly not ground floor, if it's a safe house," Breen observed. "And if Salehi's there, every possible access point will be covered."

Breen half-turned and opened the sliding panel that separated the cab from the back of the ambulance.

Rivette peered through. "Why've we stopped?"

"We're down the block from the target," Breen told him. "Didn't want to talk strategy without you two."

Williams hadn't been waiting for them; he'd been thinking. "If Salehi's there," he said, "the question is what do they plan to do next? They can't keep him indefinitely. This isn't something that the U.S. would just lose interest in."

"No, and they have to be thinking of the bin Laden raid," Breen said. "That was a guarded complex, too."

"Question is, do we go in or wait till they come out?"

"Why waste an opportunity?" Grace asked. "There's no guarantee one way will be safer than the other."

"If we split up, we get two shots at him," Rivette said.

While that hung in the air, Williams said, "The other question is, if he's there, what do we do with him?"

"You know where I stand," Breen said.

"Yes, and a trial would put a lot of our enemies in Iran and elsewhere squarely in the crosshairs," Williams agreed. "But the diplomatic wrangling between Tehran and Washington would be a major distraction."

"Not our problem," Breen pointed out.

"I would also have to arrange for transport out of here if we're seriously considering an extraction," Williams said.

"Lieutenant?" Breen asked.

"Dead," she said. "He killed, he dies."

"I'm on that page, too," Rivette said. "This ain't some guy floundering in the swamp. This is a terrorist who attacked our homeland and killed our citizens."

The four fell silent.

"There are still a lot of 'ifs' between then and now," Williams said. "We should consider asking the Fourth Fleet for surveillance, eavesdropping."

"That process can take hours," Breen said. "If he's there, he could run. And we *are* riding in a stolen vehicle."

"Commander, we are a covert *attack* team," Grace said. "This is what we trained for."

This was the first whiff of cold feet that Breen had gotten from the man. It gave him a hint of what may have gone down between them: Williams may have been worried about casualties, but he did not want Salehi to get away . . . again?

"We won't be able to pass as pizza delivery guys dressed like this," Rivette said. "We just go in?"

"Works for me," Grace said.

Breen just nodded. Williams wasn't wrong; they had been lucky on the river. An apartment was a very different animal. But Grace was right, too. The team had trained to move with surprise, get in and out with lethal force. If they did it Williams's way, they had no business being here.

"We'll need a getaway driver in case we have to abort . . . or if we get him," Breen said. "Commander?"

Williams nodded at the suggestion. "Let's see if we can park on-site," he said. "Then I'll figure out where we are, let my contact know."

As the ambulance moved, both Rivette and Grace exchanged looks.

They were seated on the floor and the lance corporal scooted over.

"I feel like we lost the heart of the major a little," Rivette said quietly.

"Traditional military rising, settings restored by the commander," she replied. "I always felt that's why they went with you and me at all. The brass *wanted* to shake things up."

"So why the major, then? And why Williams, now?"

"Age and caution aren't bad things," she said. "Not in my world, anyway. But even the major knows that if we're within striking distance of Salehi, we have to go for him."

The ambulance turned and descended a ramp. Grace got on her knees, rapped on the partition.

"Don't stop—but we're getting out here!" she said.

"Affirmative," Breen said, rolling down the window. "I'll let you know what's what."

The two crawled to the back of the ambulance, popped the door, and backed out. The incline caused the door to shut. They hugged the concrete wall and made their way down; Breen remained where he was but crouched lower and drew his handgun. Williams pulled on the bright headlights so it would be difficult to see past the glare, then put his Sig Sauer 9mm in the cup holder between the seats, grip facing up.

The ambulance slowed; Rivette and Grace kept pace with it, the woman in the lead. When it stopped at the end of the ramp, they stopped as well.

Breen said very quietly, "Two men, thirty-odd feet, row of cars between us. Semis on the hips." He looked up. "Security cameras by the door, angled to see most of the interior."

"I got those," Rivette said.

The lieutenant's knives were still sheathed; she stood facing in the same direction as the van, elbows nearly together, tapping into her energetic core, her forearms in a snake posture: hands floating, right hand slightly higher and extended like the head of a water snake.

Williams rolled down the window, called out to the men. "Dr. Newallo to see a patient," he said. "Are you here to take her up?"

Grace was already in motion, running low and hard; if the man called up, they'd be exposed. Rivette was also moving, but only so he could see the cameras. He stopped, legs apart, and took out the cameras with two shots. He jumped back just before the men could fire in his direction.

With the two guards distracted, Grace did not stop behind the cars but dashed between them, her arms moving in front as if they were pulling her along. Standing side by side in front of a door, the men drew their semiautomatics. Grace attacked the guard on the left first, her snake-arm shooting out, wrapping over then under the man's right arm, the arm with the gun. She wrenched up when she was coiled around his arm, causing the gun to point down. At the same time her left arm shot out across his Adam's apple, stiffened, and banked his head back hard against the metal door.

He dropped the gun without firing. His companion, meanwhile, had turned toward Grace; while she had the first man locked up, she kicked out with her right foot and sent his semiautomatic flying from his grip.

Rivette was there to pick it up and put his own weapon under the man's chin.

"Are there any passwords?" he demanded as Grace continued to restrain the first man, slamming his head back any time he moved.

"No, man—nothing!" the second man said.

Rivette pressed harder into the soft tissue under his jaw. "Who are you protecting?"

"Foreign dude, man. I dunno."

Rivette pressed the muzzle even harder. "Who is up there?"

"The guy," the man said. "The Iranian."

"How many guards?"

"Two in the hall . . . three in the room."

"Room number?"

The man hesitated. Rivette kneed his gut, hard.

"Three!" he gasped.

Breen had joined them by now; behind him, Williams was parking the ambulance and looking at the other vehicles.

Rivette pistol-whipped his man unconscious. Grace grabbed a handful of her man's beard and rammed his head hard into the door. His knees went liquid and he dropped.

"I'll take care of them," Williams said, running over.

"We've got to hurry," Grace said. "There may be a radio check."

Rivette and Breen dragged the men from the door and Grace yanked it open. The other two men followed.

CHAPTER TWENTY-EIGHT

Diego Martin, Port of Spain, Trinidad
July 23, 8:55 a.m.

After hearing from Avinash, Vincent Rowley-James lit a cigarette then made a call to the airfield. The United States could very well have sent some crazy SEAL Team Six guys in one or two waves. His own boys were good, many having trained, like himself, in the Philippines. But they would be no match for trained commandos with state-of-the-art weapons.

Ahmed Salehi was more alert than he had been since his arrival, and the Iranian seemed greatly relieved when Vincent communicated that they would be leaving. Vincent strapped a sheath to his arm and slid a hunting knife into it; the blade was serrated on both sides. He pulled on a black vest and selected a semiautomatic pistol from the weapons locker. The letters VRJ were painted in gold on the wood-paneled grip. He slid a pair of additional clips into his vest. Stepping beside him, the captain held his own weapon point up; a professional, not eager to shoot his own teammates by accident.

"Tell the men downstairs to be very, very alert," he told Nik.

"I'm taking our guest and Anthony to the stairs. Join us when you've spoken with them."

Vincent went to the monitors. He saw nothing in the hall, at the stairs, or by the elevator. The only ones out there were his two men, watching both.

"Let's go," he told Anthony, stepping boldly from the apartment. He had found, when hosting VIPs, that it was best to act with assurance; it instilled confidence in others.

The men had only taken a few steps when Nik thrust his head into the hallway.

"They do not answer!" he hissed.

Vincent stopped the others and considered the situation. Whatever the Americans were planning, he only had one real course of action.

"Nik, come with me," Vincent ordered. "You, too, Anthony."

Nik ran out, leaving the door ajar in case they had to fall back in a hurry. Anthony was ahead of him and, with Vincent, they hurried to the stairs where the two others were waiting. The gunmen were grave and attentive. "There may be Americans coming up," Vincent said. "Stop them."

The men acknowledged and cautiously entered the staircase ahead of the others. Vincent hoped he could trust them. He knew them only passingly and he had a saying about many of the hundreds of JAM members who had passed through this building: if they were still alive, their hearts were not in it. Vincent did not exclude himself from that equation, though as a known liaison between local politicians, law enforcement, and service providers—like gunrunners and Dr. Newallo—his superiors rarely let him in the field to fight. His blood racing, and drawing breath between tightly locked teeth, he was primed to do so.

The two lead men took up positions on the landing below, one behind the iron railing, the other pressed to the outer wall so he could see down the stairs. With Vincent in the lead and Anthony behind, Salehi was ushered slowly up the steps. As they ascended Vincent wondered if commandos could have climbed the outside of the building or come down by parachute as they had in the swamp; it wasn't likely but he could not dismiss the possibility and he moved cautiously. As they ascended he was impressed by the cool of the man they protected. The captain was over forty and from what Vincent had seen on the internet Salehi had survived many years in the field. He had escaped after planning and executing a major operation.

With all his heart and spirit, that was the kind of jihadist Vincent Rowley-James wished to be.

The staircase was growing warmer by the moment as the rising sun beat down. All three men were perspiring by the time they reached the door that opened onto the roof. Vincent motioned for the others to stop, placed his ear to the solid metal panel, and listened.

He heard nothing. That was not what he wanted to hear.

Slowly, carefully, Vincent put his left shoulder to the door. Still holding his semiautomatic, he lowered his hand onto the handle and pushed down. He opened the door a crack.

"Let our eyes adjust," he said to Anthony. If there were enemy forces outside he wouldn't have time to squint around picking targets.

Vincent did not realize quite how tense he was until he heard what he had been waiting for. He looked back at the others, a line of sunlight running down the center of each face. Salehi gave him a questioning look and Vincent nodded. The captain allowed himself the faintest smile.

The drumming increased steadily. If anyone was upstairs, the sound would have stopped where it was, somewhere in the distance. It did not.

Vincent waited until the beat was so loud that the door shook. Only then did he open it slowly—just in time to see the Mi-8 twin turbine tour helicopter drop a roll-up ladder from its cabin door.

The three Americans left the fourth-floor landing when they heard activity above; feet shuffling, a door creaking, weapon stocks hitting a belt clasp or button. They did not slow but kept up their steady pace. Grace was in the lead; Breen, in the rear, was shining a pocket flashlight ahead of her, sweeping it back and forth, looking for a tripwire. For all they knew JAM owned the entire building and had rigged it with booby traps. It was a strange thought for Grace to have at that moment, under the circumstances, but her admiration for Williams unexpectedly spiked; she knew without a doubt if something like that happened, the commander would charge up to try and salvage the mission or save his people. That gave her own determination a boost.

Behind her, Rivette was listening. During survival training, General Lovett's team had noted his attention to audio detail; probably a result, the lance corporal thought, of having to survive dark streets at night and heavy-footed gang members in school lavatories.

Rivette was the first to hear the helicopter. He stopped Grace with a tap on her arm and motioned for Breen to wait. A moment later the others heard it, too.

The lance corporal listened, tapped Grace again. She turned. He had detected two overlapping sources of sound: the squeak of new basketball shoes and the rattle of a bracelet. He held up two fingers. Grace nodded. Then he held up seven fingers; she nodded again. The guards were on the seventh floor. She indicated for the men to wait.

Breen frowned. Grace removed a hand grenade from her pocket. Breen stopped frowning. He knew he would have to kill the flashlight anyway, since it would give their position away.

Grace turned ahead and began moving up in the same fluid movement. The men could see her as far as the fifth-floor landing and then she was entirely on her own.

The lieutenant had calculated the height of each set of stairs, used the sixth-floor landing above to ascertain he best place for two men to fire down. She would have to throw the grenade while she was still under the sixth-floor landing in order to remain shielded from gunfire. That meant facing away from the target and making an arcing toss up and over her shoulder.

It wasn't doable. She was going to have to bring them to her.

Rivette and Breen would come running but she would be there to stop them. Pulling the pin, she lay the explosive on one of the steps, swore loudly, and vaulted over the railing to the adjoining staircase from the fourth floor. The wall to her right would

be peppered with shrapnel so she balled herself low and tight
against the rail.

The grenade exploded deafeningly, metal shards gouging the
concrete walls and pinging loudly off the handrail. Smoke filled
the stairwell and she began moaning—while looking down, waiting for the others. They arrived in moments, saw her, understood.
She held her hands up for them to wait.

Footsteps descended on the staircase. There was muted
talk. Rivette eased around Grace. He saw bare legs and color-
ful footwear in the haze. He fired a shot each into different pairs
of shoes. The two men went down, screaming. Two more shots
and they were silent. Rivette motioned to the others.

The explosion and the shots had turned the *whup-whup* of
the helicopter rotors into a dull drone. Grace jumped over the dead
men and ran up a flight. She slowed but did not stop, peered
around the corner of the final set of stairs, and saw the door that
opened onto the roof. She could actually feel the beat of the
rotors here.

"Clear!" she shouted down and went to the door. She waited
until the others arrived before turning the handle and pushing
lightly—

The door didn't budge. There was no lock, no key, nothing
that would seem to prevent it from opening. Breen's flashlight
caught a glint and she looked down. A knife blade was jammed
under the door, point facing in, serrated edges digging into both
the bottom of the door and the rubber wind guard. Rivette hurried to her side and they pushed together. There was a grating
sound; their efforts only seemed to make the serrations dig in more

firmly. The lance corporal studied the door. There was nothing in his arsenal that would punch through the metal.

Grace pushed here and there in quick succession, looking for vulnerable spots—even as the beats of the rotors began to withdraw.

Breen had been looking up at the skylight but it was too high to reach, even if he boosted Rivette.

The lance corporal looked up. "What if we shoot out the glass, toss a grenade?"

"Slopes to the sides," Breen said, pointing. "That's probably where the storm drains are. Blast won't touch them."

Within moments, the sounds from outside told them that the helicopter—and their quarry—was out of reach. Grace elbowed the door hard, not a tactical move but sheer frustration. They had failed by no more than a minute or two.

Breen called Williams with the update.

"They could be going to the airport," Williams said.

"Wherever they're going we'll never catch them," the major said, his voice sullen.

"I'm outside now," Williams said. "Airport is in the direction they're headed."

"Anyone you can call to meet them there?"

"No," Williams replied. "But there's someone who might have a damned effective way of stopping them."

CHAPTER TWENTY-NINE

The White House, Washington, D.C.
July 23, 8:24 a.m.

Matt Berry was relieved to receive the call, distressed to hear Williams's report, and uncertain about what he was suggesting.

His small office was dark in the morning, as much from the sun being on the wrong side as from the wildfires that had to be put out from the night before. Dealing with the hunt for Salehi—which was front-burnered at every intelligence agency in the free world—also devoured a large chunk of time. So far, no one had anything concrete.

Berry was relieved to finally hear from Chase Williams, and what the commander had just told him on their secure line seemed like their best lead . . . but not definitive. Berry was busy typing a message to Darla Price at the National Reconnaissance Office while they spoke.

"No one actually had eyes on the guy?" Berry asked Williams.

"No, but all the arrows pointed in this direction—armed guards, safe house, and some key player was definitely airlifted out of here as we moved in."

"What happened to the guards?"

"Black Wasp happened," he said.

"I'll have a boat for you," he began typing a second text. "You have to vacate. Will let you know where."

"I've got a new vehicle," Williams said. "We'll leave as soon as the others arrive. But I'd rather stay on Salehi until there's no chance of getting him."

"No. I requested eyes on the chopper and Piarco Airport asap," Berry said. "If he's been ferried to an airliner, hopefully we can spot it in time and ID it."

"And then what?" Williams asked.

"See where it goes," Berry said.

"Jesus, he'll go to a hostile nation! No one else would have him!"

"Then we'll pick this up there," Berry said.

"Why not shoot the bastard down?" Williams asked. "No one but Iran would fault us."

"Take down a commercial airliner?" Berry asked.

Williams was silent.

"That's not gonna happen," Berry went on. "You have—*we* have—zero evidence that Salehi was the guy they moved or that he's actually onboard. For all we know this whole thing was staged to take your eye off the ball. The SOB could have gone down an elevator and out through a laundry room or something."

"Hold on," Williams told Berry. "The others are back." He switched the phone to speaker. "Major, is there any chance that Salehi wasn't upstairs?"

"No," Breen told him. "They booked in a hurry, all hands on

deck. The apartment door was open—we took out the hallway security cameras, got a computer and a stack of smartphones. Only reason to collect the devices would be to maintain strict silence from rank and file. And they left without them—meaning in a hurry."

Williams turned off the speaker. "You get that?" he asked.

"I did," Berry replied. "Chase, you and the team did a bang-up from the jump to now. But you're being extracted. Head to the gulf and before you get there I'll give you the rendezvous point. Got it?"

"Yes," Williams said. "But we're not done with this."

"Didn't say you were," Berry said. "But we need to catch our breath and assess."

CHAPTER THIRTY

Port of Spain, Trinidad
July 23, 9:07 a.m.

Berry was not wrong. But it hurt to be this close and have to re-group.

The others climbed into the bright orange Jeep Wrangler Williams had procured.

"Nice ride," Rivette said, trying to lighten the mood.

"His." Williams pointed to one of the dead men. "Had the keys on him."

With the phone in his lap, the commander drove from the parking area. Beside him, Breen was booting the laptop. As they turned onto Ajax, both Grace and Williams looked out the window for any trace of the helicopter. It was long gone.

"Iranian websites," Breen said, scrolling through a drop-down menu.

"Salehi must have been reading about himself," Williams said.

"That—and, I suspect, whatever he could find out about JAM," Breen said. "His survival depended on them and he is not someone who seemed deeply plugged into the terror network before today."

"Good points," Williams said. Working with this man was like having a one-person Op-Center at his side; and what the others did at the apartment, getting to within a few feet of their target, was every bit as extraordinary as what Mike Volner and his JSOC team did on past missions. However much Williams might disagree with Matt Berry's caution, the man was smart enough to have conceived of putting Williams together with Black Wasp to create a lean, mobile version of the personnel-heavy, office-bound operation that was being terminated.

"Scary to be on the wrong side of the road," Rivette said, his knee braced against the back of the driver's seat.

Considering what he had just been through, Williams found that amusing.

Berry texted Williams, instructing him to head five miles south along the coast to the Caroni Bird Sanctuary. It was situated in the twelve-thousand-acre Caroni Swamp; moving swiftly in and out, a Naval Special Warfare Rigid Hull Inflatable Boat should not attract any actionable attention.

The ride down the Uriah Butler Highway was quiet, both inside and outside the Jeep. There were billboards, low-lying structures, and a great many long, grassy spots along the major north-south thoroughfare. When Williams received word from Berry that the RHIB was five minutes from shore, he informed Breen. The major was already watching the gulf with his binoculars and simultaneously spotted the charcoal-gray boat racing toward them, the forward section of the motorized vessel rising a sharp twenty-five degrees or so from the water.

"Not flying a flag," he noted.

"Sad when the U.S. Navy is more likely to get checked-out or shot at than smugglers," Rivette noted.

Williams pulled onto a patch of dirt and scrub, parked the Jeep, and while Breen, in the rear, watched the highway for police or anyone who might have followed them, the team marched toward the water. They reached the boat without incident and, within five minutes, were in international waters.

The U.S. 4th Fleet was established in 1943 as a means of protecting shipping against enemy submarines, blockade runners, and self-interested pirates in the South Atlantic. The fleet was disestablished in 1950, its duties transferred to the U.S. 2nd Fleet. The 4th was reestablished in 2008 to operate the Navy's surface vessels and submarines in the U.S. Southern Command, which encompassed the waters of the Caribbean and Central and South America. The stated purpose for the move was to underscore our commitment to those partners-for-peace in the region. The actual function was to make sure Russians, Chinese, Iranians, North Koreans, and the terrorists they either sponsored or ignored did not gain a strategic foothold in the region.

The Black Wasp team was taken to LCS 10, Littoral Combat Ship USS *Gabrielle Giffords*, where each of the Black Wasps personally thanked each of the four rescue team members. It hadn't been a particularly risky mission but it was a very welcomed one.

After that, the four were taken directly to the sickbay, where a pair of hospital corpsmen gave them a quick examination, handed them bottles of water for dehydration, and left them in the care of a petty officer first class. The young woman took them to the mess hall where they were joined by Lieutenant Commander Dylan Hyson. The silver-haired officer excused himself and Williams, citing security matters. Grace and Rivette were too tired to be annoyed but Breen seemed to hang on this development, this new information. Williams did not personally care what Breen knew or deduced, though the oath he took prevented him from answering questions or adding to the major's data bank.

"Sorry about that." Hyson gestured to the others as they sat at another table. "You're the only one with operational security clearance."

"Sure," Williams said. "Though it does seem a little rigid after what we've just been through."

"I know that you're a former CENTCOM commander, sir, so you now that 'fair' is not in the DoD lexicon."

"True enough," Williams said.

"We're supposed to take you to the communications center for a secure debrief from D.C.," Hyson said. "You first, the others down the line. Is there a problem with that?"

"None. Though technically, while I'm the ranking officer of the group, I'm not the leader. Have you been briefed?"

The lieutenant commander shook his head. "Only names and ranks. Commander Bacon—who's on the bridge—got her orders directly from the chief of naval operations. You have powerful allies."

Williams said nothing. It was both fascinating and disturbing that the president and Berry were running what amounted to their own shadow government.

"We know that you were on the trail of terror operations connected to the *Intrepid*," Hyson went on, "and I want you to know you have our thanks and support."

"Appreciated," Williams said. "Let me ask you: do you have any intel from Trinidad that can help us?"

The officer sighed. "The activities in Trinidad are monitored," Hyson told him, "but only electronically. Those communications are stored and reviewed by the Office of Naval Intelligence and turned over to Homeland Security. What happened this morning won't be read and plugged into the terror database for days." He shook his head. "It's meticulous, I assure you, but not terribly efficient."

"Lieutenant Commander Hyson, we are still on the trail of the attacker," Williams said. "What are your orders regarding my team?"

"Frankly, beyond the debrief sessions, we haven't any," Hyson told him. "We're continuing our patrol."

Williams explained to the others what would be going on. Leaving the team behind, Tyson took Williams to the Integrated Strategic Resources Suite, which adjoined the Integrated Command and Control Center. Williams was introduced to the captain and commander at the request of the latter.

"Commander Bacon likes to know who is on his LCS," Hyson explained.

"Perfectly understandable," Williams assured him.

Hyson escorted his charge to a small room with a laptop displaying the 10's insignia on the monitor. It was a cactus and anchor in a shield with an eagle on top and the motto *Je Suis Prest* below—"I Am Free," he knew from four years of French at Tufts.

The computer sat on a gunmetal desk pushed against a wall; there was a swivel chair in front.

"Must be fun on sharp turns," Williams said.

"I'm informed they will be contacting you," the lieutenant commander said. "Oh, and your phone won't work in here. Electronic scrambling," he added, indicating the walls.

Just like the Geek Tank, Williams thought.

"No one I need to text," Williams said.

"When you're finished, press Command Y and I'll come and get you," Hyson said, shutting the door with a click.

The fortysomething officer was efficient and polite, but nothing more. He had not seemed put out by the rescue and Black Wasp's presence, but perhaps his superiors were. Unplanned rescues were not an officer's favorite kind of mission.

Except for the purr of a ventilator, the room was quite silent. There was only a slight sense of motion, as there was throughout the vessel; these new ships were beyond what he was accustomed to. He remembered, when the ships were being designed, that by using above-the-waterline waterjets instead of the combination of underwater propellers, shafts, struts, and rudders, the LCS would be ideal for missions in which a shallow draft was required—such as rivers and near-coastal waters. The jets came with an added benefit of a smoother, quieter sail.

The clock on the computer said 9:30 and, promptly, Matt Berry's face filled the screen.

"We've got the chopper at the airfield," Berry informed him without preamble. "And a private jet on an approach path. Point of origin, Sana'a International Airport. Owner, Sadi Shipping of Yemen. Unless Salehi's is planning to go fly—" He checked a tablet. "—Caribbean Airlines to Haiti, JetBlue to Fort Lauderdale, Copa to Panama City, Surinam to Curaçao, the jet is there for him."

"Sadi," Williams said. "He's been tied to Al-Qaeda in the Arabian Peninsula."

"Reportedly," Berry said. "Large amounts of cash have been recovered by Mossad agents working undercover in the city of Dhamar, Yemen. The Israelis say the courier was tracked back to an area where Sadi is thought to be hiding. But a direct connection wasn't made."

"Saudi operatives in Jizan also mentioned him in a report—"

"That was an interview with Amnesty International," Berry said, once again consulting the tablet. "Women reportedly tortured—one of them talked. She went missing after that."

"So a man who clearly does not have Western interests at heart is likely escorting Ahmed Salehi to safety," Williams said. "What do you do? What do *we* do?"

"You were correct to make those two separate questions, Chase," Berry said, finally showing a little smile. "What I do, while the jet is en route, is make sure it's going back to Sana'a. What you do is connect with Amit Ben Kimon, who is based in Dhamar, and wait."

"For what?"

"Location of the jet," Berry said, "and something else. We're still working out the details."

"Photo of Amit Ben Kimon for confirmation?"

"Mossad won't let us have one," he said.

"Jesus, Matt."

"I know. They don't trust us a whole lot. I had to work hard just to get the guy for this. You choose the password—I will personally text it to him before you meet."

"Janette," Williams said. It was the name of his late wife who died of ovarian cancer.

"Good," Berry said respectfully. "It will be sent in English. If something goes wrong, very few Yemenis would be able to read it."

"You're not going to tell me anything more?" Williams asked.

"Black Wasp will be heading into very hostile territory," Berry said. "The less you know. . . ."

The DCS did not need to finish the statement. *The less we know, the less we can reveal if we're captured.*

"If you need to communicate with me when you're there, use Amit's phone. Uses an uplink that—well, the Israelis have one that's pretty untraceable. And Chase," Berry went on, "I *can* tell you this, though. No one in the intelligence community pursued Salehi the way you have."

"What *do* they have?"

"State and MI5 are both in Antigua, sniffing around," Berry said. "They got a tip from the Russians—seems they're pissed at him about something. But all of that is unconfirmed and not entirely reliable. Dow thinks the Kremlin wants him to ask about that nuke deal in Anadyr. Anyway, that's one reason we can't consider taking the private jet down. No one but us thinks he may be there."

"*Thinks* he *may* be there?" Williams said. "Is that the best you'll give me?"

"You did not have eyes on, so yes," Berry said. "You'd do the same if you were—" He did not bother to finish the sentence. "All right, parallel track," he went on. "While everyone looks for him, there's already talk about what to do with him when he's found."

"I guess that would depend on how he's found," Williams said. "Saddam preferred to be taken alive in a hole outside of Tikrit. His sons went down fighting in Mosul."

"The consensus here and Homeland Security's strategic psych assessment is that Ahmed Salehi is not Qusay or Uday Hussein."

"No, he's a veteran military man," Williams said.

"Who did not go down with his ship after the strike from Elmendorf-Richardson AFB."

"Correct," Williams said. "He set fire to the *Intrepid* instead."

Berry's mouth twisted with annoyance. "All of which is premature and beside the current point. My feeling, frankly—and yours, too, I'm sure—is that it doesn't matter whether he's taken or taken down. We just want to get him."

Williams did not dispute that.

"So, when we are done here, I will patch through to General Lovett so he can debrief his team," Berry said. "While that's going on, you rest while we arrange for you to be choppered to Leeward Point Field, Guantánamo Bay, and flown to Saudi Arabia. You will be equipped with local civilian clothes, cash, and a military escort to the Yemeni border where you will be met by Amit Ben Kimon. Any questions?"

"Is Amit your man? Apart from being Mossad?"

"He's completely mine," Berry said. "Converts large sums of cash for me while doing his thing for our friends at the Institute for Intelligence and Special Operations."

"Without their knowledge?"

"On the contrary," Berry said. "He gets a cut of every transaction and invests it with the Mossad's venture capital division. Everyone benefits."

Williams knew, from his work at Op-Center, that the Israeli spy organization invested heavily in cyber security and antiterrorism start-ups. It was an arrangement that gave them their own dark money funding and access to bleeding-edge tech.

"Money," Williams ruminated. "Has Ben Kimon ever transported people?"

"I don't know," Berry admitted. "But I wouldn't send you to him if I didn't think he could handle this. And before you ask, I'm not paying him for this. If you get Salehi, Amit's stock goes up in Tel Aviv. He's been in Yemen for three years and change. He really needs to shake up his routine."

Williams understood. At CENTCOM he had been in on debriefs of sleeper agents working with coalition partners, especially Tajikistan, Kuwait, and Nepal, among others. The phrase that always came to mind in these interviews was "burned out." The psychological description that emerged from their medical checkups was more often than not "paranoid." It was not just difficult living as someone else, it was difficult not developing sympathies with the people on whom you were spying. Even Saudi operatives who had infiltrated ISIS found themselves more militantly devout when they returned.

At the same time, Williams felt that one thing Op-Center had always lacked was deep-cover operatives. It was the ages-old battle between HUMINT and ELINT—human intelligence and electronic intelligence. Without the former, data and people like Salehi slip through any number of the digital surveillance. In this business, gut feelings were essential.

"So," Berry said, "safe journeys, Chase. If I was a little hard on you about the pinpoint recon, I'm sorry. You did a helluva job in Trinidad." He chuckled, but it sounded flat. "I thought that by this time you'd still be getting the lay of the land."

Williams ended the video call. He couldn't tell if there was a message between the lines: that maybe he should have taken it a little slower, that maybe it was their blitzkrieg approach that caused Salehi to leave early. And he might not be wrong to think that. Personally, Williams thought the operation was messy at worst and jury-rigged at best.

If we're to have a safe journey, he told himself, *Yemen will have to be better than that.*

CHAPTER THIRTY-ONE

Dhamar, Yemen
July 23, 5:19 p.m.

Three years before, upon his arrival in Yemen, the first thing Ben Kimon did was prevent the rape of a teenage girl who was working on a coffee plantation. The act was not entirely altruistic; the attacker was Amit's size and build and the Israeli wanted his clothes and Chinese-made motorbike. The seat was made from an old rug and the tassels that hung from the handlebars were sunblanched and sand-blasted; no one would doubt that the owner had been driving through the rugged north country for many, many years.

The thirty-year-old Haifa native had entered the country in May 2016 posing as a Saudi oilman who was offering a fat suitcase filled with riyals for qat. There was a total of 100,000 riyals in 500 riyal notes; $26,666 in American money. Amit knew that because his new American friend Matthew Berry had told him so. Berry wanted to get the money into Yemen so he could track the banks in which they were being deposited.

The deal was made shortly before midnight, under a half-moon that provided some light but little exposure. Once it was concluded, Ben Kimon returned to the SUV he had driven into Yemen, hummed off toward the horizon, and stopped when he reached the foothills of the Sarawat Mountains. There, he spilled a bottle of lamb's blood on the seat, smeared it across the door and handle, fired three 9mm rounds into the driver's side door, and then let the vehicle roll off a cliff. If anyone found it—and if anyone wondered—they would surmise that the driver had gotten out and died somewhere else. The SUV would be stripped for parts and that would be the end of the matter.

Ben Kimon began walking then, pulling on the short beard he had grown, glad he had broken in his sandals and happy for the ventilation of his loose, ankle-length white cotton *thobe*. Though he had worn the clothes for weeks before his mission began, the operative was less happy with his headgear—his *tagiyah*, a white-knitted skullcap; his *ghutra*, a square silk scarf worn over it; and the *agal*, a thick black cord that kept the two in place. The simpler yarmulke of his Orthodox brother was less burdensome, though being as devout as Yossi came with burdens of its own. Ben Kimon's rabbi father was openly surprised by his youngest son's choice of careers. The young man did not have the *chutzpah* to tell him he would rather face terrorists than Talmudic scholars. Because then he would have added, *"At least you can shoot terrorists."*

It was the very early evening of the next night when he happened upon the assault. The man was preoccupied with pinning the girl's arms to the ground and did not hear Ben Kimon's stealthy approach, did not feel the tight chokehold favored in Krav Maga combat, did not see the girl nod not once but twice when her savior presented a questioning look asking if he should finish the job.

She redid her headscarf and brushed down her dress, then ran off with a bow and a *shakkran*, a Yemeni expression of thanks.

Ben Kimon would have killed the man anyway. He really needed the motorbike, clothes, and possibly papers and family photographs the man might be carrying. Anything to build himself a life here and also remain mobile. Motorbikes were difficult to obtain since the government restricted their sale due to the proliferation of shoot-and-scoot murders of prominent politicians, businessmen, and foreigners.

That was then. The challenges were new, exciting. The potential to impress his superiors and to build a relationship with an American ally—a man who somehow knew where he was going and what he was intending to do—was something he had never dreamed of. From there, the future could be so many things. But Ben Kimon had not counted on the crippling burden of suspicion of everyone he met. Of having to watch human trafficking operate in the open, girls sold at home and abroad as slaves, boys turned into companions for depraved older men. Of being murdered when he laundered money for Matthew Berry. Every poor Yemeni— every poor soul he met from anywhere in the Middle East and Africa—wanted cash. All it took was one greedy man with a gun or knife to decide he wanted more than had been agreed upon.

Ben Kimon missed women. He missed open, talkative, gregarious, sexual women who had not been beaten down physically and emotionally or were themselves afraid of a chance encounter with some man who felt they were shameless by his interpretation of Sharia law. The government in Sana'a had made token, occasionally sincere efforts to improve their lot. They created a Women's Development Strategy and a companion Health Development Strategy—which they failed to enforce and which the rigidly patriarchal society failed to acknowledge. The worst part of it all was that Ben Kimon had to act like a Yemeni man or risk exposure. He could not court anyone, not with his itinerant and dangerous lifestyle—and the knowledge that he would leave them and any children at some point. There were options, of course. Almost daily he was offered girls, teenagers and younger; sex slaves who were often sold or offered by their parents. Suffering was burned into their eyes and their miserably strained smiles made it impossible even to think about them. But there was another, less heinous option. For that reason, he had finally broken down, this past year, and created a separate identity as Hisham Nuwas, a wealthy hotel owner from Qatar. With Matt Berry's cash, it was an easy disguise to maintain. He did not have to use it all, just show a little of it to men he knew would not rob him. Six times over the years he had gone to prostitutes for what were called "tourist marriages" with Somalian refugees. Though prostitution was illegal for Yemeni women, punishable by three years in prison or worse, the government looked the other way when men from the Gulf states came for sex. They also came with a great deal of cash.

These occasional encounters were necessary biological experiences, emotionally dead, but those were times when there was very little to keep him going other than the body of a woman—and he took some consolation that these poor women were able to feed their children. They were closer to their families than he was and

Ben Kimon was surprised to find himself missing them. The Mossad occasionally sent him updates, events like his brother's marriage and first child and his mother being one of the winners of the prestigious Dan David Prize. One million dollars was part of the honor. After that last one, he would lie in bed at night, in the room he rented from a man who worked at a diesel-run power plant, and muse about his very different road to wealth. The more he thought about it, the more degenerate he felt. She was teaching history, he was moving contraband and occasionally cutting throats.

After these three years he felt like his conscience was drowning in a sea of brutish, suspicious, aggressive physicality. And he saw no way out as long as he remained here.

Unfortunately, before he was accepted for training by Ha-Mossad leModi'in uleTafkidim Meyuḥadim—before he was taught colloquial Yemeni Arabic, exhaustively trained in the psychology and culture, and shown how to use all the weapons he was likely to encounter or purchase on the black market as well as how to send messages without being discovered—Ben Kimon had to agree to stay in-country for five years. Then, within weeks, his superiors signed off on the deal with Berry in exchange for an added year. At the time, it seemed like a wildly sensible trade-off. It mocked the old saying, "*How do you make a million dollars in Israel? Start with fifteen million.*" With the venture capital investments, the young man would come home wealthy. Only later did it occur to him that the six-year tenure had always been the plan. Berry did not randomly appear. There had probably been another Ben Kimon before him.

He never asked about that. There really wasn't a way for him to ask any of his contacts anything. They sent messages via a sophisticated receiver disguised as an old cellular flip phone that no one would bother to steal and which would survive being run over by a truck. The screen was pre-cracked and inside that crack was a powerful fiber optic wire that received messages that were announced with a loud beep one minute before transmission, two beeps thirty seconds before transmission, and then lived on the screen for a minute then died. When Amit was on his motorbike, or asleep, he did not have a lot of time to stop and get to it. The tone had been pulled from a 1980s videogame so that it would be authentically archaic. Even if the nation's brigands, terrorists, and corrupt officials had the sophisticated technology required to receive the signals, the communications were all too brief to be traced or tracked.

Ben Kimon heard from Matt Berry far more than he heard from his own people. When he did, it invariably meant a trip to Jizan or thereabouts to collect money. The Saudi courier was a banker who would physically remove the Israeli's portion and show him the Bank Leumi, Haifa, receipt from his previous deposit. This time, however, the mission was different. Ben Kimon was to meet four Americans at the border and bring them to Sana'a. The Israeli made that trip often, was known in cafes along the way. It wouldn't be difficult to come up with a cover story for the others. What puzzled him more was why they were here. Europeans and Americans stood out in Yemen—unbearded, uneasy, mute because they did not speak the local jargons and dialects. There had to be a powerful reason for coming, and it did not take a Mossad agent to figure out what that was.

The Americans attacked Yemen's terrorist leaders with drones and occasionally piloted aircraft. He knew of no special forces operating here. The only target that required boots on the ground was Sadi in his bunker. And the only reason the Americans would suddenly want him was if he had something to do with the terror attack in New York.

And he didn't, Ben Kimon knew. *A shipping titan did not attack a ship. The reprisal would be swift, obvious, and very bad for business.*

No, if Americans were here it meant that Ahmed Salehi was here. And if that were true, his capture or assassination would mean more to the Israeli than simple justice. If Amit Ben Kimon were the one to get him, he would have a ticket to wipe a year or two off his stay in this pit of hell.

Amit Ben Kimon had left his room and set out to make the 150-mile journey at a somewhat leisurely pace. If word of their presence had become known to the Yemeni intelligence forces, he would know by the additional traffic and gatherings of watchful outsiders in public places. It had been his experience that Yemeni intelligence operatives worked in groups of three or four—enough to offer some degree of mutual protection, but too few to merit a suicide attack.

As he mounted his motorbike in the sharp, slanting sun of early evening, Amit Ben Kimon did not see, hear, or feel the bullet that entered his brain from behind and ended his life.

Bader Abu Lahem of the Counter-Terrorism Unit, Ministry of Defense, stood over the corpse of this Yemeni who posed as a

Qatari and moved around with large quantities of cash. The dead man was lying facedown with a corner of his head still rocking on the ground nearly a meter away.

"The price of sin," he thought—not with judgment but as a matter of practicality. Local men should know their place and it was not in Gulf state whorehouses.

It was Lahem's job to make sure Gulf state men who entered the country for sex left the country after sex. Given the tolerance of the government for that particular corruption, it was an easy way for Sunni insurgents to enter the country and then blend in with the populace.

The thirty-eight-year-old Shia agent—who had begun his career studying to become a translator before being recruited by the CTU—was one of the few holdovers from before the Shia insurgency began in 2004. Most intelligence agents were smart enough to collect and share intelligence information on the upward chain of command. They called it the Secular Barricade. For most of them, who were products of the slums, protecting their job was more important than advancing theology. In Lahem's case, a homosexual encounter between the Minister of Education and a young friend—the friend being a cousin of Lahem's who suddenly had a great deal of spending money—was what got Lahem into university. He chose a profession that, he hoped, would actually get him out of the country, possibly an embassy appointment. But his father was ailing and he needed an income. Both parents were unable to work now, which was one reason he was here. His wife had her hands full with two young boys, and her small rug business contributed little to their economy.

The agent had been watching this man for several weeks after his visit to the whorehouse in the basement of a partially bombed-out brick apartment building on Almanzil Street. With a thumbnail-sized tracking device hidden under the rear fender of the motorbike, Lahem had tracked this man from a distance in his four-wheel-drive military truck, its markings painted-over. Cash came in and out from Saudi Arabia, always from the same location in Jizan, the regional airport. Lahem had come to know the suitcases and what they contained. He could earn a handsome profit from this trip, get his parents a more comfortable residence and, in the process, discover who in Saudi Arabia was providing Yemenis—most likely Sunnis—with funds.

Lahem checked the man's papers. There was no photograph, which was not uncommon; there were few institutions that could be bothered taking them, and few documents that were authentic in any case. The dead man was Hisham Nuwas, and everything was up-to-date. Lahem would make it across the largely un-guarded border with no difficulty. Twenty-five hundred riyal notes in the man's documents would ensure it. The Yemeni agent had never seen that much money in one place, outside a bank. He felt wealthy already.

He also examined the man's cell phone. It seemed old and fairly useless, but someone might call with information he needed. He had his own phone in his right pocket and put this one in his left. The CTU agent removed the tracker from the motorbike and crushed his own unit. That was not something he would wish to explain at the border crossing.

Lahem only knew by sight the man Hisham was supposed to

be meeting in Jizan at the airport. Moreover, his past trips had been erratic in terms of time and duration. It didn't matter. Lahem was a patient man. Whoever Hisham had been intending to meet, and whenever, they would meet Bader Abu Lahem instead.

CHAPTER THIRTY-TWO

Leeward Point Field, Guantánamo Bay, Cuba
July 23, 12:00 p.m.

There were endless quotes about mice and men, about human be-ings planning and God or nature or fate thwarting them. None-theless, as recently as yesterday morning, if Chase Williams had been given an unlimited number of guesses, he would never have imagined that he would be in the same country where Roger McCord had helped to prevent Captain Salehi from getting his nukes, thus teeing off this crisis.

The sad irony was that until the previous morning, that was exactly the job a highly experienced portion of his team did every day. Brainstorming the "what ifs." And they still missed Salehi and his scheme. That was troubling enough, but so was his other sharp concern: if Op-Center had missed Salehi—and their focus was greater than at the other agencies—it frightened him to imag-ine what State, CIA, the FBI, the NRO, and other institutions were missing.

Which, the more he thought about it, is what truly impressed him about what General Lovett had conceived. A mobile force too small to be noticed, able to vanish back into their respective services when the job was done. No doubt the general had cover stories to explain what happened if any of them perished: lost on a survival mission, killed in a crash, quarantined with some communicable disease.

Berry had sent Williams intelligence reports on Yemen, and the former Op-Center director had forwarded those to the team—minus the point of origin. Any question about why a DCS was running a military operation, and how he was funding it, could put Berry in prison. In principle, Williams did not approve of billions of dollars of black fund money provided by taxpayers. That had been his first reaction when he went to the Defense Logistics Agency, and it hadn't changed.

But Berry is a fundamentally honorable man, Williams believed. *And his efforts got us this far while everyone else was still in buffering mode.*

Williams watched his C-40C aircraft being fueled and loaded with the gear they would need. The jet was a Boeing 737-700 with added winglets and a variety of highly sophisticated avionics and various structural and instrument upgrades. To the lay rider, the interior was indistinguishable from one, big first class cabin. The military kept one at the ready at Guantánamo to collect and return visiting members of Congress and the cabinet. As Williams stood there in air-conditioning that was too old and too little for the heat, he pondered the dangers of a squad like Black Wasp. If they could be sent to a danger zone like Yemen and survive—still an "if"—what could stop Lovett or a successor from sending Black Wasp after a president or senator?

Then there were diplomatic considerations. Whoever was in the safe house with Salehi had obviously escorted him to the airfield. When they returned, the men would find two injured comrades in the parking area and two dead men in the stairwell. There were also the men killed on the Navet. The parachutes did not appear to have any markings to identify their country of origin, but there were those eyewitnesses they had permitted to escape. The U.S. Embassy to Trinidad and Tobago would have to take the Fifth on all of it.

Which, as it happens, would not be a lie, Williams thought.

He wondered what General Lovett would think about not having killed the smugglers. Williams did not think the general would share his thoughts with the team but it would certainly factor heavily into their mission analytics. He wondered if they would get additional instructions before they reached Yemen.

I wonder if there will be an opportunity to show mercy in Yemen, he thought.

Williams had made a point of not discussing their debrief with the Black Wasps. They had been taken to the secure room in turn—Breen, Grace, then Rivette. There was no outside discussion among them that Williams was aware of. The only conversation Williams had was with Breen, requesting that he be permitted to send the JAM laptop and smartphones to Washington. The major had no problem with that, and they were passed along to the lieutenant commander to be sent to the deputy chief of staff at the White House. Each of the Black Wasps then ate in the mess in silence, after which Williams had folded his arms, put his chin on his chest, and managed to nap. The next thing he knew it was time for the ship's MH-60 Seahawk to ferry them to Guantánamo Bay.

Whatever the team had not talked about on the LCS, there was a decided chill here. Grace and Rivette had chatted a little—about weapons, it seemed from the way they were sharing and handling them—but they had not spoken with either of the other men. Nor had Breen and Williams spoken. He could only imagine that the major—with his law-and-order background—was harboring some of the same thoughts and concerns as Williams.

The squadron commander who had brought them here came to get them a half hour later. He was a brawny young man who had a distant look; moving terrorists in and out had to wear on the soul. Not their captivity; Williams had yet to meet a single member of the military, other than one chaplain, who felt sorry for the enemy combatants held here. It had to be the hate that got them—hate coming from the prisoners, hating them back because of what they stood for.

But the squadron leader was still a professional airman, like their driver at Fort Belvoir, and the team was brought on board with care and efficiency.

After takeoff, a crewmember opened the three footlockers that had been brought aboard. These contained clothes, dictionaries and phrasebooks, and identity papers printed from emailed files—it turned out that Berry maintained a considerable documents operation at the Defense Logistics Agency. There were only rudimentary cell phones. To be seen using smartphones or tablets would invite theft.

There was a generous supply of Arab clothing at Guantánamo.

It was used to replace the worn attire of longtime inmates. Though most of the inmates were men, women were occasionally brought to the facility, which enabled Grace to select a *niqab* from what she found, since there was little to be done to make her features look Yemeni. She wasn't bothered by a partial loss of peripheral vision; she had trained extensively wearing a blindfold to give herself an advantage in nighttime hand-to-hand combat. The heat and breathing, however, would be a challenge. She started practicing at once—and suggested everyone do likewise.

"When I work out, I perspire," she said, her voice muffled by the fabric. "Nothing gets out that smell. Our clothes should be the same."

The others agreed and were soon settled in for what would be a sixteen-hour flight to Riyadh, and then a chartered flight to Jizan. They were supposed to be accompanied on the Saudi Arabian leg of their journey by Salman Al-Saud—fitting, the chief risk officer of the powerful Al Rajhi Bank. When Berry had texted the information back in the ready room, he answered Williams's unasked question: "We were roommates and played on the men's squash team at Princeton."

Williams wondered if, even then, his friend was preparing for the financial life he now led. He also wondered how, in all their dealings, he had never picked up on any of this.

Berry maintained that there would be no problem getting into the country. Williams was frankly surprised that Berry had not suggested skipping all the niceties and executing a high-altitude jump into Yemen. Or it could be that Berry had nothing to do with that decision.

Maybe Grace scared General Lovett off any kind of jumps for now, he thought.

Either Berry is that good or there was a hole in your personal intelligence radar, he decided. The last resonated unpleasantly. *Christ, I should never have made the move from CENTCOM.*

This was not the time for that . . . and, he reminded himself, as even a halfhearted Catholic, he believed there was always room for redemption. That was what he had to focus on.

Williams reminded everyone that it would be about 4:30 in the morning when they landed, and he said he intended to get as much sleep as possible. Just thirty minutes out of Guantánamo, Breen was already out. The others agreed to do the same.

There was not one of them who did not need it.

CHAPTER THIRTY-THREE

Sana'a, Yemen
July 24, 9:10 a.m.

The smartphone call from Vincent Rowley-James delivered the good news first.

A black screen looked back at the young Trinidadian as he said that Captain Salehi had been safely seen to the jet and the jet had departed without incident.

"But we lost two men killed, two men injured," he said. "Three of us returned from the airport in different taxicabs, arrived at different times, were unmolested. The attackers have fled, sir."

A young woman, who also held the tablet, translated what the caller was saying, but Sadi liked to see the faces of the people who were reporting to him. How strong were they? How afraid? How truthful. This man was too simple to be deceptive.

"How did the Americans enter the building?" Sadi asked through the translator.

"In an ambulance," Vincent said. "Stolen from our doctor. There may be clues . . . the police are looking."

"There will be no clues," Sadi said ruefully. "How will fibers and hair samples help now?"

Vincent had no answer. He appeared, in that instant, not only mute but dumb.

"Where are you?" Sadi asked.

"We are at the apartment. The police are here—I know them, sir. I explained that we were attacked. There was also a gunfight in the swamp . . . they understand that the Americans are to blame."

"You did not call on your laptop."

"No, sir. I am on the roof with my phone. That . . . that laptop is missing. Along with phones I had collected from the others to maintain security."

Sadi was not unduly concerned about the laptop. His communications were always routed through an alternate sequence of Sadi Shipping vessels and buoys, making it virtually impossible to trace the calls to him. A trace would show that this call went only as far as a tanker in Venezuela. What concerned Sadi more was the carelessness of the operation. JAM was just one of the many foreign terror groups he financed, but it had proven itself the least reliable. So many young men had left the island to join ISIS, and so few had returned, that rebuilding would take years.

"I want to know the identity of the Americans," Sadi said. "You had security cameras?"

"In the garage and in the hall—all destroyed, sir," Vincent said, his forehead now glistening with sweat.

"I want the last images they recorded," he said.

"Yes, sir."

"I want one thing more," Sadi said.

"Yes, sir."

"You very nearly lost an important asset," the terror chief said, the silky tone of his voice never changing. "And our safe house is no longer . . . safe."

"No, sir."

"To save your life, you will select a finger and bite it off."

Vincent stared at the black screen as if he were seeing the black heart behind it. He seemed to want to speak; his lips moved but he said nothing. Raising his left hand, he inserted the ring finger deep in his mouth. He did not hesitate to bite down—not from courage but just the opposite. He was afraid he would entirely lose his nerve. He bit down hard, then harder, simultaneously grinding his teeth back and forth. He applied more pressure, then more. He was wincing and a guttural sound gurgled from his throat—a cry of anguish modulated with blood. The soft tissue did not resist as much as he had expected, and soon there was just a bit of skin and sinew holding the finger to his hand. A forceful bite finished the job and he simultaneously dropped his hand and spit out the finger. The phone image wobbled about as he put the phone on the ground in order to pull out a handkerchief and stuff it in the wound. That done, he recovered the phone.

"You may collect the finger and seek a surgeon, I shall not be needing you again today," Sadi said. "Fail again and I will have you and your parents burned alive. Do you understand?"

Fighting tears of pain, the man nodded vigorously.

Sadi cocked his head slightly toward the translator and the call was terminated.

Sadi rose from the wooden chair and relocated to a circle of floor pillows surrounded by large Tibetan singing bowls. He selected a cushion, picked up a stubby oak stick with one end wrapped in leather, and struck the bowl in front of him with the hammer. The gong resonated through his thin body. For five minutes, each time the tone died, he struck it again. Whatever negativity had collected during the call vanished. His spirit was cleansed and his mind was clear. He looked at the translator who had remained kneeling beside the chair, her head bowed, the ends of her black hijab knotted loosely beneath her throat and hanging straight down, as he preferred.

"Come," he said softly. "Bring the device."

The girl picked up the tablet, rose without lifting her head, and crossed the room. Loubna was the most fortunate slave he had ever purchased, educated in Cairo and yet foolish enough to return to Sana'a to visit her ailing mother. Though schooling for women was not forbidden, parents feared for the chastity of their daughters and refused to send them to coeducational schools. That included the presence of male teachers. An uneducated population of women made for a dearth of female tutors. Loubna had the double misfortune of having been trained in languages—a highly valuable skill in Yemen. Perhaps she was consoled, somewhat, that her situation helped to get her medical care for her mother; it was her father who sold her.

The young woman knelt before him, in the same position as before. Sadi extended the last three fingers of his right hand and ran them down the soft, smooth chiffon. Through it, he felt male and female unite in a bond that was as powerful as it was ancient. It completed the process of calming him.

The Trinidadian was correct. The main part of the mission had been a success, however hastily executed.

"I will see the path of the aircraft," Sadi told her.

The woman brought up a global map that showed the jet well over the south Atlantic. Sadi smiled. It had crossed the region of the sea where the American navy's 4th Fleet prowled like a school of dolphins—intelligent but helpless. If word had reached Washington of the identity of the passenger, they had chosen to do nothing.

For now, he thought.

He did not wish to underestimate the enemy. They were clever enough to have found Ahmed Salehi and would not give up the pursuit. They, too, could follow his path. Not just to Sana'a but to Sadi.

He would have to do something to take their mind off those prizes.

The first move had been Salehi's. The next move, in Montreal, had been Sadi's.

Forgive me for going out of turn, Captain, he thought playfully.

"Loubna," he said softly. "I wish to communicate with Ibrahim Abdullah."

CHAPTER THIRTY-FOUR

Aden, Yemen
July 24, 9:26 a.m.

For Ali Abdullah, the tactic was born from the videos watched by his followers. The men, fighters all, were fascinated by the martial arts movies that were sold on the black market. The Bruce Lee, Jackie Chan, Jet Li films—and also the Japanese movies about samurai and ninjas.

When he had a moment to watch the fuzzy videotapes and bootleg DVDs over their shoulders—films to which he had not been exposed when he attended Oxford University—the ninjas were what appealed to him. Though important, it was not the skill with sword or dagger or pike that was the key to success. It was stealth. The key was not just to move silently but also to torture and kill silently.

That was four or five years ago, early in the Houthi ascension. Now, with both the old and new recruits, it was policy.

In the waning hours of the night, Abdullah and three men had waited in the dark—dressed in black robes and black facial coverings, not minding that they had the aspect of women in mourning. They were concealed apart but within eyesight of one another on the dark dock, behind crates that were waiting for light to be loaded. And they did not use the weapons of the Japanese warriors but their own tools: wire, gun, and thimbles with the ends removed and the edges razor-sharp for putting out eyes. Several nights of reconnoitering had told them that this was the route their target took. A young man on a bicycle traveling the same place, the same way, the same time every night, had to be a courier carrying messages. And no one would need to behave in a clandestine way unless he was bearing reports from a spy to a Saudi agent.

The courier himself was of no importance. He probably worked for the money; otherwise, he would be out fighting for one side or the other. But the men on either end of his journey were of great interest to Abdullah. The job of his team was to undermine enemy forces. That meant everyone who was not a Yemeni and a Houthi.

The men arrived a half hour before the boy on the bike. They took their positions, and waited. When they heard the squeak of his unoiled wheels, the team knew where he was and which of them would have to make the first move. It happened to fall upon Shaher, the biggest and broadest of the group. Abdullah had reminded them all that the boy must be stopped in a way that did not permit him to cry out or allow the bicycle to clatter to the cement. Waiting until the boy had just past and smothering him with his body and massive arms from behind and to the left, the big man was able to accomplish both.

As soon as one of the other fighters had dashed over to grab the two-wheeler, which was resting on Shaher's hip, the large man hoisted the boy up bodily and, his hand over his mouth, walked him back into the buffering darkness of a cargo container. The other men moved quickly around the boy who was shouting into Shaher's massive, muffling hand. One of Abdullah's men relieved the boy of the switchblade in the pocket of his Western trousers. Another punched him hard in the belly to keep him from squirming, and also turning the cry into a moan. The third squatted, pulled off the boy's sandal and wrapped a wire around the right ankle, just below the bone. He inserted a pencil in a loop formed by the two ends and remained in position.

The panicked youngster was still upright, sucking air through his nose, his feet off the ground. Shaher's belly held most of the boy's negligible weight.

Abdullah approached him. He could see the whites of the boy's eyes become slightly more expansive. He knew that whatever was coming, this was it. The eyes searched for Abdullah's hands, found them. The warlord held them palms up to show the boy he was unarmed. The eyes did not, however, relax.

"*As-salāmu ʿalaykum*," Abdullah said, though peace was clearly not upon the boy.

Whatever the boy said in response was lost in the meat of Shaher's hand.

Abdullah smiled at the effort. "I would like you to nod if you understand what I am about to tell you," Abdullah went on. "Did you understand that?"

The boy nodded.

"Very good," the warlord replied. "On my command, the wire around your ankle will be tightened. When it is, you will lose your right foot and your livelihood. Your right hand will follow, making it difficult to find any work other than begging. You may not bleed to death . . . but then again, you may. Do you understand?"

The boy nodded his head vigorously, nearly shaking off Shaher's grip.

"I offer you a far better alternative," Abdullah went on. "Answer my questions and we not only let you go, we will pay you. You will work for us. Do you understand that?"

The boy nodded again. Abdullah indicated for Shaher to remove his hand. Slowly, incrementally, the big man loosened his fingers. The boy made no sound, other than to pant as quietly as he was able. The Houthi leader raised his palm. The boy remained cooperative—and attentive.

"What is your full name?" Abdullah asked.

"Mūsá Basha, my lord," he replied.

The boy had used a traditional honorific for a fighter-chieftain. He might be young but he was worldly.

"Mūsá," Abdullah said, "you will whisper to me the identity of the individual whose information you carry."

"My lord," the boy said, "my employers will take my sister and sell her in Riyadh. That is what they told me and my parents."

"They will not find out," Abdullah promised him. "But if they find you here, with amputations, perhaps dead, they will assume you gave up the name and they will take your blessed sister anyway. Yes?"

The boy did not deliberate long. He told them the man was a Sunni and a scholar of languages. Mūsá did not know his name but he told the fighters where they met at the University of Aden and at what time—at midnight. He did know the name of the Saudi who received the messages, but only because he heard it spoken when he handed envelopes to one of the seamen. It was Mahdi. The boy had seen him only once and provided a description.

Abdullah thanked the boy and pressed a one-riyal note into his slender fingers.

"You will be given more when we meet again, but you are cautioned to tell no one but your father of your newfound wealth, and then to spend it cautiously." Abdullah signaled for Shaher to put the young man down and for the wire to be removed. He told the others to leave and moved from the darkness so that his eyes could be seen. "I will not tell you when and where we shall meet again," the warlord said. "Inform anyone of what has transpired and it will not go well for you."

The boy said, "My lord, my family is Shia. Nothing has gone well for us since I was a child."

Ibrahim Abdullah had not brought his phone with him. None of the men did. Sometimes, even warriors on the side of Allah lost battles.

It wasn't until several hours later, after they had slept, that he checked for messages. There were rarely any because of security concerns; this time there was one. He returned it at once. The call was very brief. It consisted of Abdullah listening while the man on the other end spoke.

Abdullah spit after completing the call. He did not spit once but twice. He wished he had enough saliva for a third spit. His dislike of Sadi was as intense as the Houthis' need for his finances.

The feeling did not arise from their different points of view. They were both Shia, who believed that the son-in-law of Muhammad, Ali, was the Prophet's true successor and that the three caliphs who came after were not. Sadi was profound in his faith. But he used his inherited money, not bravery, as a cudgel. And because they all needed it—the fighters and the politicians, even the ayatollahs—Sadi acted as if he were himself a caliph. A true Shia, a Muslim of any kind, should possess humility as much as he possessed faith and courage.

I survive day to day, sometimes hour to hour, Abdullah reflected, *while he can plan for the future. A man with that blessing should show more respect for the men on the front line.*

Abdullah had not taken the call—or spit—where his men could see or hear. He trusted them all, but torture could break even the most loyal warriors. And their enemies, the Saudis, the Sudanese, were experts.

Despite the ever present dangers of his militant existence—in addition to the daily risks of living in a generally lawless state—the thirty-nine-year-old Houthi warlord had lived long enough to be known as the "old man" among his fighters. He had survived years longer than most of his fellow field commanders in part because his strikes were invariably bold and unexpected, and in part because of his conviction that he was destined to be an even older man among the triumphant Shia.

Bareheaded and wearing a black Western-style blazer over his traditional white robes, Abdullah and seven members of his two-hundred-strong personal fighting force were oiling and cleaning their guns. As his second-in-command Khaled once observed, the weapons collect more sand than footwear on the beach.

They were based in the Khormakser district of the port city where Sadi Shipping had many interests—as well as a storage facility where Ali and his people maintained cots, along with their Iranian-supplied weapons and communications systems. The Sadi warehouse gave him and his fighters cover to strike at the Sudanese troops backed by the Hanbali-Sunni Saudis, who had been trying to secure the city for four years. Sadi was also close to the Iranians, and in one way or another he was responsible for running both legal and illegal shipments to and from that nation.

Ibrahim Abdullah understood the man's importance to their cause. But the warlord had been ordered—not asked, *instructed*—by Sadi to break off his present plans and meet his private jet, which would be landing at the Hodeida International Airport at approximately two o'clock the following morning. After that, he was to bring the passenger to the warehouse, see to his needs, and wait for a call to take him to the tanker *al-Wadi'i* in the nearby port of Al Hudaydah on the Red Sea. There, they were to wait—to be attacked by a team of commandos.

That was all the information Sadi had provided. It meant, of course, that there was no opportunity to go to the University of Aden and reconnoiter the Sunni scholar who was spying for the Saudis. He would survive to commit treason for another few days.

Abdullah selected three men to go with him, told them to rest while the other four continued watching the professor's movements. The four petitioned their leader to be permitted to carry out the assassination. But the plan they had just been working out called for eight men. They were going into an area heavily patrolled by Saudi puppets and a university where loyalties of the young were variable. He would not risk the others needlessly.

No one argued with Abdullah. No one who served the man *ever* argued with Abdullah. Not because they feared him but because he commanded that level of esteem. Sadi's wealth and the aggressive tactics of men like Abdullah had helped the Houthis to corner the black market on food and oil in Yemen. That had given them an enormous power base. That had allowed the Houthis to secure a great deal of legitimate power in the country. When the men in the field were finished, their grip would be absolute.

But first we must nursemaid a friend or colleague of Mohammad Obeid ibn Sadi, he told himself.

Abdullah resumed cleaning his weapon, trying not to become consumed with self-reproach for agreeing to something that would not permit him to plan and could conceivably endanger the lives of his men.

He hoped that the visitor was worth the risk.

CHAPTER THIRTY-FIVE

McMark Residence, Washington, D.C.
July 24, 2:01 a.m.

"You understand," a hoarse President Midkiff said over the phone, "that what you're doing could not just explode in your face, it could tear down my administration."

Matt Berry had left the Oval Office at 10:45 p.m. He had an important stop to make on the way home, but he had stayed long enough to fully brief the president on the activities of what he had dubbed Op-Center 2.0.

"God save us from 'semantic versioning,'" the exhausted president said as Berry had begun his briefing.

The DCS had made it sound very positive, very much under control—as he felt it was, more or less. The part over which he had no control was the future, which the president understood.

"What do we tell Hewlett?" Midkiff had asked.

Abe Hewlett was the secretary of Homeland Security. To the annoyance of January Dow, the president had named him the point person on all incoming intelligence regarding Salehi. Midkiff had done it precisely because it did not sit well with January.

She was jockeying too hard, too openly to make this operation her own. The mission itself seemed to be taking a backseat to that single-minded effort.

"Let's not tell him anything right now," Berry said. "We have four people squarely in harm's way. A leak could cost their lives and lose us Salehi."

The president had said he would go along with that, for the time being. If nothing else, it would give the other agencies time to triangulate their own intel, hopefully arrive at the same conclusion Williams and his team had reached.

But Midkiff had obviously considered the potential blowback during the last hour and it was not sitting well.

When the president called, Berry had been sitting on his new sofa, paid for by petty cash from the DLA. He was perched in front of the TV, still in his street clothes, watching a home renovation show to tire his eyes and mind. He muted the show but kept his too-wide eyes on the screen.

"Mr. President, we have the same two objectives as we did when this started," Berry said in the low, reassuring monotone he affected when he had to mollify the commander in chief. "The first is to capture or kill Salehi. We have the best opportunity to do that with the team that is en route to where we believe the target is headed. They are way downfield with the ball, no opposing players in sight," he added to appeal to the football enthusiast. "If we rustle the leaves too much, he will vanish. Our second objective is to give General Lovett's experiment, Black Wasp, a chance to work."

"You're close to Chase Williams," Midkiff said. "How much are you being influenced by that?"

"Frankly, sir, not as much as I should be," Berry admitted. "So far, he has supported my faith in him by giving Black Wasp its head. Consider, Mr. President: they went into and got out of Trinidad without a plan—just the four of them, two of them kids by comparison—and came away with more actionable information than our entire intelligence network! At the moment, their discrete nature is our greatest asset in this. They are following the trail in real time, not tracking it after the fact. That's a very new tactic and I understand, sir, why it's disconcerting."

"What did you mean about not being as concerned as you should about Chase?" Midkiff asked.

"He's a sixty-year-old military traditionalist who is running a democratically operated special ops force," Berry said. "He's not trained for this."

"Shit, Matt, that's a big part of what *concerns* me here," the president said. "He's already dropped one ball—"

"Making it vitally important to him that he doesn't do it again," Berry said. "Which, to answer your question, is why I should be concerned. I think he would trade his life to take Salehi down." Berry watched a wall get plastered by a woman in very tight shorts. He shut the TV. "And the truth is, I'm okay with that."

The president was silent. Berry was troubled by the fact that he could even read the president's moments of quiet. This was the impatient thoughtful Midkiff, breathing slowly through his mouth, not the unconvinced Midkiff breathing hotly from his mouth or the times-up Midkiff who had decided to move a plan in another direction and was exhaling fire from his nostrils.

"All right, we give this quarantine—what? How many hours?" the president asked—as Berry had expected.

"Flight lands around two-thirty p.m. Saudi time, that's six-thirty a.m. our time—let's revisit at noon after I've heard from my contact and hopefully Chase himself."

"I can go along with that," the president said. "But don't try and 'revisit' this in twelve-hour chunks. Barring an extraordinary or imminent development, there has to be a hard stop on the embargo sometime tomorrow."

Berry had picked up his tablet, was scrolling through files. "Do you remember what General Lovett said last month when we met with him for a preparedness update on the Wasp program?" He had opened a file and scrolled to a yellow-marked note. "'The team burns through fuel like a Hummer. They will get results fast or not at all.'"

"I remember," Midkiff said.

"I do not see this lasting very long at all, Mr. President."

Being reminded that there was a top military officer behind this program, this approach, that it was not just the bureaucrat Matt Berry, caused the president to exhale—tension gone, course maintained.

"All right, Matt. It's this day—the kind you don't expect and you can't screw up."

"We won't," Berry assured him.

The president clicked off and Berry went back to the television. Like a flagellant, he went to the twenty-four-hour news channels and watched their coverage of the *Intrepid*, what they had somehow unanimously agreed was to be called "Assault on a

Queen." The same ghastly footage was shown over and over, with a "graphic content" warning.

"You're all milking this," he muttered accusingly.

There were images of the makeshift memorials in the street, the flowers, the notes, the teddy bears in sailor uniforms. There were services on other vessels and naval bases. Then—inevitably, every few minutes, cue more "graphic content" warnings of the carnage in Montreal. A crib photo of the dead Pakistani child, Amna, had been provided by her father and had somehow become the go-to image to illustrate the tragedy of the day. The anchors and reporters had stopped pointing out that she was not a victim of the *Interpid* but the granddaughter of the terrorist Dr. Akif.

There were interviews with weeping family members, stunned neighbors of the victims, bicycle messengers and cabdrivers and passersby who had witnessed the attack. And, of course, there were the pundits. The terror experts, some of whom said we had brought this on ourselves by our reckless actions against Iran off the coast of Alaska—which they did not reveal because they did not know what those actions were. One woman actually trotted out, as legitimate, the explanation Tehran had provided for their vessel being there.

"They were a geological research ship studying the undersea earthquake that occurred 155 miles off the shores of Chiniak, Alaska," she intoned.

"The assholes," Berry thought.

Then the intelligence and military experts cycled through, saying nothing new because there *was* nothing new. Some talked over Google maps revealing where the attack was planned, explaining how the attack was pulled off, speculating on how the terrorists escaped and where two of the three of them went.

"To hell," one anchor said—the only comment Berry liked. The others were all exhaling hot air.

"Salehi will go back to Iran, where we must work to extradite him. . . ."

"Salehi will go to an Iranian community in the United Kingdom or Austria, possibly even in Israel, where he will be hidden. . . ."

"Salehi could only have gone to an Iranian community in the region, in any of the five boroughs, or he would have been found and arrested. . . ."

There was, of course, speculation on "what's next." What new attacks, what military response, what sanctions. And then there were updates on "The Hunt for Salehi" illustrated with the security camera photo and one other Fox News had dug up, of the captain some ten years ago on the bridge of a ship.

"I've been in the Oval Office during situations like these," said one former national security advisor who had been there so long ago the photos of him were even older than the shipboard image of Salehi. "The trail is cold and the hunt is stillborn," the man said. "We have a diligent intelligence service, but they dropped the ball going into this and they are not equipped to quickly find a needle in a haystack. The system is a behemoth."

Berry clicked the TV off. It was bad enough to be living events with this carousel of noise, color, and nonsense. Terrorist acts were jarring enough, but the fear-mongering was how it spread and continued to breathe. And there was no useful reason other than it grabbed eyeballs, fueled ratings, and earned profits for the networks. Like so much of government, the goal was not serving the citizenry. It was personal enrichment.

He peered into the now-dark den and drowsily reflected on the call from the president. It was a rare moment of candor and vulnerability from the normally collected, even courtly man. He was very clearly a leader who had reached the end of his endurance for governance . . . and for this day. And not just because the buck stopped on his desk.

Everyone else was running a side operation. January, Allen Kim, Trevor Harward, Abe Hewlett, Berry himself—they all wanted first and foremost for the terrorist to face one kind of justice or another. But, as with the aftermath of September 11 and the long pursuit of Osama bin Laden, the republic would endure. Berry knew from years of watching the History Channel that nations and empires were invariably destroyed from within, not from without. A populace always rallied to repel an enemy—then gnawed each other to death. At the end of this chapter, each one of them wanted to be standing tallest or with the best balance or, preferably, both. Berry was the dark horse, the deputy who had very little real authority but, unknown to all, had more power than any of them. He had cash, which, in the right hands, could destroy not just lives but small nations.

In that respect, Berry actually gave himself credit for being as even-keeled as he was. A drop of money could end the career of any or all of those jockeying for power. And the success of Chase Williams—or at least, of Black Wasp—would ensure that.

"God help us, Chase," he said to the walls. "I do want that prick Salehi, whatever it costs."

He fell asleep on the sofa, which, unlike the pursuit of Ahmed Salehi, seemed so comfortable because it had cost him nothing. . . .

CHAPTER THIRTY-SIX

Hodeida International Airport, Yemen
July 24, 2:52 a.m.

Salehi had not truly missed home until the jet touched down and he set foot on Arab soil. As he emerged in the darkness of Yemen, the distinctive heat that had a touch of the sea; the jet fuel that smelled—fresher?—in the region of its origin; the attire of the few locals he saw as he was escorted to the terminal; all reminded him that he had been away from an ancient region ripe with his people, his culture.

Torn by sectarian rivalries, he lamented, *and yet that, too, is part of the character of the Middle East.*

Not being devout, Salehi felt somewhat apart from that strife. Though he knew that being in unhappy Yemen, and not in Iran, he would probably experience that very differently now. Hopefully, he would soon be on the sea and away from religious and political turmoil.

A middle-aged male flight attendant had been the only other person onboard beside the pilot and copilot. He escorted the captain to a yellow pickup truck and left with a bow and a blessing. Salehi stood a few feet from the front of the battered vehicle. The headlights were off and the back was covered with a canvas canopy. The left-side passenger's seat was empty and the driver looked around cautiously before he opened the door—reaching across himself awkwardly with his left hand. When he emerged from the right side driver's seat, Salehi saw that his right hand was in the pocket of his robe—no doubt holding a gun. The driver was a tall man dressed in black, including his *keffiyeh*. His short beard was also black. The driver approached the new arrival as the white jet sat silently beside them like an angel that had just performed a task for Allah.

"*Ahlan wa sahlan,*" said the robed figure, offering a neutral welcome that was courteous but no more.

Salehi thanked him with an equally secular "*Sabah al-khayr,*" a simple "good morning." It was as though a password had been tendered. In a land where men were shot simply for possessing a particular religious alignment, or for professing no affiliation, greetings were careful things. Though the driver's short beard suggested he was Shia, his words had not been a test.

Sadi was unlikely to have sent a man who would shoot an honored guest over that, Salehi reasoned.

The driver personally escorted him to the vehicle, looking around the entire time not with sudden, obvious turns of his head but with his eyes. The interior light had been disabled and the men drove away without having identified one another or said anything beyond the greeting.

They drove southwest along Airport Road, according to the signage. Every now and then they hit a dip or bump that caused the truck to rattle. There were extra rattles in the back; armed men, Salehi surmised.

"We are driving to the sea," Salehi asked after several minutes. "What is our destination?"

"You are Iranian," the driver observed, answering in his language.

"Yes."

The driver was thoughtful for a moment then turned on a dashboard reading light. He looked over briefly then shut the light.

"That is why he was so secretive," the driver said. "You are Ahmed Salehi."

The passenger was silent.

"I am Ali Abdullah, leader of the Supporters of Allah."

"Houthi," Salehi said. "Aligned with my nation."

"We are brothers at arms," Abdullah said. "You have bloodied the cursed allies of the Saudis. I am honored to be escorting you to a vessel owned by our benefactor, where, I understand, we are to await further orders."

"Were you provided with any information, Ali, about the team—presumably American—that came after me in Trinidad?"

"Nothing," Abdullah said, "though—that was very quick work."

"It was, I discovered, a highly compromised plan."

Once again, Abdullah reflected on this new information. "That is why we were assigned to you. Several of my fighters are in the back, as you may have realized. We are to keep you secure until further orders are given."

"You are taking me to a ship," Salehi said. "I was promised a ship."

"Then that makes even more sense," Abdullah replied. Despite the unexpectedness of this mission, and the impact on his ongoing plans, he was clearly honored to be a part of this undertaking—and was also suddenly more forgiving of Sadi. None but he could have plucked this man from danger and brought him swiftly to the other side of the globe, and relative safety. "But you say there was a team pursuing you. We must assume they have not, will not, give up the chase."

"They were very capable and relentless," Salehi acknowledged. "More so than I would have expected."

"There are any number of fighters who could have been enlisted to protect you," Abdullah said. "I suspect our role may be more than guard dogs."

"Attack dogs?" Salehi suggested.

"At night, in places where we are not expected," he said.

"Does our 'benefactor' know where the Americans are?" He did not use Sadi's name because Ali Abdullah had not. Whether that was out of respect or security or both did not matter. Salehi simply followed the lead of his host.

"Very little happens within our borders of which he is unaware," Abdullah said. He smiled at the new prospect and would alert his bands of followers throughout the country. "I have no doubt that we will be hearing more very, very soon."

CHAPTER THIRTY-SEVEN

Jizan, Saudi Arabia
July 24, 4:40 p.m.

Chase Williams had thought that no civilized place on earth could be more oppressively hot than Washington, D.C., in the summer. He could take the discomfort; survival training in the desert had been part of his training. He actually found it cleansing to sweat, to purify his body inside and out. It was a strictly aesthetic observation.

The flight, the landing, and the meeting with Berry's banker associate—accomplice, Williams corrected himself—had gone off flawlessly. They transferred to one of the bank's fleet of private jets for the trip to Jizan. Salman Al-Saud did not make this trip with any of his aides, there was no flight attendant, and the pilot and copilot did not emerge from the cockpit. He explained, though it was self-evident, that he felt more comfortable that none of his aides knew where he was going, or with whom. Though if the chief risk officer was comfortable, Williams would have hated to see him when he was uncomfortable. Even on the jet, between conducting bank business on his tablet, he would look out the window, toward the cabin, listen to every bump as though he expected terrorists to emerge from the lavatory or the aircraft to be taken down by a missile.

None of which was entirely impossible in this part of the world, Williams knew. *Especially with us as passengers.* But there was no sense worrying about it when there was nothing one could do.

Al-Saud had agreed to turn them over to Amit Ben Kimon and then depart. The men covered their unbearded faces with the ends of their head coverings after which the banker personally escorted them to the curb of the small but modern one-story Jizan Regional Airport.

Al-Saud stopped short when he saw the familiar figure pull up curbside several meters away, behind a line of taxicabs and a pair of Conquest Knight XV SUVs.

"What does he expect to do with just his motorbike?" Al-Saud wondered.

"Not attract attention by changing his m.o.?" Major Breen said.

"Maybe one of those other vehicles is his," Williams suggested.

"No," Al-Saud said. "Those are Saudi Amoilco stickers on the license plates."

"Smart," Breen said to his teammates. "They don't have to open the windows and show IDs until they're in a secure area."

The banker took several steps from the group, fetched his smartphone from an inside pocket of his Western suit jacket, and began reading emails. He seemed to want to be doing anything other than this. He was here often enough so that it shouldn't arouse suspicion from the police—they were probably on his payroll—but that might not include showing up with strangers whose faces were covered.

Wiping perspiration from his eyes, Williams turned his attention to Ben Kimon. The Israeli did not move to the other side of the line. In fact, he seemed to hesitate even when the first limousine pulled away. Perhaps the Israeli was waiting to make sure everything was all right. He was in a foreign land, there were Saudi police inside and outside the terminal, and this was not at all a typical mission. He had to have a plan for transporting them.

"I'm going over," Breen said suddenly and started toward the man. "Is there a password?"

"Janette," Williams said. He felt almost unfaithful giving it to him. "Do you even know what greeting to use? The police may notice."

"I'm just going to shake his hand," Breen said. "I read that's acceptable here, plus I don't trust my accent."

Williams stayed with the others, silently cursing the damned SITCOM imperative. If Breen were taken for some reason there were still three of them to go to Yemen. Berry had already informed them that the jet had landed at Hodeida International Airport where it was met by a pickup truck. The configuration of the truck was being image-searched and color enhanced. But it was night, nearby field lights had been turned off, and both were problematic. Berry had no additional information.

Lahem had been waiting for the better part of the day for his contact to make his appearance. The only excitement, if one could call it that, was receiving a text on the dead man's phone. The message was an English name, Janette, which appeared and then vanished in moments. He did not know why it had appeared.

Now that the man had appeared—with three persons and no suitcase full of cash—he did not know what to make of it. He considered aborting the undertaking—but he was in a foreign country with police all around. Any sudden, suspicious action might bring a response . . . and his scooter could not outrun a car.

He waited, and then one of the new arrivals came toward him. Lahem had been wearing a scarf across the lower half of his face, and sunglasses. He watched the other man carefully as he removed them. The fellow did not react. It was possible he had no idea what Hisham looked like. Smugglers and money launderers did not like to be photographed.

The newcomer offered his hand. Lahem shook it and nodded—slowly, his eyes on the other, as if he were acknowledging something tacit that they both knew.

The man continued to hold Lahem's hand. He looked him in the eyes, leaned in, and whispered, "You have something to tell me?"

Without thinking, Lahem answered, "Janette."

Breen released his hand. "We must get to Aden."

Lahem started slightly. He had not been expecting these people . . . and he had not been expecting English.

"Aden," he repeated.

"Yes, I thought you would have been told. Dhamar is no longer the destination."

It took a moment for Lahem to respond, in English, "I see." He was an experienced enough agent to have, as his default action, one of the first lessons he had learned in training: saying little and listening much. And what he was listening to was like lightning in his ears and coursing through his body. "I have transportation nearby," he said. "I first wished to make this connection."

Breen nodded. "We will wait on those benches." He pointed to steel seats in a glass gazebo.

Lahem nodded and drove off, his brain—a good brain, he knew, capable and logical—struggled to make sense of what he had stepped into. Part of him was afraid. He had gone home to tell his family he would be on assignment a few days and left them with one thousand riyals—causing them to worry that he was involved with something illegal. He assured them he was not. Stopping currency smugglers by any means necessary, and confiscating their goods, was his job, not a crime. If he ever had to defend his actions at the CTU he would plead—also truthfully—that he had been drawn into a larger undercover action.

And that was the only thing that weighed on him: what in the name of everything sacred *was* this operation?

The only way to find out was to continue to act the part of Hisham Nuwas.

If this were Yemen, he would steal a vehicle. He had to show up with something to transport the four of them, and quickly. The answer was a tour bus. There were three waiting, possibly for a group. If so, this would cost him more. Lahem stopped by the open window where the driver was smoking a cigarette.

"Are you engaged?" he asked.

The man's big sleepy face caused his big beard to puff outward with a smile.

"I am most inexpensively at your service," he replied.

"Into Yemen?" Lahem asked.

The man's smile weakened. "I . . . I have a wife, a mother, a grandmother, and four children," he said. "This is dangerous."

Lahem passed up three five-hundred riyal notes. "Get us there and I will tell you when you can leave," he said. "It will be soon."

"That . . . that sounds safe enough," the driver said.

"There is another thousand riyals if—and mind me—if you assure my guests that you had been engaged by me previously."

"I will tell them whatever you wish them to hear," the driver replied.

The new arrivals might not understand the language . . . but then, they might.

"Just follow me and remain mute, unless I ask you something," Lahem said.

The man touched his forehead, started the bus, and flashed the bills at his fellow drivers as he swung past them.

"How did he seem?" Williams asked quietly when Breen returned.

As passengers walked behind them, a mildly anguished look from Al-Saud implored him to keep his voice quieter still.

"Cautious," the major answered.

Rivette wandered over so he could listen. Grace maintained

her distance, as was expected of a Saudi woman. Under her robes, her hands had pulled into leopard paws; she felt less humiliated that way.

"That's not a bad thing," Williams said.

"No," Breen agreed.

The men stopped conversing when the man they thought was Israeli returned with a tour bus. Al-Saud had not looked up from his phone until now. He hastily wished the four well and excused himself. Williams knew that Berry had to use the assets he had, and he also knew—from the daily Op-Center intelligence and news reports—that even prominent Saudi billionaires were not immune from arrest for corruption, as the case of Prince Alwaleed bin Talal had demonstrated just two years before. But this man was a red flag if ever he saw one.

Within minutes, the passengers having boarded and the motorbike having been hoisted into the aisle, the bus drove off. The growl of the old engine ensured that, as long as they spoke quietly, they would not be overheard by the driver.

The border crossing proved not to be a problem. Williams knew that a border wall consisting of pipelines filled with concrete, stacked ten feet high along eleven hundred miles of border, had been constructed in 2003. He also knew that it became a source of frustration for Saudis who did business in Yemen—particularly in qat and other drugs. That was a war the kingdom did not want to fight, and large sections were removed a dozen years later. Guards patrolled intermittently, more for the drilling practice than for actual policing.

The bus driver simply took a route where he knew the border

guards did not patrol at twilight. Williams quietly asked Lahem why they stood down at dusk.

"It is when they are most vulnerable," the Israeli imposter explained. "It is too late for sunlight and too early for night-vision glasses."

Williams nodded. After they were more than a kilometer into Yemen, the man went to the front of the bus to talk to the driver.

Rivette was sitting in the seat behind Williams. He leaned over.

"Did you notice he hasn't even looked at Grace?" the lance corporal said. "Even though she's hidden?"

"Deep cover will do that," Williams said. "The sexes don't intermingle in public. He can't afford to slip."

"They can stone their women, and sell them, but they can't talk to them," Rivette said. "Place is messed up."

Shortly after going up front, Lahem came back and bent over Williams. "The driver has only been engaged this far," he said. "We must get off the bus."

Williams looked out the window. They were in a hilly, desolate region with night closing in. "Amit, this mission is time sensitive. How much more money does he want?"

That was another surprise. They thought he was an Israeli.

"It is not a question of money but of getting home safely," he said. "I will talk to him."

"Please convince him," Williams said.

The agent went back up front. A few minutes later, Lahem came back. He made a point of returning a revolver to his pocket.

"Our driver is not happy, but he has agreed to continue with us," he said. "This is not a time or place for us to be wandering through the foothills."

It appeared, to Williams, that Black Wasp now had a fifth member of the team, one who was as improvisational as the others—which, given the nature of his business, did not seem a good fit. It also did not fit the careful methods of any Mossad-trained agent Williams had worked with at Op-Center. He knew what Berry had told him but—just to put the question to rest—someone, somewhere at the Israeli agency had to have a photo of Ben Kimon. Berry himself should be able to get a college photo . . . something. Even a description.

Maybe you should just ask him what year it is on the Israeli calendar, Williams thought. *But then, he might know.* People out here lived and breathed religions, even those of infidels and blood-enemies. Or the man might shoot two of them before they could return fire, or before Grace could reach him. *No one expected what happened to the* Intrepid, *but, Christ, this thing had not been sufficiently thought through.*

Williams motioned Lahem over. "I'd like to borrow your cell phone," he said.

The man fished out the device he had taken from the body of the dead man and handed it over. He did not ask why. He was probably supposed to know.

Williams thanked him and waited. "Access code?" he asked.

"Sorry, my mind was elsewhere," the other man said. "It is 226AX," he said.

Williams punched in code. The screen did not come on. He tried again.

"That's odd," Lahem said. He took the phone back, tried it himself, played with the battery, then tried again.

"When was the last time you used it?" Williams asked.

"While I was waiting for you," he said.

Berry's words echoed in his head. "*Very few Yemenis would be able to read it.*" Williams hoped he was just being overly cautious, though he found himself wishing that Aaron Bleich and the team of the Geek Tank were here. They'd have this thing working.

He handed the phone back to Lahem. "All right, thanks," Williams said. "It wasn't urgent."

The guide went to a seat in the front of the bus and Williams broke protocol by trying his smartphone. Because of the terrain—the mountains and lack of an uplink here—he was unable to get a signal. Maybe he *was* being paranoid, but he couldn't shake the feeling that something did not sit right about this man and his plan. It all seemed a little makeshift for someone who was trained by the Mossad, had spent three years in-country, and taken this route countless time.

Williams looked up the aisle of the dark, bouncing, diesel-permeated bus. Then he looked back. The rear door was padlocked—probably to help thwart attacks—and the motorbike blocked the front exit. It probably meant nothing—all of it. But he wished he could be sure.

Breen was in the seat across the aisle. He leaned over. "What did you need?"

"I wanted to reach my contact in D.C.," he said.

"Not just to say 'hi.'"

"No. Is it just me or do you feel okay about all this?"

"We're headed in the right direction for Aden," he said. "That's the main thing."

"On a hijacked bus."

"'Commandeered,'" the major said. "You did say you wanted to stay on it."

"True," Williams admitted. "But just now, our friend didn't know the damn code."

"Or his reception is screwed here, too."

"Wouldn't he know? He's traveled this route."

Breen frowned. "On a motorbike, not in a bus with three kinds of metals used to repair the roof." The major pointed overhead. "I also saw the driver admiring a five-hundred riyal note. Ben Kimon would deal in nothing smaller, I suspect."

Williams suddenly felt like a mulish hybrid between a tenderfoot and a prophet of doom. Breen certainly seemed relaxed enough, as did Rivette and—as far as he could tell—Grace as well. Maybe the SITCOM approach was more ingenious than he had realized. Maybe that was the way things *should* work in a world of terror cells, tribal chieftains, and black market economies powered by smugglers. Maybe Matt Berry was the harbinger of a new kind of global power, the government as multinational financier embodied in the shape of one quasi-responsible man.

You're no longer behind a desk, he told himself. *Stop overthinking and trying to micromanage.*

He put his phone away. Major Breen was right. They were going where they needed to go. As for the rest—since this region was the birthplace of many faiths, it might not be a bad idea to do something he had not done since Janette's death.

Closing his eyes, Chase Williams prayed.

Lahem informed the driver that Highway 10 lay ahead approximately five kilometers.

"You will take it to Aden," he said in Arabic, making sure the passengers heard their destination.

"We will need fuel," the driver replied.

"In Harad," Lahem said and gave him another five hundred riyals. "I promise this will be worth your time. You may keep the change."

The man seemed less appreciative than before; from the way he listened for knocks and coughs, nursed the wheel, he was apparently calculating the cost of replacing his bus.

Lahem did not feel too bad. Considering the injury this man's nation had inflicted on Yemen, he was lucky the CTU agent did not simply shoot him and kick his body out the door.

Moving to the back of the bus, stretching as he walked past his passengers, Lahem flopped into a seat and slumped low. He felt that he had not managed the exchange about the cell phone as well as he could have. He did not blame himself; he had passed the most crucial tests and brought the enemy into Yemen. But the oldest of the men seemed guarded now, if not suspicious, and they still had a journey of some 742 kilometers ahead of them. That would take at least ten hours and he was concerned that he would not be able to continue the charade.

The CTU agent took out his own smartphone and switched

the light to dim. The device was linked to the Ministry of Defense communications system in nearby Harad; that was as far as he had to reach. He addressed his text message to outpost Commander Salim al-Shaabi:

> **Have infiltrated 4-person elite terror unit in blue bus. Soon to intercept Highway 10 south. Require hard mission force to intercept. Capture occupants for mission interrogation. Bader Abu Lahem**

CHAPTER THIRTY-EIGHT

Harad, Yemen
July 24, 6:15 p.m.

Commander Salim al-Shaabi did not know Bader Abu Lahem, but his CTU dossier was on file and there was no reason to doubt the authenticity of the text message or its contents. Even Saudi agents—who were plentiful in the Hajjah Governorate, secretly advancing their Sunni cause—were not well organized as a military force. It had been six years since Al-Qaeda attacked the Defense Ministry in Sana'a, using a car bomb to blow a hole in the compound wall and then mercilessly slaughtering soldiers, medical personnel, and other civilians. Since then, enemies of the state and foes of the Shia faith had chosen softer targets to hit.

The bald, six-foot-two-inch al-Shaabi was not a soft target. His outpost was not a soft target. If terrorists were planning a paramilitary action in his command, they would be stopped.

The commander had two armored fighting vehicles in his arsenal. He ordered those and his two armored personnel carriers to take up positions on the side of the highway. They were to allow traffic to pass until the blue bus was sighted, after which they were to block the road.

"I do not want air coverage that might alert them," al-Shaabi told the captains of his two, American-made, light observation Bell 206 helicopters. "Be prepared to provide air cover if required."

That meant a man leaning from the open hatches of each helicopter. That was the way they hunted insurgents in the field—a blue bus with nowhere to go would be a canary in a cage.

Only a quarter of his complement of 125 troops was deployed along the roadside, west of the chokepoint. He did not send them all because there was a part of him that feared this was a Sunni ruse to attack the depot itself. He alerted the rest of his men to don full body armor and be prepared to repel such an attack.

Within a half hour everything was in motion. Fifteen minutes later, the troops and vehicles were in place. Standing at the front of an AFV on the southern edge of the highway, Salim al-Shaabi watched the horizon with binoculars, eager for a fight that, for once, would be more muscular than a holding action against the accursed Saudis.

CHAPTER THIRTY-NINE

Major Breen was sitting back in the lumpy seat, having found the bodily impression made by decades of riders. He was concerned about the mission. His issues were not whether the new man was simply careless, a double-agent, or something else they had not even considered. To Breen, this was like a parachute jump. The condition of the equipment really did not matter until impact, when you either landed successfully or did not. The progression of every legal trial was important but nothing mattered until the jury or panel rendered its verdict. And even then, it was just a pause before the inevitable appeal process. Until there was something to concern Black Wasp, until there were actionable facts or leads, they should not be burning energy on "what ifs." That was one of the mandates General Lovett had hit on over and over again.

"A wasp is fast when it strikes," he had said. "You must be, too."

That unorthodoxy was the very reason they were created and the reason SITCOM had been designed. That bold new vision, though dangerous as hell, could signal a major transformation for the American military. The idea of amassing overwhelming numbers had been invented millennia before to line and protect borders. With drones in the air, satellites in space, and thousands of pockets of specialists ready for sabotage, assassination, infiltration, and other highly targeted missions, the financial and human cost of the military could be greatly reduced. For Breen, that future savings in lives, treasure, destruction, and suffering was worth this risk.

What worried Major Breen was not the concept, was not Amit Ben Kimon, was not who or what they would face in Aden. It was Chase Williams.

The man had obviously been the leader of a group of some kind, most likely from behind a desk. He was not sure-footed in the field, was not willing to risk his team the way any field commander must. He was also unwilling to cede command.

When Breen was named to Black Wasp, it was understood if not expressly ordered that being the oldest of the three original members by more than a decade, he was the nominal leader. SITCOM trumped that, but in survival training in Alaska and in Death Valley, the other two specialists had deferred to his broader knowledge and experience.

Chase Williams did not know how to do that and that struggle, along with the mission, seemed to be stripping his gears. Along with something else that he had not shared with them. But he clearly had a personal stake in this. He did not seem to be a man in mourning—though uttering the name "Janette" seemed to shine a brief light on an old wound, a lost wife or daughter perhaps. It was not likely he lost someone on the *Intrepid*. What pushed him forward had all the colorations of a vendetta. He had been boldest in Diego Martin at the apartment, when they were closing in on Salehi. No recon, no curbside caution. The major suspected—strongly suspected—that this was personal. And, as in a trial, when emotions were factored into the mix, results tended to spill out of control.

Breen had been debating, for the last half hour, whether to discuss this with Williams. He had not yet decided on that when the bus slowed, climbed slightly, and turned toward the west—still in the direction of Aden but now on a paved highway.

"Yay," Rivette said from two seats back. The lance corporal had seemed to groan and grunt with every bump; for a man whose survival depended on a steady surface for a steadier hand, the discomfiture was understandable.

The driver finally turned on the headlights and the team rose in their seats, almost as one. They were no longer protected by wilderness. They had to be prepared for anything.

CHAPTER FORTY

The National Reconnaissance Office, Washington, D.C.
July 24, 11:12 a.m.

It was her first day on the job. But in the aftermath of the Assault on a Queen, it was all hands on deck—and, if nothing else, Kathleen Hays had proven herself as a highly adept visual analyst during her tenure at Op-Center.

The night before—a dozen hours before, in fact—after having been given security clearance to take her new, junior position, the thirty-four-year-old had been home reading a history of the NRO when there was knock at the door of her Silver Springs, Maryland, studio apartment. A laminated credential was already in the eyepiece. The caller was a man named Matt Berry and he was the deputy chief of staff for President Midkiff. Anyone could have had a fake ID printed, but if someone wished her ill there were numerous other ways to accomplish that. She palmed her small can of pepper spray and opened the door.

Berry asked to come in. She permitted it; her visual analysis of the man was that he had the tired face of a bureaucrat, not the desperate expression of a lunatic. The two were not wildly dissimilar in the visual lexicon, but after eight months at Op-Center she had learned to quickly tell the difference.

Matt Berry faced her in a suit as creased as his expression and said without preamble, "The president arranged for you to have this position and for you to be assigned to the Yemen Surveillance Team for a particular." He gave her a business card that had no name, only a cell phone number. "I want you to watch the triangulated territory from the Jizan Regional Airport, Saudi Arabia, to Dhamar and then Aden in Yemen," he told her. "In particular, I want to know two things. One: Moving south, off-road, any vehicle large enough to carry five people. Two: Any sudden military or police activity in that region. You will text me with any information, at that number, from your private phone."

"I was told, Mr. Berry, that my private—"

"A forty-eight-hour window has been opened for you to place outgoing texts from the NRO," he cut her off. "Get there as early as you can and give me any information you pick up, however trivial you think it is. Questions?"

She shook her head and he turned to go.

"Mr. Berry," she said suddenly. "Do you have any idea how Director Williams is?"

Berry shook his head and closed the door.

Kathleen had slept four hours because she had to rest her eyes, and was at her bullpen-style station in a windowless room in Chantilly, Virginia, by five o'clock in the morning. The thirty-three-mile drive was traffic-free at that hour—reason enough to embrace an early-to-rise work ethic.

To Kathleen's surprise, from nine a.m. to the present her

communications with Berry had been more or less constant. He had acknowledged each with a simply TY; she had not expected thanks from the brusque man she had met. That alone suggested to her the stress he was under and, thus, the reason her information was vitally important. They were on the trail of Ahmed Salehi. Since she was including no other recipients, including the NRO, she could only imagine how highly classified were the things she had *not* been told. That was underscored by the fact that no one, not even her superiors, had come by to oversee or ask to see her work.

Kathleen felt like she was somewhere near the center of the known universe and found her mind, eyes, and spirit glinting with a sharp, new edge at the challenge.

The woman reported what looked like a bus departing Jizan for the border. The dark silhouette of the bus crossing the border and heading southeast without lights.

And then the movement of four vehicles and dozens of troops along the sides of Highway 10 in Harad.

Mr. Matt Berry did not acknowledge that message. Kathleen hoped he had received it.

CHAPTER FORTY-ONE

Highway 10, Yemen
July 24, 7:13 p.m.

If Grace Lee had not used the rancid toilet in the back of the bus, she would never have heard the quaint, muffled beep outside the door. It did not seem indigenous to this old crate of a bus, it was not something she had heard before, and it did not seem like something that should be ignored.

She opened the door, the squeak of it lost in the rattling over the rear wheels. She shut it in time to see the Israeli, sitting two seats ahead, reaching into his robe. He pushed the mute button, but that did not stop a two-chime beep from sounding seconds later.

Chase Williams had heard it, too, and rose.

Fussing with the phone, and accustomed to ignoring the woman, Lahem did not see or hear her as she moved stealthily behind him and saw the LED message:

Troops massed on highway in Harad.

The message evaporated and Lahem thrust the phone back in his robe. He looked at Williams coming toward him, but did not notice Grace easing into the empty seat behind him, leaning over, and throwing her right arm around his throat. She did not pull back but sunk back, her own weight tightening the choke-hold and causing him to gasp audibly.

Now the others were on their feet and hurrying back behind Williams.

"It's a trap," Grace said. "Military blockade in Harad."

Williams asked Breen to have the driver stop the bus. He did not steer the vehicle to the side of the highway but off it, resting slightly lopsided on a slope. He killed the headlights. Vehicles occasionally sped by at a high rate of speed, none of them showing any curiosity in the bus.

When they had stopped, Williams loomed over the man in back, whose clawing, kicking struggles to free himself had proven useless. Even in the dark, Williams could see the man turning red. "Let him breathe—once," Williams said.

Grace obliged then retightened her grip. Her captive sucked air down his raw throat before the hold was reapplied—tightly but enough so he could gasp . . . and speak.

"Who are you?" Williams demanded as the bus made an ugly stop that brought a shifting, grating protest from every part of it.

"CTU," he wheezed.

"Name?" Williams asked.

"Bader . . . Abu . . . Lahem . . ." he said with as much pride as he could muster from his constricted voice box.

Williams held his pistol at the man's forehead and asked Grace to release him. She did, pulling off her head covering and glaring at the man who was hacking to clear his compressed windpipe.

"Where is the man we were to meet?" Williams asked.

"Dead."

"You killed him?"

"Yes."

"Why?" Williams demanded.

Lahem hesitated.

Breen said over Williams's shoulder, "You didn't know about the phone or who he was meeting. You wanted his money route. We were a surprise."

Lahem hesitated again . . . then nodded.

"Our friend here communicated with the Yemeni military using his own device," Williams said to Grace.

She understood and reached across him, slapped his pockets, found the smartphone along with the dead Israeli's papers. The man seemed repulsed by her familiarity with his body, by her hair touching his cheek.

Williams pocketed the phone in his robe. He glared at the prisoner over his gun. "The only reason you're still alive is we may need you. You move, you speak, you die."

Rivette had returned and removed his headdress. He used the cord to tie the man's wrists, tightly, to the metal armrest of the seat. Breen's cord attached the man's ankles to the leg of the chair in front of him.

"I'll watch him," Grace said, drawing one of her knives from under her robe and sitting on the handrail across from him.

The other men moved a few steps forward. Breen was facing the front of the bus, keeping an eye on the driver; the man sat very still, his hands on his knees. If he hadn't seen the weapons he had heard the English. He was also Saudi; he had no reason to become involved in whatever was going on, only to survive it.

"We can't stay on the highway, obviously," Williams said—surprised how good it felt not to have to whisper anymore. He felt like a commander again.

"We also can't continue off-road," Breen contributed. "This thing can't take it."

"My ass can't take it," Rivette said. "No joke. If my lower back is off, I'm off, my aim is off."

Williams had known snipers, had known their artistic idiosyncrasies. He did not dismiss the complaint. He looked back at the Yemeni. He knew that something had been off with the bastard, and was not gratified to have been right. But the man gave him an idea.

"The military is off-road until they see a blue bus," Williams said, thinking. "When they see one, they will converge on it, on the highway."

"Assuming they don't just shoot the shit out of it," Rivette said.

"Unlikely," Breen said. "They'll want to interrogate the passengers."

"Right," Rivette said. "How much distance you think we got? I can pick 'em off—"

Breen ducked down, looked out the windshield. "City lights look about a mile, a mile and a half away. They wouldn't park too far from HQ in case this is a feint. And they're not using air cover, probably to keep from scaring us off."

"Good gets," Williams said.

"Too far without an M107, which we don't have," Rivette lamented.

"Not sure guerrilla war is what we want out here," Williams said. "We still have to get to Aden." He thought for a moment.

"There's no chance they've seen us yet. It's nearly dark. The bus moves forward, headlights will keep them from seeing inside."

"We can't run through or around this," Breen said.

"No. But I have an idea."

He told the other two what he was thinking. The plan seemed to self-blossom, parts of it emerging as he walked them through it. Breen was stoic as usual but Rivette's smile broadened as he listened.

"I like it," the lance corporal said when Williams was finished. "I want to be the one to stay with this guy." He indicated the Yemeni.

Williams shook his head. "Anything goes wrong, we will need your firepower."

"And I may need cover," Grace said from the back. "I'm staying with the prisoner. I'll meet you on the other side."

If this were Op-Center, Williams would probably not have approved the plan. It made him realize how his limited field experience had made him think that JSOC was recklessly out of their skulls most of the time. They weren't. Still, Williams hesitated.

"It's her call," Breen reminded Williams.

That was something he needed to hear—again. "All right," Williams said, easing around Breen. "I'll try and communicate to the driver what he has to do to survive this."

CHAPTER FORTY-TWO

Harad, Yemen
July 24, 7:48 p.m.

The dump truck was filled with potatoes grown in the highland regions of North Yemen, roughly one thousand meters above sea level where the temperature, sunlight, and water supply favored their growth. Qahtan al-Beid had worked the fields since he was a young boy, growing as they did, encouraged by the government's establishment in 1980 of the Seed Potato Production Center. Today, he and his two sons and both of his male grandchildren had a successful business; successful enough so that they only had to grow the vegetable and not participate in the drug trade. Illegal operators did not pressure him to surrender land; they, too, liked potatoes with their meals.

For the past sixteen years al-Beid had a contract with the government to provide potatoes for the military outposts and depots in the north. They did not pay very well, but what the family lost in profits they made up for with regular visits from military patrols as well as fly-overs by helicopters. That helped to let bandit groups know the fields were not to be molested. By and large, the tactic was successful. Bandits could only carry so many potatoes in any case; they were acceptable losses and some of them had even become al-Beid's eyes and ears in the region, warning about clandestine operations by Saudi invaders. That information, passed to Commander al-Shaabi, made the officer seem prescient to his own superiors in Sana'a. In all, it was a successful and synergistic relationship. The old but vital driver flicked his hand-rolled cigarette through the open window and sipped tea his grandson poured from a thermos. Though al-Beid carried a shotgun beside the door—the military could not be everywhere at once—he felt quite safe on Highway 10.

It was for that reason the grower and his son Nashwan were surprised when a blue bus suddenly, slowly struggled across the highway into their headlights, blocking the road.

Having moved two hundred meters to the west along the slight incline athwart the highway, Major Breen had flashed Williams's smartphone twice to signal the approach of the target. That was the sign for the frightened, greasily perspiring driver to move his bus onto and across the single east-running lane of the two-lane highway.

The dump truck would have plowed through it, had the driver not applied his brakes; though the impact would have done considerable damage to the cab and its occupants, who had not bothered to install seat belts.

The driver pulled up a shotgun but remained seated. His companion, sitting on the left, drew a revolver and rose up slightly, looking to the side and behind—as much as he could see over the stacked potatoes.

He froze when he saw the guns.

Rivette had been lying belly-down, facing the road. As soon as the truck stopped, he was on his feet, crouching, two guns drawn, moving forward in the deepening blue twilight. He hurried silently onto the running board, quietly cursing his cramped lower back, and pointed both weapons into the cab—one on each of the occupants. The shotgun remained at the height it had been raised.

That was when Breen stepped up. He pointed his own weapon at the driver and relieved him of the .12 gauge.

Rivette opened the left-side passenger door to pull the man out. There was not a great deal of traffic but the team did not want another vehicle to stop here now.

The lance corporal had warned the others not to fire unless they had to. Even a single shot would be heard a mile away. He broke that rule when he had opened the door and a light came on and he saw the young man's revolver pointed at him. The passenger's finger tensed and Rivette fired into his shoulder.

That was it, he thought unhappily. *The clock is really running now.*

Rivette pulled the young man out while Breen did the same on the driver's side. The two Americans jumped into the cab of the truck, Rivette at the wheel. They turned off the road, back into the rugged plain, while the old man ran to see to the other.

"Wait!" Breen said to Rivette. "We can't leave them. The military will know where we've gone.

Rivette swore and, together, they got out and pushed the two Yemenis up the rear swing gate and into the back. Williams arrived then and pulled himself up beside them. Grace followed. The plan had been to stall the army by driving the bus to the checkpoint where Grace would slip out and rendezvous with the truck. That plan was dead; even now the horizon was bright with lights racing in their direction. The woman jumped from the driver's side running board to the dumping bed then on to the potatoes.

"Hold on!" Rivette shouted out the window as he tore into the countryside, the passengers sliding over the high, unsteady load. The jostling was extreme; Grace buried herself deep, facedown, to keep from sliding around. Williams followed her example.

"What did you do with Lahem?" he asked the lieutenant.

"He killed Ben Kimon, saw the banker, heard us talk," she said. "I had no choice."

Williams did not, could not, approve of field executions; he also did not blame her. "The driver?"

"I gave him some of the money for his trouble, kept the rest in case we need it. He actually seemed okay."

Breen was lying on his side near Williams, his gun on the Yemenis. He was facing the back of the truck. The old man had removed his *keffiyeh* to try and bind the bullet wound of the other. He was on his knees, more skilled than the rest at keeping his balance.

"Lance corporal—is there a first-aid kit in the cab?"

"There is!"

"I'll cover him," William said, grasping the major's intention.

Breen handed him the gun and elbow walked to the front of the truck. He extended an arm through the open window, took the kit from Rivette, and squirmed his way back. He gave the kit to the old man—who seemed both surprised and grateful.

The major turned back toward the others and recovered his

gun. "The soldiers are still going to see the tracks," he said. "And the potatoes that are bouncing out."

"If we abandon the truck they'll hunt us down," Williams said.

"End run!" Rivette shouted from the cab.

The other three had no idea what he meant until he swung the truck into a dramatic turn back in the direction they had come—but to the east.

"Shit," Grace said. Then, to Rivette, "Nice one!"

"Thanks!"

The other two realized, then, what the lance corporal meant. He would get back on Highway 10 below the military checkpoint.

"Choppers'll spot us," Williams said.

"Not in the city," Breen said. "We abandon the truck."

The other two agreed as Rivette steered them back toward the highway. They thumped onto it well below the spot where the original checkpoint had been. When Harad was just a turnoff away, they stopped.

Williams said something to the old man in English. He replied in Arabic, made a show of not understanding. That was good enough. Even if they'd heard what the Americans were saying—potatoes proved to be surprisingly sound-absorbing—they couldn't tell the troops anything. Blindfolding them with their own headwear and tying them back-to-back with their rope belts—gently, so as not to pop the younger man's hasty bandage—the team slipped from the truck and moved silently toward the city.

CHAPTER FORTY-THREE

Aden, Yemen
July 24, 9:00 p.m.

Ali Abdullah did not spit when Sadi called again. This time, he was consumed with fire. The Quran relates how it is the djinn who are created from flame; if so, then Abdullah was now himself a being of the supernatural.

Upon returning to Aden with their prized passenger, Abdullah had brought him to the warehouse to await further instructions— and also to introduce him to his fighters. The experience put most of them on their knees, threw some into prayers of thanks, the *du'a* from the Quran. Abdullah had never seen his fighters like children, like women, but he did not begrudge them that. He had wanted to bring Salehi here to stir their passion, and that had happened. The Iranian was openly embarrassed by the spontaneous display, but he was also poised and present enough not to dismiss the respect he was being shown.

Afterward, Abdullah offered to give the man privacy in one of the sleeping areas that had been set up for the fighters. Salehi asked, instead, to go outside in the sun, to smell the sea. The warlord understood and, fixing him up with headgear to conceal his features, went outside with him. Abdullah always carried a Walther P-99 in the pocket of his robe and, for added security, had quietly sent two men to the roof of the warehouse to watch over their guest. He did not wish to crowd the captain but to see to his protection.

The warehouse was just fifty meters from the water and Salehi approached with quiet reverence. It was a rare moment of balance for Abdullah, he was with an ally who had achieved a great victory against an enemy of Islam, someone who had done, in a minute, what the Supporters of Allah had been struggling for years to achieve.

They remained outside for nearly an hour, after which Abdullah allowed Salehi a quiet meal in their galley—and he informed his men that their mission was not yet complete.

"We will review maps of the port of Al Hudaydah," he said. "It is there we will be taking our honored guest—and protecting him from a strike I have been informed is coming from a team of commandos."

The information roused the men anew.

For several hours, they studied maps of the port and of the ships presently in the harbor. They learned about the tanker *al-Wadi'i* to which they would be bringing Captain Salehi. Their benefactor had sent over the plans and they ascertained access points for themselves . . . and an unknown number of commandos who might come for them. They did not look for exits since each man would die rather than retreat. They studied the corridors, stairs, elevators, and charted routes that afforded the greatest protection. After making their plans they slept, while Salehi did the same.

Abdullah was awakened by the call from Sadi, informing him that the commandos had gotten as far as Harad, where they had apparently evaded a roadblock.

The news of the foreign team evading another force in their own land should have been concerning to Abdullah. But it had just the opposite effect. Ahmed Salehi had pitted himself against the greatest odds a man could conceive and had won a great victory. Abdullah and his core group, the best of his fighters, now had a chance to do the same.

"I do not have information on their exact number," Sadi said. "But they are small and mobile and should not be underestimated."

"They will not be," Abdullah assured him.

"The *al-Wadi'i* docks are at high tide tomorrow morning, 11:09," Sadi said.

"Overcast with rainfall," Abdullah reported. He always made it a point to know the weather where he would be fighting.

"You please me," Sadi told him. "I do not know that I will have further information. From now until the encounter you must be vigilant. These invaders have proven difficult to predict and resilient, as have your own fighters. Perhaps Captain Salehi can contribute observations from Trinidad."

"An excellent thought," Abdullah replied.

"*Fi Amanullah*," Sadi replied before hanging up.

"May Allah protect you as well," Abdullah replied, throwing off the vestiges of sleep and going to see Captain Salehi.

CHAPTER FORTY-FOUR

Al Luḥayyah, Yemen
July 24, 10:08 p.m.

It was not the lights of Harad that Rivette had seen. He had traveled further south, paralleling the highway, and had reached the coastal town of Al Luḥayyah.

"Read the signs next time," the lance corporal muttered as they entered the town.

"This is actually good," Grace said.

"How do you figure?" Rivette asked.

"Because the chance we have of getting to Aden quickly—and at all—is by sea," Breen said.

"The Red Sea," Williams said.

His remark had the effect of putting the team into a new and different state of mind . . . and spirit. It hit them, to varying degrees, that this was not just a region of religion. It reminded Williams of the feeling he had whenever he went to the Oval Office. Regardless of the occupant, it *was* the Oval Office. This was immediately bigger. It was a place where God Himself hammered prophets with suffering, raised them when there was need.

Now that Williams had given them time to catch their breath somewhat, to take stock, to save the peace of the nighttime, it was humbling on an entirely new level. He could sense, from their silence, their almost reverent tread, that the others felt it, too.

The men walked shoulder to shoulder, Breen in the center, Rivette on the right. Grace had repaired her outfit and was walking behind the men. She did not mind; it left her better able to keep tabs of anyone who might be around them. She had been amused, on the flight over, that the military had prepared backpacks for them: more weapons, more ammunition, medical supplies, and radios. Except for power bars tucked in pockets, they had left it all behind. She carried only what she had when she left Trinidad, hidden beneath her robes, the knives still tight in their sheaths. She had choked Lahem to death rather than cut his throat as he deserved. In Ancient China, a literal coat of blood was a warning to others who aspired to enter a community and become murderous "entrepreneurs."

The short, potholed exit ramp opened to a bleak vista where the spotty electric lights seemed to be accompanied by the sound of generators. The only nearby lights came from two campfires about one hundred yards ahead. They were lit in the ruined foundations of buildings that once stood on two empty lots. There were burned vehicles on the road beside those lots and the firelight revealed craters averaging a yard or two in diameter. Williams had seen enough combat photos to recognize the damage caused by rocket-propelled grenades.

Several men were gathered around each fire; driven by a gentle sea breeze, the cottony smoke floated toward the new arrivals. Some of the men had rifles slung over their shoulders. Two were standing, using binoculars to try and ascertain what was going on up the highway. All turned to look at the ghostly white trio coming down the road followed by a woman.

"They're probably self-appointed militia watching for Saudis or insurgents," Breen said.

"We should go some other way," Rivette suggested.

"We turn, they may fire," Williams said.

"We don't turn, they will ask us questions we can't understand or answer," Breen pointed out.

Williams desperately sought a third option—splitting up, turning back, opening fire. None of it ended well.

"Lieutenant—you're rattling," Breen said.

"I know," Grace replied.

All of them flinched as two helicopters passed over the highway, headed east from the direction of Harad. It wouldn't be long before they split and started zigzagging over the terrain to the south and this city to the north. They had to move.

Rivette had been looking around. "Hey," he said. "There's an old pickup facing the exit—right side of the second lot. See it?"

The others looked.

"Their troop transport," Breen said.

"Yeah, probably with keys already in the ignition," Rivette said. "Our ticket through this no-man's-land forbidden zone if we can get to it."

The lance corporal had a point. The port city was spotted with fires like these. The blazes, fueled by wood that used to be homes or carts or trees, could be families trying to stay warm in the cool air of the ocean—or it could be more men watching for trouble.

The gatekeepers of Al Luḥayyah were only fifty yards away

and most were now on their feet, facing the newcomers. The group
was not walking toward them, but they had come from the wilderness, in the night. Williams knew there was no way to get out of
this cleanly. He knew that there were two priorities: the mission
and the team, in that order.

*If we fight and kill men who are simply protecting their homes
and families, how are we any different from Salehi?* he asked himself. But he quickly reduced that larger philosophical question to
a practical one: *If we do not, we are likely to die here, now or slowly.*

"Let me handle this," Grace said, walking around Breen before anyone could object.

That move alone caused the onlookers to stiffen with shock.
They spoke one to the other, one of them shouldering his rifle and
aiming at Williams, who was the tallest man. Another raised a
walkie-talkie. Williams and the others stopped.

"Grace, what's the plan?" Rivette asked.

"You be prepared to take on the boys to the right," she said
to the lance corporal without taking her eyes off the Yemeni force
straight ahead. "There may be one or two left standing."

"One or two?" a disbelieving Rivette said.

"And they may be calling for backup," she added, "so we'll
have to book."

The militiamen must have heard the lance corporal, heard the
English, because the men were in motion now, spreading out and
raising weapons, targeting all the men. Grace was moving away
from her companions, appearing to be saving herself for the inevitable shootout to follow. Williams fought the urge to raise his
arms in surrender. Whatever Grace was planning, the wall of

Yemenis would cut the three men down before she could reach them and before Rivette could get his hands into his robes.

Williams saw the silhouette of her arms moving beneath her spacious robes. She couldn't attack all of them with her knives; that couldn't be her plan. It was only a moment before she made her move that he understood.

"*Get down*," he hissed at the others.

Grace had already pulled the pins on two of the hand grenades she had taken from the boat on the Navet. She flung them in two simultaneous, arcing moves. Gunfire spit from one handgun but it went wide as the man was knocked over by a neighbor who recognized the threat and was diving for cover.

Grace took a flying somersault behind a pile of stones, hunkering down as the grenades exploded. She raised her head at once, searching for a target, was just in time to see Rivette, on one knee, firing at anyone who tried to get back up.

Williams raised his face from the cracked asphalt beneath him, peered through the smoke of the blast that was thinning and expanding in his direction. His head ringing, he could not hear the shots but he saw two men drop with new, bloody holes in their hips.

"Move it!" Breen shouted over the team's temporary deafness. "That's going to draw reinforcements!"

As one, the group was on its feet and running toward the rusted pickup, Rivette slightly behind and covering their escape. There was no one left to fire at them, though Williams saw a pair of youthful faces behind what used to be a basement window behind the truck. He refused to think about the kids. He couldn't.

Williams got behind the wheel, suspecting—correctly—that the old truck would be a stick. The key was there and the truck started as the others jumped in the back.

"Hopefully," Rivette said breathlessly as Grace pulled him in, "anyone who sees us will recognize the pickup and let it pass."

Grace lay flat beside a small cache of canvas-covered weapons. She pulled the fabric over her so she would not be seen. Rivette crouched by the tailgate, guns in each hand.

"They've got an RPG here," Grace said.

"Nice," Rivette said. "The Lord provides."

"Not for these people," Breen remarked.

The hell behind them was duplicated in front of them as Williams picked his way through a ruined city toward the sea. At the speed they were going, in the dark, the robes and head coverings the men wore raised no suspicion from other men who were protecting women who were scavenging for canned goods or fabric—banners made good patches—or collecting water from faucets that still worked. The destruction here was probably recent, or most of the food would be gone.

The flat, dark expanse of the Red Sea grew, as did the trappings of civilization. Buildings were in better repair here, probably because the port was active and was needed by both sides in the struggle. It reminded Williams of the old NAP—the Neutron Attack Plan, first conceived in the 1960s—which involved deploying a weapon that killed troops and population with a blast of enhanced radiation but did little damage to terrain or infrastructure. Though it was designed for antitank strikes, the minds at the Pentagon imagined scenarios they called "area denial" where geographical regions could be poisoned to prevent enemy troops from moving in . . . or out.

The port of Al Luḥayyah was like that. Shoot, starve, or bludgeon the resistance or invaders without damaging the ships, maintenance systems, or housing. It was an insidious tactic designed to support and prolong war, not to end it.

They reached the port unmolested. Breen was standing, leaning on the panel in back of the cab, facing forward. He and Williams saw it first: there was just an abandoned container ship and several rowboats in the port. No fishing boats, no tugs, no patrol vessels. Nothing with a motor to get them where they needed to go.

The major looked around.

"What's wrong?" Rivette asked.

"We have to find a place to bunk down," he said. "This plan isn't going to work."

Williams heard him and had reached the same conclusion. Open channel or no, he had to contact Berry. There was a burned-out grocery store on the road that ran along the coast. The shop would have a basement. If there was no one inside, that was where they would go.

His spirits sinking, Williams turned the wheel and headed for the bleak, unlit shell of a building.

CHAPTER FORTY-FIVE

The White House, Washington, D.C.
July 24, 2:30 p.m.

Berry sat in his small office, the door closed, his mind open, his hopes somewhere in the middle. He was looking through a database of the Yemeni Shia insurgency. Whoever met Salehi would also have the resources to protect him. That meant Shia fighters.

"That means a force of Shia fighters large enough to repel an attack they have to suspect is coming," he murmured.

The bloody country had more factions than Washington had lobbyists. The trick to locating the right group was the same as Black Wasp had managed to achieve in Trinidad: find the safe house or hideout. The key to *that* was identifying a spot where the enemy did not go. Possibly because there was intel, possibly because they had lost people, probably both.

He looked up Saudi and Sudanese movements in Aden. The port city was a relative Sunni stronghold due to the fact that insurgents could infiltrate from the north and by sea, and the men did not do much to disguise their clothes or the cafes they frequented. Those hangouts had already been identified by Sunni operatives hired by the U.S. eight years earlier during the secular civil war that was part of the wider, poverty-and-politics-fueled uprising of the Arab Spring. Unfortunately, the Yemeni recruits were not professionals and suffered a high mortality rate—or else they took their profits and left the lethal gaming table.

Berry sent his request for a wardrobe identification scan to Kathleen Hays, asking her to search using a variation of facial-recognition software. The program identified clothing and tracked it over days to create time-lapse images tracking the movements of individuals. When enough individuals in a group were charted, then group patterns became known.

Moments after he sent his request, he got a response—but it was not about the clothing.

Likely match for Hodeida International Airport truck. Seen 23 minutes later, Sadi Shipping sector, Aden seaport.

That was something, and Berry asked for the exact coordinates. Satellite views showed a large complex of nondescript structures, with dockworkers moving about. That wasn't enough to help Black Wasp.

"They can't go door to door," he said.

The desk phone rang and, unthinking, Berry picked it up without checking the ID.

"Rumor has it that you authorized two off-the-book military flights," said the caller.

"I did, January," Berry replied smoothly.

Her voice thick, low, and unhappy, January Dow went on: "The flights were to and from Trinidad, where there was a dust-up with JAM terrorists—the group likely involved in the Montreal murders; and then from Guantánamo—which happens to be in that very same Caribbean neighborhood—to Saudi Arabia. Is there intel you are not sharing, Matt?"

"Where would I get intel that didn't originate with you or one of the other agencies?" he asked.

"Don't be a shit," she said. "I know you have personal dealings with the Mossad, with MI5, with General Intelligence in Riyadh to name a few. What are you not telling me?"

"You?"

"Us," she corrected herself.

"Why don't you ask your boss, the president," he said.

"*Our* boss," she corrected him. "Why the hell would you run a secret operation on something this important?"

"So far, you're the only one who has said anything about secrets and missions," he said.

He could hear her breathing through her nose. "All right, Matt. Play your hand. But I promise you, if you are violating one word of the Homeland Security Act then you will follow your friend Chase Williams out the window."

"If I'm lucky, then, I'll land on him, cushion my fall."

January hung up and Berry knew that time was as short as the president had suggested the night before.

At least he has plausible deniability, Berry thought. *I'm the only one with fingerprints all over this.*

He prayed that Black Wasp had received the message he sent

to Amit Ben Kimon, and that everything had worked out in Harad. If it had not, he did not risk texting to the cell phone in case it had fallen into the hands of the Yemeni military.

The only thought left was an oath, which he uttered, then went back to see if there was any intelligence on the Sadi warehouses. Nothing came up.

He wondered, with a stabbing moment of irony, if he should call January Dow to find out what she knew.

If I thought it would help them, I would, he said as he looked at his stubbornly silent smartphone. . . .

CHAPTER FORTY-SIX

Williams parked the truck in front of a boathouse down the road from the grocery, and they made their quiet way along the deserted street. Nighttime was for smugglers and most people had no reason to come here. Given the active search for Black Wasp, smugglers might not come here tonight either.

Hopefully, if the team needed the truck, it would still be there; if anyone found it, they would likely assume the people who stole it were gone, out to sea, and not hiding down the block.

The grocery store was seven aisles of empty shelves, spent ammunition, shattered glass, and blood. There was dog feces on the floor; it was old, indicating how long it had been since there was anything edible here.

At least, Williams thought, it did not smell of rotted meat. The animals had made off with that.

The cigarettes were gone but there were matches, and Williams used them to find the basement. They weren't as bright as the light on his SID and, though the battery had a forty-hour life, he saw no reason to waste any of that.

The basement was located down a short flight of stairs. It was stuffy and hot; during the heat of the day it was probably stifling. The room was nearly the size of the store above and it had obviously been used as a prison, possibly as an interrogation center. There were empty beverage cans, cigarette butts, chairs with rope tied to the armrests, two pairs of handcuffs on the floor, and more blood.

After checking to make sure it was sturdy, Rivette dropped into one of the wooden chairs. Grace stood and removed her head and face coverings. Breen sat on the stairs. It felt good to plant himself on something that wasn't jostling.

As soon as everyone was settled, Williams dropped the match he was holding and turned on the SID. He used the text function to minimize noise. It also occurred to him that the others had no idea who he was working for or with. Though it wasn't high on his list of concerns, Berry might want to keep it that way.

Amit murdered by Yemeni who took his place. Killer is dead. We are safe in Al Luḥayyah cellar with no way to get to Aden.

It took nearly a minute for Berry to respond. Silence had never sounded so deep, and so deeply unsettling; they not only had no way to get to Aden, they had no means of getting anywhere safe.

USN won't go there. Can you put to sea at all?

Williams replied, unsure if his not-so-mild sarcasm would translate:

Rowboats.

A longer silence followed. Williams picked up a few greasy rags and found his mind drifting to the men they had killed back at the exit ramp. It was not guilt but profound regret, and he tamped it down by telling the others that the Navy wouldn't come here.

"It's too incendiary," Breen said. "The Red Sea, I mean."

"Why?" Rivette asked.

"These are major Saudi shipping lanes," he said. "I read the intelligence reports on the plane. The corridor from Hodeida to Harad is still a Shia stronghold but the Saudi Sunnis have been probing for soft spots."

"That explains the all-out effort against us on the highway," Rivette said.

"Exactly," Breen told him. "The Houthis have been threatening to attack crews and blow up shipping, make the waterways unpassable. The Saudis are American allies—"

"So a Navy ship would make them go crazy," Rivette said. "Even a dinghy."

"It's happened before," Breen explained. "The U.S. Navy transport HSV-2 Swift was hit by an antiship missile in October 2016. The destroyer USS *Mason* was fired at but not damaged after that. We responded with a Tomahawk missile and other armaments—"

"Which is why there's nothing legal going on out there," Rivette said, cocking his head in the direction of the sea.

"That, plus oil spills," Breen said. "The older tankers leak. It washes ashore here. Fishermen can't earn a living."

"So, economy, too," Rivette said.

"There's a big cash conflict going on below the surface," Breen said. "Saudis are building the world's largest oil tanker fleet. That threatens the big player here, Sadi Shipping. This isn't just about Shia versus Sunni. It's about the economic resources to keep Yemen afloat."

Williams was impressed at how much Breen had read, retained, and most importantly contextualized. He finally understood why this man was part of the Black Wasps.

Berry answered then.

Arranged pickup at sea, Saudi tanker Dima, +/-2:15 a.m. Going Aden. Speak English to lookout. Spot ship passing at +/-1:00 for distance.

The clock on the phone had just scraped past eleven. That was a lot of time to avoid being spotted. But it was the best offer on the table and they had to take it—even if to just get out of Yemen.

Williams was about to acknowledge and sign off when Berry wrote:

Kathleen Hays at NRO has update. Wardrobe ID Puts +/- dozen supporters of Allah Houthi at dock. Top stealth fighters. Likely guards for target.

Williams texted back:

Acknowledged, understood.

Berry wished them Godspeed, and Williams knew he meant it—maybe, even, for more than just his job.

You are getting too cynical, he thought. *Lose your humanity in this place and you will never find it.*

Williams lit a match and ignited the rags to give him a larger—but not too large—fire. Then he updated the others, earning universal scowls from the team. Not only would they have to reconnoiter and survive here for over three hours, they would have to row into the Red Sea, at night, in a rising wind.

"And—hold on," Rivette said, creeping back upstairs. He paused at the top of the steps. "Yeah," he said and came back down. "It's drizzling and blowing in."

"It has to rain here, what, twice a year?" Grace said. "Lucky us."

"It actually might be," Breen said. "Should keep the patrols down. Even soldiers need to collect drinking water."

"Lance corporal, why don't you—" Williams said, then checked himself.

This was a military democracy. He had to get used to that. "We should rest, eat, maybe collect some of that water ourselves," he suggested. "We'll also need a sentry."

"I volunteer for that," Rivette said with a knowing chuckle. "Also," he lay down one gun and reached into his robe, "got a few potatoes if you don't mind raw."

Williams smiled as Rivette tossed them to Grace.

"I'll come with you to get the water," the lieutenant said, picking up two empty cans that once held peas and shaking them out. Dark particles dropped to the floor. "I'd save some matches, commander. We should boil before drinking."

He nodded in the flickering light, then sat back.

"I can't tell you anything more," he said to Breen, holding up the phone as the others moved cautiously to the grocery. The statement was half-explanation, half-apology.

"As long as it doesn't impact Black Wasp directly, I don't need to know," Breen assured him. "But you look a little more relieved than I've seen you."

"If you could apply that word to anyone at the Alamo or waiting to cross the Channel on D-Day—yeah," Williams laughed. "My liaison did something good for someone I used to work with. Probably for others as well."

"Good to know," Breen said, without prying. "I'd hate to be partnered with a dick."

Williams noticed that the major had said "partnered with" and not "working for." Breen was an attorney, careful with his words, and that was an important distinction, a useful reminder as they awaited what might be a final showdown—and their last day on the planet.

Working in Washington, at Op-Center, it was easy to forget the old World War II rallying cry, "Why we fight." This operation was not for Matt Berry or President Midkiff or the future of Chase Williams.

It was for the American people.

Just then, Rivette bounded back inside, taking all the steps in a handrail supported jump.

"Grace is upstairs—we got company."

CHAPTER FORTY-SEVEN

Al Luḥayyah, Yemen
July 24, 11:20 p.m.

Crouched in the doorway where the door no longer existed—it was just a metal frame with tiny glass shards along one side—Grace Lee watched the brightening sky to the west, then heard the beat of the helicopter.

That information about the Houthis and their stronghold explained why it was here. The team had avoided the roadblock, abandoned the potato truck, killed Houthi fighters and stole their truck—which had been described, most likely in a radio communication. Now it had been spotted. The helicopter rotors did not have the familiar, deep beat of a military vehicle; most likely it was a repurposed police chopper without built-in armaments.

Still, they would be able to call for ground support.

She raced back down the stairs where the others were already on their feet.

"We have to get into the sea," she said.

"Now?" Rivette asked.

"Now. The chopper is going to pin itself on the pickup we took and rally the troops. We can't be here."

No one disagreed and they raced upstairs just as the helicopter arrived. As Grace had predicted, a spotlight fixed itself on the abandoned vehicle. Fortunately, the vehicle was far enough away so that the grocery store was not an obvious next step.

"West along the road, into the nearest rowboat," Williams said.

He left the fire burning; stamping it out would produce and spread smoke that might be spotted. It would go out on its own in a minute or two.

Following Rivette, the team left the grocery through a shattered side window, opposite the hovering helicopter. There was a paved road that was dark and had to be crossed slowly; it was covered with debris from the store and they did not want to make any noise. There was a light drizzle, which seemed to amplify every sound, at least in their vicinity. The drone from the helicopter was loud, but somewhat muted on this side of the grocery. They did not know who might be in the abandoned, three-story brick building ahead. The goal was to put more distance between themselves and any team that might be directed from the helicopter.

The team hugged the front of the brick building and crossed the street toward the concrete dockside area one at a time: Breen, Williams, Grace, and finally Rivette. It was up to the two with guns and, more importantly, recent firing-range training to cover the others. Reunited, they crept to the row of six wooden wharfs that were in various stages of neglect and disrepair.

Williams ushered them to a boat he had noticed earlier. It was an old wooden rowboat with seven-foot paddle oars. There was a broken mast but no sail just behind the pointed bow and, aft, a squared transom with the end of the boom jutting a foot beyond. It seemed to be in good repair and was probably used by arms smugglers; the tools onboard, a crowbar and hammer, as well as removal of the center thwart suggested a cargo of small crates.

Grace boarded first, being the lightest, most agile, and least likely to make a sound. The boat was slick in the rain, and rocking in the wind, and she pulled in the mooring line to help steady it. Breen got in next; Rivette last. The major had already taken up the oars and Grace released the rope. Williams took his Sig Sauer from his robe and sat on the port side of the stern athwart, watching the men pulling up around the glow of the helicopter spotlight. Rivette covered their retreat from shore by sitting at the stern. Grace sat starboard, opposite Williams, her sharp eyes backing up Rivette. Williams's heel kicked up against something under the seat. It was a long, rubber-surfaced box with a drop-down front panel. It was most likely waterproof, possibly for food but most likely for weapons. He opened it, was not surprised to find it empty. He returned to watching the retreating shoreline.

For Williams, the Red Sea no longer had a sense of majesty; it was a disagreeable body of water, instantly and completely impacted by the wind and rain. He could not help but think that a strong wind might, in fact, part the waters.

That would certainly make our passage easier, he reflected.

The water was not rocky enough to make them seasick, but the air was cold enough to make everyone but Breen shiver.

The shivering increased when Williams noticed the spotlight

suddenly turn from the car as the helicopter moved out over the water.

Maybe they decided we did *go out to sea*, he thought unhappily.

Rivette saw it, too, and turned, aiming his guns in that direction.

"No!" Williams said. "The men on shore will pick us off."

"You have a better idea?"

"Give me your guns."

"Oh no," Rivette said. "I—"

"There's a locker—under you too, probably," he said quietly but urgently. "Put them in there. We have to flip the boat, get under, play dead."

The team was fast, economical motion. Breen made sure the oars were secure in the locks then handed Williams his own gun and went over the side. Grace dropped off the back, unconcerned about her knives. After securing the firearms and SID phone, Williams and Rivette went into the water. Breen and Grace had already organized that they would tip the boat toward starboard and the others joined them from both sides. They pulled and pushed, but the boom and two surviving feet of mast helped to center the rowboat, making it difficult to invert; Williams finally pulled himself partway from the water, grabbed the boom, and dropped back down causing the hull to roll. As soon as the boat was keel up, the four got underneath. Breen and Grace held on to the front thwart, Williams and Rivette grabbed the boom. Williams took a moment to fish out the mooring line and force it up to the surface as if the wind had knocked the boat loose.

"Nice one," Grace said.

"There sharks in this water?" Rivette asked.

"It's an inlet of the Indian Ocean, so probably," Breen said. "Try not to move."

"How much air you think we got here?" the lance corporal asked.

"About fifteen, twenty minutes if we don't kick and we don't talk," Breen calculated.

The four hung in silence, fighting the added weight of their waterlogged robes and occasionally knocking their heads against the boat when they were raised by swells. At least, thought Williams gratefully—after being baked all day by the summer sun—at *least* the damn water was mild.

The searchlight threw a moving white circle on the sea. It crept toward them like a luminous jellyfish, creating an eerie light under the surface as it suffused and writhed in the currents of the water below. The team saw fish for the first time, more than they had expected. The sound of the chopper was amplified by the water and by the hull; it stopped when it was directly above them.

"Please God don't shoot," Rivette said.

"They won't if they're well-trained," Breen said. "There could be explosives in the lockers."

Only then did it occur to Williams—helped by a critical look from Breen, illuminated by the subsurface glow—that those lockers could have been booby trapped.

The helicopter hovered for what seemed far too long. Either they were getting ready to lower someone or calling HQ for instructions. Whatever the reason, the battering of the rain on the hull had picked up steadily and that, it seemed, was finally what turned the helicopter back to the west, to Harad.

The sea was once again dark—the air under the hull decidedly warm and rank.

"I'll go out and look around," Williams said. "See if there's anyone watching from shore."

"Hold on," Breen said. "I saw the shadow of a derelict tanker on the sea bottom. Another minute or so and it'll be between us and the shore. No one will see us."

It was another sharp call from Breen, and Williams gave an appreciative nod. As they continued to bob and drift, Williams found himself wishing they could stay where they were. Assuming they could right the rowboat, it was going to be a damn cold couple of hours.

CHAPTER FORTY-EIGHT

Sana'a, Yemen
July 25, 1:33 a.m.

Ordinarily, Mohammad Obeid ibn Sadi found it easy to sleep. Sprawled in safety and comfort on his pillows, his soul at rest, having read from the Quran—there was no reason for a man to lack for peace. But tonight was different.

It was not just the fact that he had Ahmed Salehi as his guest, or that within a very few hours Ali Abdullah would destroy the team that had been sent to apprehend him and post video of their remains on jihadi websites—adding a second fresh wound to the arrogance of the infidels.

Sadi was aflame with the vision he had for Yemen, for his people. In 1881, Muhammad Ahmad bin Abd Allah of Sudan had declared himself the Mahdi, the redeemer of Islam, and set about to oust foreign powers from the region—including the wicked English. He was not just a religious leader, but a military campaigner who succeeded in building a short-lived Mahdist state. Had he not died of typhus shortly after the fall of Khartoum, the history of the region—of the world—would have been very different.

Others had tried and failed to emulate the Mahdi. Saddam

Hussein was a Sunni, doomed by Allah not to succeed. Abu Bakr al-Baghdadi had taken, then lost, a caliphate in Syria and the Levant. Osama bin Laden was another Sunni who was more interested in celebrity and sexual sin than in conquest. Even the pathetic ayatollahs in Iran were so caught up in preserving their power base against rebellious youth that they had lost their external vision.

Rebellious youth! Sadi thought. *They shatter the Ten Commandments of the prophet Mûsâ ibn 'Imran and they are not punished!*

Sadi's bony hand closed around an imaginary switch. His sunken eyes looked across the room, which was lit by a single lamp in the corner. He vividly remembered many of the sinful young who had been blindfolded and brought here and taught how to live a virtuous life. He remembered it not just with pride but with undiminished enthusiasm.

Unlike his fellow Shia in Tehran, Sadi had the wealth to carry out his ambition. He had the ships that controlled the flow of oil, and when the Saudis and the Sudanese and the Americans were gone, he would command the Red Sea—the waterway that controlled the ships that carried the oil. Because he had wealth, he had also been able to grab, quickly, the man who would become the public face of his war. And while America and Europe chased him around the globe—constantly stymied by his resources—he would win his war at home, build and arm the military with resources from Iran, and then foment Shia uprisings everywhere, toppling the House of Saud and the Sunni nations of Pakistan, Turkey, Egypt, and, to the east, the former Soviet republics.

While contentedly imagining a new map of the Middle East, Sadi was finally able to fall asleep.

CHAPTER FORTY-NINE

The Tanker Dima, *Red Sea*
July 25, 2:12 a.m.

Saudi captain Bandar Al-Sowayel became interested in the sea after reading about the proud biremes of the Ancient Phoenicians, the ancestors of the Syrians and the Lebanese, who were known to have traded with Egypt at least as far back as 1400 B.C.E. It was incredible that these peoples had cut cedar from their hills, constructed galleys with two tiers of oars, and cast themselves into the oceanic void.

And yet, the fifty-year-old seaman thought, *it was less treacherous sailing those millennia ago than it is today.*

The long-range tanker *Dima* was one of eighty or so ships to sail the Red Sea each day, a body of water 2.250 kilometers long and just 355 kilometers wide. Thanks to the sophistication of modern electronics, he could sail at night and in inclement weather with the same confidence as on a sun-bright afternoon; and with the same concerns, since Yemenis with RPGs had been equally adept striking targets day or night.

Because of the unrest between his nation and the one off his port side—and not as far off as he would like—there were few Yemeni ports where he could dock. Aden was not one of them, but it was on the way to the port of Trivandrum, India, which was his destination. Within five minutes of agreeing to the mission— which would appear to be spontaneous and accidental, the recovery of Americans at sea—his associate in Washington known only as Blackberry, had transferred $50,000 American to an account with the Al Rajhi Bank, an account that had personally been set up by their chief risk officer, Salman Al-Saud. The captain had immediately sent $5,000 of that sum to ship's second officer Fareed El-Hashem, who spoke English and would handle the recovery.

Captain Al-Sowayel had been instructed to watch for a rowboat that would be some five kilometers from shore. He had extra men on watch because of the rain, and he had personally remained on the bridge to scan the waters.

"For Yemeni vessels," he had told the bridge crew, which would give him an excuse to look for and find a vessel the size of a rowboat.

The call from El-Hashem was made to the captain's wireless phone on the command console.

"Yes?"

"We've spotted a rowboat roughly fifty meters from starboard," the second officer reported. "There seem to be occupants— that is all we know."

"Full stop," he told the first officer. Then, to El-Hashem he said, "Dispatch the rescue team. I'm coming down."

Williams was shaken by sudden turbulence. Then, suddenly, there were hands moving here and there in the dark. Not his hands;

those were numb. The hands belonged to people who were pulling him from the sodden bottom of the rowboat and placing him in another vessel. One that was upright and mostly dry, afterward a thermal blanket was placed across him. Other hands were helping and moving Grace, Rivette, and Breen—all of whom were conscious, though just barely.

"The boat," Rivette was alert enough to say. "We need the boat."

Williams heard Arabic words and a line was attached to the breast hook. Then they were moving again, pushed now by something other than increasingly uncooperative oars and even less cooperative currents. Upon reaching the tanker they were taken to sickbay where they were hydrated and given a quick checkup; Grace was brought to the medic's office by a male nurse, where her examination was more cursory than the others.

Upon the arrival of the captain and the second officer, everyone else was asked to leave. The sickbay door was closed. Grace came from the office on unsteady feet, having pulled a hand towel over her head—an imperfect but earnest show of respect to their rescuers. Williams and Breen were on examination tables; Rivette was on his feet, leaning against a well-stocked cabinet.

The second mate introduced himself and the captain. The captain spoke and El-Hashem translated.

"Captain Al-Sowayel wishes me to express that he is glad you are safe, but wonders how you came to such a state," the second mate said.

"We had to turn the boat over and hide under it to escape Yemeni officials in Al Luḥayyah," Williams said. "It took—I don't know how long, but a while to set it right in the wind and rain."

"Impressive," El-Hashem said after he had translated for the captain.

"How did you get us here?" Williams asked.

"A hydrofoil minesweeping sled," he replied. "A necessity in these waters."

Mentioning the vessel reminded Williams of their own craft, the mission. "There are things we need in the boat—"

"It has been lifted aboard and is safe," the second mate assured him.

The captain spoke.

"It is thirty-five hours before we are in the Gulf and can put you ashore by motor launch," said El-Hashem. "The captain recommends—"

Williams sat up sharply. "That won't work," he said.

"Your pardon?"

"We have to get to Aden as quickly as possible," Williams said, not sure he could even sit let alone stand, let alone participate in a commando assault.

"But you have experienced—I think the word is 'exposure'?" El-Hashem said.

"That is true, and we still need to be in Aden." Williams listened to what he was saying, could not believe he was willing to push himself and the team onward—though no one contradicted him. "How did you communicate with the man who engaged you?"

El-Hashem asked the captain, listened, then answered.

"A text," the second mate said.

"Then text him back—*please*—and tell him about my request.

I am hopeful, I pray, you can think of something." He looked at the captain when he said, "We have a rendezvous that, I believe, has a very short expiration date."

The captain considered this, then shook his head. He spoke to El-Hashem, who seemed disappointed.

"The captain says that if he talks to this person, he will convince him to do something stupid."

"Something to help your country," Williams fired back.

El-Hashem shrugged. "If the day has come that the royal family needs our help, then the country is already doomed."

Williams could not and did not dispute that.

Besides, Breen had a better idea.

CHAPTER FIFTY

West Wing, The White House
July 24, 7:00 p.m.

It was said that spies knew when some important offensive was being planned at the White House by watching the number of food delivery trucks coming and going. Tonight, Matt Berry would have advised them to watch for unlicensed pharmaceutical dealers—of which there were more than a few—dropping off amphetamines. Even interns were handling crises with the media, every agency including the Department of the Interior and Housing and Urban Development needed immediate funding for added security, and the security organizations were tripping over one another following clues.

Most of them still had Ahmed Salehi in or having left Antigua—including one rumor that he had been extracted by Iranian submarine. Which would not have been a bad scenario if Tehran were suicidally inclined to be surrounded by American and European sea power and caught, or sunk, with Salehi onboard.

That was the kind of scenario that precipitated this shitstorm, he thought. Iran, a ship, a nuke, and Captain Salehi.

His SID sat in his open left hand. Coffee rested in his right. Behind him was an invisible army, troops of hard cash. He had thrown it at every aspect of this mission. That had been easy and effective. But it was crunch time now, with the president set to turn his information loose on the other intelligence agencies unless Berry could give him not just a progress report but, as the president had put it:

"Something really encouraging, Matt. Something with a clock ticking a very short countdown."

The damn thing was, when he arranged for Black Wasp to rendezvous with the *Dima*, there had been only a faint glimmer of a chance that Berry could finish what he had begun. The oil tanker was a day and a half from Aden. He did not believe, could not believe, that Salehi would stay tucked in some safe house for long. Like bin Laden, he would have to get lost somewhere, not by accident but by design. And if the design were good enough, it would take years to find him—if he could be found at all.

The reason for the rendezvous was that Berry was beginning to feel the cold breath of failure on his neck. He had stuck that neck out for the first time in a long time—impulsively due to a confluence of the *Intrepid* attack, Op-Center being shut down, and General Lovett having called the president to implore him to let Black Wasp loose on this. First and foremost, relocating the team to the tanker was about getting them into a position of safety. He had been impressed by their dogged perseverance, especially Chase Williams, who had not been trained or prepared for any of this. He was driven, Berry guessed—and the DCS knew him well enough to speculate—by one part patriotism to nine parts flagellation for the intelligence failure that permitted the attack.

But their deaths or, worse, their capture on top of the failure of a black ops mission would not only end his career, it would have him on trial for money laundering, suppression of intelligence, and whatever other vindictive charges the Justice Department, January Dow, and even the "I knew nothing" president could hurl at him.

Berry had not actually used speed since his college days, but he knew he should probably be taking Valium instead of swimming in caffeine. But as much as he wanted to relax, he dared not.

Better to think in fast motion, he told himself, downing the final gulp of lukewarm black coffee.

It had also not been since his college days that he wanted a phone to ring so damn bad. Back then it was Patty, whom he stupidly thought he could woo from the team quarterback with the lurid appeal of his off-campus poker games. He was wrong because he did not understand women. He still didn't, though now he could buy whoever or whatever he failed to otherwise persuade—

The SID played "Ride of the Valkyries."

Williams, he thought, upending the empty mug as he rushed to poke "answer."

"Go!" Berry said.

"We're going to need a lot of money," Williams said without preamble. "The tanker has a helicopter deck with a helicopter. It's the only way we get to Aden while we can be sure—relatively sure, anyway—that the target is still there."

That was a lot of qualifiers. And Williams was right: it would cost.

"Chase, are you and your team even in any condition to continue?"

"I honestly do not know," he admitted. "I'm lying down, talking to you. But we are still the only ones in striking distance, yes?"

"Short of Tomahawk missiles flattening the port," Berry acknowledged, "which would cause immense collateral damage, including Saudi, and cost us the proof of a body, just scraps of DNA that no one would believe."

"All of that," Williams agreed, "plus your ass on a public griddle for sitting on this information."

"Yeah," Berry agreed. "Yeah. But if you are taken—"

"Bad PR," Williams agreed. "And it doesn't do the four of us a world of good either. But taking the target, getting him so soon—that's worth the risk."

Berry wasn't about to disagree. Covert ops was always a risk, which is why he had always preferred the safety of money to buy the disloyalty of foreign nationals.

"Look, I know Kathleen Hays," Williams said. "Tell her it's my ass and she has to narrow the target. And thank her, for me. But before you do that, text Captain Al-Sowayel and pay him whatever he wants to buy that helicopter and a pilot."

Berry said he would try and clicked off.

Five minutes later, having spent a half-million dollars of the government's money, Berry had hired himself an MH-6 "Little Bird" and pilot.

CHAPTER FIFTY-ONE

The Tanker Dima, *Red Sea*
July 25, 4:14 a.m.

While the Black Wasp team recovered in the infirmary, a pair of seamen brought the lockers from the rowboat. They openly expressed surprise and a respectful but clear delight to see Grace with the men.

"I think we just created a pair of potential émigrés," Breen said, not entirely in jest.

The return of the gear proved to be potent medicine for the group. While Williams had called Berry, Rivette had checked the guns and found them in good working order. Grace had discarded her sheaths—taking care to put the forbidden leather items in the locker, so as not to offend any devout crewmembers—and used elastic bandages to hold the blades to her legs. Cotton balls and bandages kept the points from stabbing her.

El-Hashem came down to inform Williams that they had their helicopter and a pilot. The name of the volunteer was Oudah, a short, round-faced weightlifter who was former Saudi Royal Air Defense. The only English he knew were a few aviation terms. El-Hashem said that Oudah did not have to be persuaded to take the assignment. His younger brother had been a relief worker in Syria when he was captured by ISIS, placed in a cage, lowered by crane into a pool, and drowned. The underwater video was posted on a jihadi website. All Oudah asked was that, in the event he did not return, whatever fee the captain offered him be sent to his mother in Medina.

Through the second mate, Oudah informed them that the helicopter was compact and maneuverable. It was able to seat six and had a range of 430 kilometers—a little more than enough to reach Aden. At a maximum speed of 282 kilometers an hour, they could make the trip in just under ninety minutes, given the rain and seven-mile-an-hour wind speed coming at them from the Gulf.

They would have to have a place to land and also to refuel for the return trip and, working through relationships rather than channels, Captain Al-Sowayel had contacted an officer with the Royal Navy who agreed to obtain clearance for them to use a helipad that the Saudis had constructed off Sira Island in the Gulf of Aden.

"But there is a—*hitch*," El-Hashem said, after searching for the right word.

"There is presently a disabled helicopter on the pad, its tail rotor chipped by gunfire. But Captain Al-Sowayel was assured that there is probably enough room to land a Little Bird."

Oudah seemed unfazed, convinced that he would find a way to make the Little Bird fit.

"If not," Rivette quipped, "we'll just jump into the sea. Not like we haven't been there before."

With preparations made, the team agreed that they should

get to Aden as soon as refueling could be arranged—if it could be arranged. While they waited, Berry called back.

"Kathleen has a likely target," he told Williams. "There's a pickup a few blocks from the dock that seems to match the outline of the one that met the jet in Hodeida. She only found it because one of the wardrobes she was tracking went there from a Sadi Shipping warehouse."

Berry sent over a satellite photo of the area, from directly overhead. There was an arrow pointing at the structure.

"Good map for going in by air," Williams said. "Did you thank Kathleen for me?"

"I did not," Berry admitted. "I got a qualified woman a job— that's all I'm supposed to do."

It seemed odd for an international money launderer and feedbag for black operations to show such precise scruples, but Williams had to accept it.

"What time did she ID him?" Williams asked.

"About five minutes ago," Berry said. "She hasn't left her post."

"If I get stuck here," Williams said, "you *will* thank her."

"You're coming home," Berry assured him. "Because I want you to stay with the chopper."

The suggestion was ludicrous. Williams said so.

"These people have trained for this kind of takedown," Berry said. "You have not. And friend—you get caught, you know pretty much everything."

That was true. But he still had no intention of staying behind. Not on a mission to get Salehi.

"Tell you what," he said. "I'm going to use just one thing the Wasps have taught me—SITCOM."

With that, Williams hung up. The others were all looking at him.

"Someone tell you to sit this out?" Rivette said.

Williams nodded.

"You're a good man," the lance corporal said admiringly.

"Hey, my contact was not wrong," Williams acknowledged.

"You'd be a high-value get," Breen speculated.

"That's right. But I won't get 'got.'"

It was the first time Williams truly felt like a member of the team, the more so because no one made a fuss about it—he was the one who had put himself on the outside. The rest just went on with their preparations.

"So, we've got our Little Bird," Rivette said as they rode the elevator to the helipad on the oil deck. "What's that *giant* bird they have out here? The one from the Sinbad picture?"

"A Roc," Grace answered. "From the Arabian Nights stories."

"Right," the lance corporal said. "So that's about the only thing we haven't ridden since we left home. Though I have to say—fishing boat, plane, chutes, tanker, chopper, bus, dump truck. A freakin' *elevator* is the last thing I expected to be taking."

"Don't forget the ambulance," Grace said.

"The RHIB and LCS 10," Breen added dryly.

Williams had not gotten to know Rivette, had spent no downtime with the man, and couldn't say whether his comments were whistling past a graveyard or represented bona fide astonishment.

It wasn't the first joking remark he had made since they pinned down the passage to Aden. Given the dangers and constant, unexpected sharp turns the mission had taken, it probably would not be the last.

He was feeling none of that. He was arm-weary, leg-weary, his eyes tired, and jet lag did not even begin to describe his disorientation. At least they had eaten on the tanker, so hunger was not an issue.

But the dominant feeling he had was a wrathful kind of focus. He saw that image of Salehi in his mind, remembered what the man had done and why they were here, and he knew without question that nothing short of death was going to stop him from apprehending the man.

And he could live with death, he had already decided, *as long as he took Salehi with him*. Williams could not speak for the others, but he sensed they would all act first and think about consequences later.

Except for a generous spin in the dryer, their robes were as soiled and creased as when they had been pulled from the sea. Williams suggested, and the team agreed, that wear-and-considerable-tear would make it easier to blend in with the majority of the dockworkers if necessary. The weapons and SID were in the same places as they were before. Williams and Breen had both gotten used to keeping their right hand in their pocket, where the handguns were.

The rain added a fresh touch of ruin to the robes as they hurried to the helicopter.

The chopper lifted swiftly from the helipad, cutting through the low rainclouds but remaining below its flight ceiling of five thousand feet.

"Steer clear of military traffic," Breen noted when they leveled off under a sky rich with early-morning stars.

How many early poets, astrologers, astronomers looked at these very lights, Williams wondered—once more, albeit briefly, contentedly in awe of where he was.

The flight was uneventful and, save for the beat of the rotors, blissfully quiet and smooth. The chopper dropped through the clouds in time to give them a view of the entire port, which faced the very tip of the Red Sea on the west and the Gulf of Aden to the south. This gave the team a chance to peer through the rain-splashed windows and put three-dimensional images on the flat maps and photographs they had seen.

The port was large and, at least geographically, Instagram perfect. Their approach took them over the Sira Fortress on Sira Island. Lit by the rising sun, the eleventh-century edifice looked particularly photogenic in the rain, its brownish stones standing out on a promontory of green trees and lower foliage. To the southwest, the island was connected to the mainland by a short stretch of highway. Shipping was clustered on the northwest side of the island, on the Gulf of Aden. The primary activity seemed to be among the fishing fleet, which sold their produce—peace permitting—at the fish market, also on the southeastern coast.

Their destination, the Gulf warehouse area, was new, built and owned by Sadi Shipping. An ambitious port had been under construction when hostilities between Shia and Sunni flared; it was unfinished and marginally accessible to small cargo ships. It seemed to Williams that the tankers in the Gulf were a symbol of the failed state; they frequently bypassed the tortured city for safer ports.

The helicopter landed artfully on the pad. The helipad crew had maneuvered the grounded UH-1 Huey as far to the side as they could pull it by winch and powerboat. There was just barely enough room to accommodate the diameter of the main rotor; as it was, the backwash against the Huey rocked them when Oudah set down. The helipad was vulnerable to the wake of every ship that came by, making it difficult for the team to cross the rain-slickened surface and adjacent walkway to the dock.

Oudah stopped Williams and pointed to a small aviation-fuel tanker. It was dwarfed by a ship-fuel tanker that would sail into the Gulf and resupply vessels that were just passing through. Williams nodded with understanding as the pilot threw him a salute and hurried off to see to the refueling.

Williams caught up to the others and noticed Grace looking at him critically—not directed at him but at the world. To her, Oudah had assumed Williams was the commander. Williams had not walked a lifetime in her boots, had not had to endure ageism, did not want to judge her reaction.

Only the timing, he thought. Social offense was not something one should nurse before going into battle. Nothing that might impact focus should find purchase in a soldier's mind or heart. In his experience, that was something the younger generation of soldiers had not learned.

The rain kept activity on the dock limited to the pair of small cargo ships. With so few people—all of whom wore gloves and work boots—mingling was not an option.

"The warehouse," Breen said, pointing ahead. "Second of four."

The others looked at the row of plain, gray cinderblock structures. They were built to withstand gunfire, possibly an artillery shell, perhaps even a sustained drone attack: heavy cinderblock walls, no windows, and a flat roof of a metal alloy that would probably not become superheated in the sun. There was an air-conditioning unit on the roof of each building along with a generator and a large water collector. No one saw any exterior stairs to the roof; those were probably securely inside the structures. But they did see security cameras in every visible corner of each building. The four of them stood waterside, studying the structure.

"Built for a siege," Breen noted.

"Against the Saudis or antiterrorists?" Williams wondered.

"You mean Sadi himself?" the major asked.

"Couldn't rule that out," Williams said.

"Spray paint on the side," Rivette said. He was at an angle to notice a section of graffiti. "Anti-Saudi or anti-Yemeni, I wonder?"

"Could be workers angry at their employer," Breen said. "The Arab Spring unleashed a lot of rage."

"Except for knocking on the door, it doesn't look like there's any way in," Williams said.

"Even if we got in, we don't know their numbers or how the place is guarded," Grace said. "We go in there, we have to fight their fight. I was just thinking—surveillance showed they make trips to their vehicle, which would be at the far side of the complex. I wait inside—"

"How will you interrogate the man?" Breen asked.

Grace hadn't considered that. She swore.

"They have to move Salehi some time," Rivette said. "Out here, we can target them."

Williams shook his head, said, "We don't have 'some time.'"

"What do you mean?" Breen asked.

"No one knows where Salehi is probably hiding except us," he said. "We were in the field, we were on his trail, we were given a lead time. That status downgrades in about four hours when the intel goes wide through the global intelligence system."

Breen seemed to brighten. "That could be a good thing," he said. "We wait for backup."

"What, we just sit here and point?" Rivette complained.

"I read about the Supporters of Allah on the tanker," Grace said. "They do not engage in firefights. They own whatever turf, whatever enemy they have to fight."

"Not if an M-162 Evolved SeaSparrow missile comes sailing in from the Gulf," Williams said. "One of our destroyers could punch big holes in those walls."

"That's not what I'm saying," Grace replied. "They won't let it get that far. To them, we are spotters."

"If they know we're even here," Rivette said.

Breen was looking up at the roof of the warehouse. "We are four people who arrived by helicopter and are standing in the rain. They may be harboring the world's most wanted fugitive."

"Exactly," Grace said.

"Spotters," Williams caught on. "We can use that," he said suddenly.

"How?" Rivette asked.

Williams told them. A few moments later, Black Wasp was in motion.

Ali Abdullah was sitting at a card table, looking at his computer, streaming Al Jazeera. Ahmed Salehi was taking breakfast after having spent, he said, a restful night in his quarters. Abdullah himself had not retired, had not slept much as he watched the clock in anticipation of the launch from Sadi's tanker—but more immediately, the anticipated attack. It did not seem strange to him that the news he watched showed worldwide intelligence services being uncertain about Ahmed Salehi's whereabouts or his pursuit. No one knew that the attack on Osama bin Laden was coming until the first shots were fired.

That must not happen here.

His radio came on with the sound of rainfall and wind-rustled canvas. The observer was lying beneath a tarp on the roof. It was one of many with silicone-treated, waterproof fibers that covered exposed vents—except for his, which was reserved for spotters that watched the grounds around the clock. He had a rifle at his side, which gave him an advantage the security cameras lacked.

"Four new arrivals were looking this way," said his caller. "There's a woman among them. They are walking toward us."

"I'm sending two men out," Abdullah said. "Come down—we may need you."

The leader turned and went to two men who were napping in folding chairs, their chins on their chests. He woke them by calling their names. The pair were instantly alert.

"Go out, find three men and a woman," he ordered. "Approach but do not engage. They may be the team we are waiting for—most likely there are others, possibly Saudis in concealment."

The men picked up their semiautomatics, did not bother to conceal them as they hurried to the door. Abdullah switched the computer to security camera access to see what the spotter was seeing.

Grace was standing apart from the others, nearest to the door of the warehouse, when the two men emerged. They were incongruously wearing robes and Western windbreakers. They did not come directly toward her but dashed from the building to an idle forklift and hopped into the cab.

Observe from a different perspective, she thought. *Running their playbook.*

Grace would upset it. She immediately walked over to the door facing away from the warehouse, rapped on the window, and began speaking to them in Mandarin. They might not recognize it, but they would know it wasn't English. They might let their guard relax just enough.

The nearest man opened the door. Grace reached up and slapped her palm on his arm, her strong fingers grabbing through the two layers of sleeve and digging into the meat of his arm. She turned her hip, he flew from the cab, and she drove her right heel hard onto his gun hand. The metal caused the bones to shatter.

Pushing off that heel, she launched herself into the cab and used two open palms to ram the other man's head into the window on his side. It went through the glass and she immediately reached for his ears and pulled him back through, lacerating his throat. He dropped his gun and, screaming with fear and pain, put his hands over the wounds. She was still holding his ears as she backed from the cab and rammed his forehead into the controls between the seats. On the way out, she put the same right heel down hard on the other man's temple.

Both were unconscious. A radio came on. A voice was unanswered. Someone was going to have to come out and investigate. Grace picked up one of the semiautomatics. She had not held a weapon in months and it felt unfamiliar—strangely weak. But the forklift offered protection from rain and gunfire, and the broken window was a perfect place to target the door.

She waited.

Breen and Williams had moved out of view of the doorway. They had circled around the warehouses to the other side and stopped. If the spotter were on the roof of any of the four buildings, he would have to watch two sectors at once. While Williams kept a lookout for Supporters of Allah who might be doing sentry duty outside, Breen had pulled the compact binoculars from under his robe and was studying the rooftops.

"I don't see anyone on any edge," Breen said. "If someone's up there and armed, it's for long distance. He'd have to move to target the nearby perimeter."

"They've probably got exits we can't see," Williams said.

"Probably. We can't let them slip out the back."

"Let's go," Williams said, starting toward the second warehouse.

Abdullah could not make out exactly what had happened in the forklift, but the woman's face was in the window and he could not see his men. He sent one man to get Salehi and rallied the remaining five fighters.

"We are under assault," he said when their guest had arrived. "Two men down." He pointed to one man. "Out the back, bring the pickup." He pointed to two others. "Cover him." He pointed to the fourth and fifth. "You're at the front door. I'll stay with the captain."

The men moved swiftly and efficiently.

Abdullah was not going to let them get their guest.

Dhu Basha jogged through the rain along the outside of the warehouse, never straying from the eye line of his comrades who shifted in the doorway to follow his progress. The pickup had been parked so that anyone going to it would have armed backup, watching.

Basha's own eyes were constantly in motion, his Uzi swinging left and right as he ran. He stopped halfway to the pickup, which was parked on the street between the third and fourth warehouses in a spot directly diagonal from the door of warehouse two.

The two tires he could see were flat. He looked to see who had done it, saw two men standing brashly at the far corner of the last warehouse, not far from the front of the truck. Neither man was armed—they were just standing there. Basha raised his weapon—then spun and dropped, dead. Moments later, the two men in the door flew inward, landing and skidding back in their own blood.

"And . . . bonus points," Rivette said, rising from behind a parked car.

The lance corporal had broken from the others and, running, circled wide around the warehouses through the border of the Saudi-controlled section. His goal was the pickup truck. He could not be sure he would have an actionable target—but the team had agreed they must anticipate a possible retreat. He had not spoken with Breen and Williams, but Black Wasp had trained for the rope-a-dope scenario: the sniper in a place relatively safe from attack, a juicy target offered to the enemy who, taking it, was vulnerable to a counterpunch.

Rivette did not stay put. Breen and Williams were already in motion toward the open back door of the warehouse. The lance corporal fell in behind, covering them.

Abdullah heard the shots, assumed his men had fired them, was enraged to see them skid inward. Salehi had been handed a pair of firearms, ready to repel an attack. There were only two ways in and it would only take two men to cover them.

The men from the door had turned at the sound of gunfire. Abdullah held up one finger and pointed to the back door. One man ran over. Abdullah remained in the central command area with Salehi. They crouched behind crates that were filled with cement and had been arrayed for an assault.

The wait was not as long as it felt to the men in the warehouse.

They were watching and also listening. The rain on the ribbed steel roof was heavy and constant. That had to be a disadvantage for a team moving toward them. Even with rubber-soled *tabi* boots, maneuvers in a squall were—

A steady spray of gunfire erupted from the front door. Abdullah had heard the sound just before the shooting started.

"The forklift!" the sentry shouted, turning briefly.

"Withdraw!" the chieftain ordered.

Before the man could do so, he disappeared outside the doorway—moments before the load backrest and mast of the vehicle rammed into the opening, blocking it.

Grace had started the forklift forward and followed behind the open door. It was parked in such a way as to draw the gunman's attention to his right. Her goal had been to get closer to the man before he thought to shoot the legs out from under her; she assumed, correctly, that he would target the cab first. By the time he destroyed the rain-covered window, saw that there was no one at the controls, and swung in her direction, she had climbed to the overhead guard atop the vehicle. She lay flat, shielded by the mast. When the man turned to alert the surviving Supporters, she had jumped off, dashed to the left side of the door, and grabbed him by the collar before he could fire again. She pivoted sharply at the waist and he sprawled flat on the ground. Grace dropped a knee to the back of his neck. Except for twitching in his fingers and feet, he did not move.

She had already discarded the other weapon, did not pick up this one, but crouched by the door. She listened for the slap of any feet that might come to investigate the gunfire. None came.

Oudah must have heard it, too, told everyone to stay put, she thought.

Grace was in a hyperalert, predatory state. Tension inhibited the flow of energy and she moved her arms like outstretched wings, with fluid, sweeping White Crane forms. That moved the pooled aggression from her gut, her *dontian*, the "cauldron," to keep her from acting on a dangerous impulse. That impulse was to somersault in and tear into anyone and everyone she saw.

But they were armed and it was better to leave a mystery outside the door—something they would expand in their minds, and fear.

She waited, confident that one of the others had taken the SITCOM initiative from their position.

Crouched at the back door, only the front site and the tip of the barrel extended beyond the metal frame, nineteen-year-old Akram ibn Hayyam was impatient to act. He burned with a need to defend his leader and the great captain, to repel the infidels who dared to set foot in their land. He did not care if he died in the effort. He would be in Paradise and able to bestow blessings on those he left behind.

Hayyam drew comfort from the men who lay sprawled behind him. Their blood honored the soles of his boots. Even now, he listened for them to whisper into his ear, to advise him.

Kill, they seemed to be saying.

The infidels were cowards. After murdering his fellow fighters from safety, they went back into hiding. Hayyam knew that his leader, Abdullah, employed that same approach—they had worked it out for the Saudi scholar, who still must die—but it had never sat well with the teenage warrior. He had beheaded Christians with ISIS, in Mosul, before joining the Supporters of Allah.

It was always warmer when they saw their killer, when they possessed fear.

Akram ibn Hayyam was drawing breath through his nose, his mouth downturned, teeth exposed in a feral contour. They were out there, somewhere, the invaders. He inched the gun forward, following it as slowly as he could with his body.

His hand exploded, the gun flew, he lurched slightly forward, and then a bullet entered his left temple and exited from the right, carrying the front of his skull with it.

Breen and Williams were at one side of the warehouse, Rivette at the other. They had been waiting behind the wall so as not to be in the line of fire when Rivette took his shot. They also wanted to be able to communicate with Grace, who stood along the same wall, just beside the jammed-up doorway.

There was only one way out now. And one way in. No one filled that opening.

Rivette had been waiting for Williams to look around the corner. As soon as he did, the lance corporal pointed to himself, then to the door. Williams was going to shake his head but realized, once again, that he was not in command. However, Williams's hand shot up suddenly, urgently indicating for the marksman to wait.

A moment later, Grace's last hand grenade flew over the forklift and exploded in the warehouse. Gunfire spat from inside, anticipating a charge. She hurried over to the two men.

"Center of the room," she said. "No cries—probably barricaded."

"And probably low in manpower," Breen said. "They haven't bothered to post anyone else back here."

"Someone still has to cover the other door," Williams said.

"I'll go," Breen told him.

Williams felt, even more strongly now, that the major was at heart a closet pacifist—here by design, he suspected. A man with a conscience was not a bad thing to have on a team like this.

Rivette came over, stood on the other side of the door.

"You out of grenades?" Williams asked Grace.

"Sadly."

"At least two prizes in there," Rivette said. "If Salehi's inside, boss would've stayed with him."

Williams nodded.

"I don't like standoffs," the lance corporal added.

The group started as they heard the sound of falling stone.

"The door I hit," Grace said, "was not in good shape."

"Jaz," Williams said to Rivette, "what do you think about going over there and shooting some more of it down. Make like we're going to come over it, or follow it in like a tank."

"Draw their fire and you go in from here," the lance corporal said. "I like it, but I got a better chance of taking them out if you shoot it down."

"Yes, but it's my SITCOM call." Williams smiled thinly.

Rivette smirked and turned back the way he came, circling the building so he would not have to run in front of the door.

Grace and Williams were standing together, the woman behind.

"How do we do this?" she asked.

"We don't, I do," he said.

"Why?"

"I honestly don't know," he said while they waited for Rivette to start shooting. He raised his Sig Sauer 9mm XM17 so it was shoulder high, pointed up, ready. "This is terra incognita for me. I just know I have to do it."

"I can respect that," Grace said. That was all she said; Williams knew she would honor that and be prepared to move in if something happened.

A few seconds later the drone of automatic fire started chipping at the cinder blocks, drawing fire from inside. Williams knew the terrorists probably did not have a clear target, were looking to create what ISIS had called a "wall of death" in their blind defensive assaults when Fallujah was retaken by Iraqi forces.

As soon as he heard the shooting from inside the warehouse—two, possibly three separate weapons, Williams judged—he risked a look inside. It was a mental snapshot that he processed immediately, tactically, the way he had done with so many surveillance photos, so many helmet-cam attacks that he viewed and studied at CENTCOM.

There were two men crouching inside an array of crates, about twenty-five feet away. The boxes were on their sides in a kind of maze-like arrangement designed to thwart a full-scale assault. But they were low enough for the men behind them to fire over.

They were low enough for their heads to be visible.

One of those heads was wearing a long *keffiyeh*. The other belonged to Ahmed Salehi.

Williams felt his insides burn at the sight of the Iranian. He had not bothered to withdraw his face from the door. They were not looking in his direction; they would within moments, though, when they realized that the shooting was a feint. Without hesitating, Williams swung in, aimed his weapon, and fired three rounds into the head covering. The man was lifted bodily to his right and fell. His weapon continued to fire, his finger still locked around the trigger. Bullets ricocheted against the crate in front of him, causing Salehi to scramble backwards, to the narrow end of the crate for protection. He had stopped firing and Williams seized the lull to stride forward behind his gun.

It was pointed at Salehi's head.

"No!" Williams shouted, thinking that was one word of English the man might understand.

Salehi had already been turning to face whoever had fired the fatal shot at Abdullah. He dropped both guns and raised his hands. Williams saw Rivette climb on top of the forklift, moving his gun around the warehouse to make sure no one else was hiding.

"You're good!" the lance corporal said, easing in through the opening he'd made. Breen followed.

The Iranian captain stood slowly and faced Williams. His face was a statement of spiritual serenity. Salehi seemed unbothered by the death around him, by the black marks on his soul, by the fact that he had been apprehended. In fact, as Williams approached and Salehi deduced that his captor was American, he almost seemed to relax. It was the look of a man—no, a sea captain—who knew he was about to take a voyage that would last for several years: a trial in America during which governments and other powerful forces would fight for his release. A man who knew that the future would not be about the act he had committed but the multifaceted symbol he had become: avenging Iranian warrior, honorary jihadist, a man who was unjustly treated by Op-Center—whose existence, whose JSOC commandos would be exposed. Salehi's single-minded defense counsel would see to that. They would defend this creature while he sat with this same look of confident, righteous serenity.

Williams shot the man through the heart. Saheli fell in a lazy half-turn and landed on his back.

"God!" Breen shouted as he made his way through the crates. "Good, good God!"

Williams just stood where he was and lowered his arm. He heard Grace behind him, saw Rivette shake a fist in triumph. Now openly angry, Breen came forward.

"You had no call or right," the major said.

"Screw this son-of-a-bitch," Rivette said.

Breen ignored him, kneeling and feeling for a pulse. He dropped the man's wrist. "We had him!" he yelled. "He'd *surrendered*. He should have been tried!"

Williams looked at the JAG attorney. "He was."

Removing his SID from his robe, Williams stood in a position that roughly matched the security camera image. Then he took a photo of the dead terrorist, his face intact, and forwarded it, and a short recap of the takedown, to Matt Berry.

CHAPTER FIFTY-TWO

The White House, Washington, D.C.
July 25, 12:00 a.m.

January Dow had been napping on the sofa in her office when the call came from the president's executive secretary, Natalie Cannon. Midkiff had called an emergency meeting of his top intelligence personnel regarding "new information" about the fugitive Ahmed Salehi. Instantly alert, January texted her driver and used the mirrors in the elevator to quickly brush her hair and straighten her black pantsuit.

It was a short trip from C Street NW to 1600 Pennsylvania Avenue, and Dow's driver encountered very little traffic at this hour. The INR head used the seven minutes to swipe through the latest intelligence reports; she did not want to show up at the meeting "stupid," as her mother used to call it back in Austin, Texas. Angel Dow was a young widow who worked as a temp. Before she went to a new office, she made a point of calling other temps to find out about the company.

"You can ingratiate yourself with wiles or with knowledge," Angel had told her young daughter. *"Knowledge doesn't run out or get old."*

"Nothing," January said hotly under her breath as she saw a

lot of speculation, a lot of cities and locations that were ruled out—but nothing concrete. A CIA team that had been dispatched to Trinidad reported:

11: 20 p.m.
JAM code name for attackers "Pack of Lions." Disorganized strike. Doctor at the clinic they hit saw an Asian woman and a Caucasian man in jumpsuits. Fits profile of river attack. JAM organizer made to sever finger with teeth. Surgeon reattached. Analysis: mob hit.

The NRO had added:

11:29 p.m.
JAM Canada team traveled Port of Spain to Munich, Germany to Sana'a, Yemen to Port of Spain to Montreal. In-country 17 months. Investigating Yemen activities through ELINT database.

The FBI had just noted:

11:59 p.m.
Surveillance of Pakistan Embassy showing only known diplomatic personnel. Shift change.

So the update was the same as always in these lone-wolf or quasi-lone-wolf attacks: methodical backtracking to plot potential forward movement. Even with computer analysis, it was a slow process. Algorithms, metrics, and all the tools used by intelligence services still required the input of raw data.

"You goddamned idiot," she said to a mental image of Chase Williams. He was the screw-up who should have had that data.

January was not surprised to see the cars of Trevor Harward and Matt Berry still in the parking lot. Part of "knowledge" was knowing who she might be facing before she went in. She was surprised that there were no FBI, CIA, or Department of Homeland Security personnel present. That was either a very good or a very bad sign. Either she was going to be asked to take point on what was clearly a stalled investigation or she was going to be fired for failing to move the ball—the sacrificial lamb.

"They wouldn't dare," she thought as she went through West Wing security. The Oval Office was notified of her arrival and, tablet tucked under her arm, she walked briskly down the corridor toward the Oval Office. There was a fair amount of activity here—some of it data crunching, she suspected, but more of it probably damage control. Blame for the *Intrepid* attack was being spread across DHS and the White House equally. Tucked in the data she had just read was a poll that said the handpicked frontrunner for Midkiff's job, Roger Levi, had seen his lead plunge from 55 to 44 percent.

January strode past the Marine sentry, was told "Go right in" by Natalie Cannon, and opened the door to find Midkiff, Harward, and Berry seated around the coffee table between the two couches. Berry sat alone, on the left.

The INR director shut the door, her eyes on the laptop facing

Berry but angled away from the empty seat. She sat beside him. No one was smiling but there was a palpable air of—*serenity* was the word that came to mind.

Berry turned the laptop toward January; slowly, as if he were roasting corn over an open flame. There was an image on the screen. It showed the face of a man who was unquestionably Ahmed Salehi, his eyes staring. He was lying on his back, on a concrete floor, his head resting just atop of symmetrical puddle of blood. There was a single bullet hole in his chest.

The photograph had been posted to the intelligence feed and marked SL-1, highest security level visibility only. The time stamp read WH 12:07 a.m., which was about the time she had passed through security.

January frowned. The image had just been posted, and from this office.

"We also got a team of Supporters of Allah terrorists," Berry added. "Including their leader, I'm told."

The president picked up the phone on the coffee table.

"Nat? Have the press secretary come in in five minutes," he said.

"Who and where?" January asked no one in particular.

Berry replied, "Chase Williams in Aden, Yemen," he looked at his SID, "twenty-three minutes ago. Firefight with the afore-mentioned Supporters of Allah."

January's skilled, restless brain assembled a timeline that did not fit. Op-Center disbanded, Williams put in charge of a com-mando unit—possibly his old JSOC team—the group sent to Trinidad off the Montreal murders, a shootout there that collected essential data, extraction by the Navy, and then either night-dropped or sea-borne into Yemen.

"Is he all right?" January asked.

"He is," Berry said. "I'll tell him you asked."

"We are not going to reveal who or how to the press," the president said. "Just 'commandos,' and that will be it. But I would like you to be the source of this information."

January's frozen look of puzzlement surprised even her. "I see. Why?"

"Because this has to have been run by one of our intelligence agencies, relentlessly following leads and fielding a team before the enemy had a chance to go underground," he said.

"Why me?" she asked.

"Because someone is going to take a storm of justifiable out-rage from the other agencies—in private, of course, but they will not appreciate how you kept this information to yourself."

"To protect the highly covert nature of the mission," Berry contributed. "Not for personal advancement."

"No," January said, looking him squarely in eyes that seemed to sparkle with caffeine-fueled life. "Who would do a thing like that?"

"You've got credibility and you've got steel in your spine," Midkiff said. "And frankly, what you don't have is mud on your reputation the way Op-Center and the high-visibility agencies have. DHS, CIA, FBI—their social media negatives are in the red."

"Whereas INS doesn't even register," she said. "We really have to up our Twitter game."

"ASAP," Harward pointed out. "Press conference has been called for one a.m."

"Yes," the president said. "I'd like you to be at the podium. Decline all questions—just look like the cat that devoured the mouse."

"I can do that, Mr. President," January said with a small Cheshire look.

"I've seen her make that happen," Harward said innocently.

January's eyes had moved from the president to the national security advisor to Berry. Harward did not seem to be in on whatever joke the DCS quietly seemed to be nursing. She was willing to bet that before the men had gotten together here, Harward had no idea what had been in motion. Realizing that she had been as clueless as the president's old football team college buddy was no consolation.

"I'm impressed," she said. "Truly. You worked two fronts and won both."

"Just doing the people's work," Berry said.

"January, Matt's right—this is a triumph for America," Midkiff said.

"And for Chase," Berry added pointedly.

She had to give Berry that, too. Whatever the details—and she would have them, somehow—this operation reeked of the DCS, right down to the kill-you-with-civility rollout of this meeting. As for Midkiff, she did not know if the president was just exhausted, blind to Berry's motives, or—as she had always suspected—more than a trifle naïve. Angel Dow would not have been impressed by him. The deep knowledge that should have been his was stored in the heads of others.

The president turned bodily to the INR head. "You will brief the press secretary and then we will have all the intelligence heads in the situation room," he glanced at his watch, "at eight a.m. to plan for possible retaliation from whoever managed his escape."

"Your press conference will probably ignite a bunch of fires," Berry said helpfully.

"We do not believe this was run by JAM," Harward said. "They haven't the muscle or reach. There is obviously a powerful player in Yemen we have to find, starting with whoever rented that warehouse from Sadi Shipping."

"Why not Mohammad Obeid ibn Sadi?" January thought out loud. "He has not been seen in public for decades."

"The Howard Hughes of the Middle East," Berry added.

"Well, that can be part of the agenda tomorrow," the president said. His eyes shifted to Berry as he rose. "This win is yours, Matt."

"And Chase's," he added.

"He owed us one," Harward said.

Even January would not have said that, even though she thought it.

"I'm going to get some rest," the president said, seeming to deflate a little, leaking whatever energy he had left. "See you all at eight."

That was all the president said to the group as he left the office and Press Secretary Suze Bender walked in.

Passing her in the doorway, and within earshot of his tired

secretary and the alert Marine, the president made a point of using the same words Paul Bremer, head of the Coalition Provisional Authority in Iraq, had used at his press conference in December 2003:

"Ladies and gentlemen, we got him!"

CHAPTER FIFTY-THREE

Little Bird, Gulf of Aden
July 25, 1:25 p.m.

"If Chase hadn't shot him, I would've," Rivette said. "Hell, that's what we were trained for!"

Leaving the warehouse, the four had made their way silently, but swiftly, back to the waiting helicopter. Sitting in the four facing seats in the helicopter, the lance corporal had to shout to be heard by Lee and Breen over the rotors as the chopper fought a headwind to get above the clouds. The refueled MH-6 had lifted off without incident and was nosing through the rain that was driving at them from the south. The mood of the passengers was grim, though none of that was directed at Chase Williams.

Williams sat quietly beside the pilot, ignoring the debate as he contemplated his own actions at the dock.

"The man wasn't shot, he was executed," Breen said.

"He's a man, now, this guy who slaughtered innocents?" Rivette said. "He is—was—a murderer who does not get to kill any more Americans, ever. I am very happy that he has joined his Pakistani brethren in whatever afterlife is the hottest."

"The Pakistani girl, lance corporal?" Breen asked with rare anger in his voice. "The granddaughter? Are you glad she's dead."

"Price of terrorists doing business," he said. "Her incendiary-device-creating grandfather should've thought of that before he took her on his killing spree."

Grace was sitting beside Rivette, the tailboom behind them. Breen was across from her, his back to the cockpit.

"Ahmed Salehi broke the harmony of the universe," she said. "He alone is responsible."

"It is my understanding, from having read his file, that he was responding to an American attack that sank his cargo ship."

"That was on a mission to collect Russian nukes," Rivette said. "Yeah, I read that, too. Some SEAL team or something stopped him. If they'd stopped him better, those people would not have died on the *Intrepid*." The marksman looked ahead in disbelief. "Counselor, are you actually defending that prick?"

"Not him," Breen said calmly but firmly. "Due process."

"We didn't 'due process' those guys in Trinidad," Rivette pointed out.

"Or the Supporters of Allah," Grace added with more than a hint of satisfaction in her voice.

"That was a question of survival," Breen said. "We are soldiers first and we were on a mission. But we had Salehi. He was ours." He pointed beside him. "There is an empty seat where he should have been sitting. Without due process, our country is no better than the one we left."

"I believe, Major, we just proved that isn't so," Grace said. "Our country targeted a man, not a museum or a school or a workplace, as they have done. Back there, Salehi had an equal chance. If that had been a school instead of a warehouse, we would have waited at our own peril. On the *Intrepid*, no one had a chance."

"That reasoning is based on a principle of retribution, not justice," Breen said. "And you are wrong. Salehi *did* hurt us, Lieutenant, possibly worse than we realize."

"How?" she asked.

"We crossed a red line," he said. "It'll be easier, now, to cross more."

The plastic panel behind Williams muted the conversation and he was glad for it. From the tone of the Black Wasps, however, he knew what the topic was. And he was not entirely convinced he had done the right thing. The dead man had attacked the *Intrepid*, but he had also cost Williams Op-Center. At least, the Op-Center he knew.

I pray to God that was not why I did what I did, he thought. *I pray that I did it for the dead.*

The remainder of the ride was quiet, save for communications between Oudah and the *Dima*. The Little Bird rendezvoused with the tanker in just under ninety minutes, not far north of the choke point where the Red Sea passes between Yemen and Eritrea on its way to the Gulf of Aden. The return flight took longer than the initial trip because the pilot took them near their ceiling to avoid rocket fire from Shia radicals.

The tension remained thick as the team exited the helicopter and hurried to the elevator. Williams knew, from debriefs, that a good deal of that was a holdover from the mission, the birth pangs of post-traumatic stress. But the shooting of Ahmed Salehi also weighed heavily on the team—all except Oudah. The gunfire had been heard and the battle witnessed and his expression and handshake before reporting to the captain told Williams that he had been proud to have played a part in the mission.

After they were shown to guest quarters in the cabin deck above the main deck, Williams paused in the corridor and faced the others.

"I'm very sorry for the dissention I've caused," he said. "You don't know much about me, and that's how some higher-ups want it. But I'll tell you this much. I was in the Navy for thirty-five years and nothing prepared me for a moment like that. I will probably never know if what I did was right." His eyes moved to Breen. "Legally, it was not. Ethically—the Supporters of Allah and whoever spirited him out of Trinidad on a private jet did not want Salehi for show. I think I'll sleep a little better knowing there's one less terrorist we have to watch out for."

"They were probably giving him a boat," Breen offered. "Otherwise, why fly him to Yemen only to sneak him somewhere else on a ship?"

"So he could pick up more warheads," Rivette suggested. "A-bomb fever."

For a flashing moment, Williams felt as if he were back in his office at Op-Center, listening to a debate between Roger McCord and Paul Bankole.

"This is a postmortem for the party planners," Williams said. "I'm going to find out how we're getting home from India and then I'm going to sleep. I just wanted to tell you that you're all exceptional people and it has been an honor serving with you—and to learn from you. 'SITCOM,'" he uttered, shaking his head and laughing. "You cannot know how important it has been being a part of a new team."

Williams supposed that the others took "new" to mean the christening of Black Wasp; from his knowing look, maybe Breen had picked up his real meaning.

"Will we be seeing you again?" Grace asked.

"That's up to the people who put me here," Williams replied, "and who I have to go contact. Let them know we're safe, headed for Trivandrum, India, and would like a ticket home."

"I—all of us, I think—hope we all get to do this again," the lieutenant said. "There is not a history text or military game plan that we did not impact."

"For the *best*," Rivette insisted, not looking at Breen.

"You're like a dog with a bone." Grace scowled. "Let's go, Lance Corporal," she said, asserting rank as she started them down the hall to their cabins.

Breen remained with Williams. "'Party planners,'" the major said when they were alone.

It took a moment. "Crap," Williams said. He should have known better than to talk to outsiders when he was tired. Especially one who missed nothing.

"You were intelligence," Breen said, "involved with the fracas off Alaska, I suspect, given our target . . . and his present disposition. Maybe you were making sure that this time Salehi did not get away." The major held up a hand. "I don't expect an answer—I only want to say that you've also given me a few things to ruminate over."

The major saluted and then the men shook hands. As he turned to go, Breen said, "There's a line in Luke, I think it is, that may apply. 'He was lost but now he is found.'" He smiled. "Welcome back."

"Thank you, Major," Williams said.

It was a fitting way to end their stay in the Holy Land.

CHAPTER FIFTY-FOUR

Sana'a, Yemen
July 25, 1:30 p.m.

Being a Shia in Yemen, and being a man of business, Sadi was not unfamiliar with losses, with setbacks. As always, in defeat, he turned to the words of the Prophet and of Allah.

"You may fight in the cause of God against those who attack you, but do not aggress. God does not love the aggressors."

The wisdom of the words of the Quran compelled him to examine his own actions. Had he transgressed, had he crossed a line that had made him an aggressor?

As fast as he was to render discipline to the guilty, he insisted on no less for himself. Failure was its own bitter punishment, but it did not bring with it enlightenment.

Sadi knelt on the rug, facing his wooden chair. His hands gripped the armrest and the top of his robe hung from his waist, his back exposed and facing the room. There were many old wounds along his backbone and shoulder, healed red marks where the lash of a switch had ripped the flesh and drawn deep-flowing blood.

His brown eyes peering from a swarthy face, the young man

stepped to the side of his employer. The youth was one of Sadi's few trusted messengers, and the only one who had clerical training to serve as a messenger of another kind—a tool of repentance to connect Sadi with Allah.

Sadi nodded once. The young man rose on his toes, his arm raised high, and the hickory switch came down with a whistling bolt of lightning.

The older man moaned from deep in his throat, his entire body rippling with pain.

"God, did I do your will?" he wept.

The switch struck again. Sadi's head rose up as his muscles contracted. His body lost its self-possession; only his arms on the chair prevented him from falling forward.

"Did I take too much upon myself?" he cried.

A third blow dropped him onto the cushion between the armrests, though his hands stayed where they were, his fingers digging into the wood.

"I . . . did . . . you . . . shame," he uttered. "I . . . will . . . atone."

The young man did not strike a fourth time. He was a medical student, studying in Iran, his education paid for by this man. He knew when a body could take no more.

The young man had been instructed not to immediately apply a balm but to leave the man where he was, in prayer and contemplation. He would be summoned when needed.

Sadi inhaled and exhaled rapidly, tremulously, each breath causing pain to shoot through his torn flesh and wounded muscle. As he slumped there, feeling the soft comfort of the cushion on his naked chest, he saw a vision of light on the closed lids of his eyes. The light was the sun and the sun was the eye of God and God was unhappy.

"But not with you," he said weakly. "It is not a flood He shows you, for such would be as it was with the prophet Nûḥ ibn Lamech ibn Methuselah and his ark, the work of Allah. Fire is the tool of men." The faintest smile broke through his physical agony, a glimmer of relief. "You did not stray from the faith. Allah is not displeased."

Sadi did not yet have the voice to summon his aide, but felt the warm trickles of blood on his skin and knew, without certainty, that they were the comforting fingers of God.

"There will be flame," he promised, remembering the holy face of Ahmed Salehi. "The man is now martyr but the fire he lit will grow."

Rising with strength that could only have come from Allah, Sadi turned and motioned to the young man who knelt with bowed head in a far corner of the room.

CHAPTER FIFTY-FIVE

Off the Record, Hay-Adams Hotel, Washington, D.C.
July 27, 9:00 p.m.

Chase Williams felt as if he were on a first date.

It was a stupid anxiety, unexpected, comprised of equal parts jet lag, embarrassment, and something he had never expected to have to do: watch what he said to a pair of former Op-Center co-workers.

But he was grateful to the president for personally okaying the meeting with Kathleen Hays and with former deputy director Anne Sullivan. Kathleen, of course, knew nearly as much as Williams about what had gone down the last few days, though Berry would not have told her about Black Wasp; Anne would know nothing whatsoever. That was how it would remain.

Kathleen arrived first at the crowded hotel bar and spotted her former boss in a corner booth. Berry had arranged for it at the trendy, crowded venue, no doubt by slinging his influence. The two hugged and sat, smiling at one another in the dim light.

"Thank you," Williams said.

"You're welcome," the woman replied, her voice breaking a

little as she said it. She sat back, collected herself, and took a sip of the water a busboy brought.

"You saved this thing, and me," he said. "You should be proud."

"Can I get a raise?" she joked.

The mood chilled as they both realized she hadn't been asking him for one and he was no longer in a position to accommodate her.

"Sorry," she said.

"No, there are going to be landmines and eggshells everywhere, as my predecessor Paul Hood warned me. We just keep moving forward."

"Eggshells?" Kathleen asked, happy to change the topic.

"He once had a team in North Korea, I think it was, half a century back. The enemy had run out of antipersonnel explosives so they surrounded their bunker with eggshells to let them know when an enemy was coming."

"Pretty clever," Kathleen said.

Anne arrived then, moving through the patrons like she held a winning lottery ticket. Her big smile caused Williams to choke up now, and he rose to catch her as she threw herself against him.

"I am *so* happy to see you!" she wept.

"Likewise."

"Even if you smell like oil," she said.

"Been working on the car," he told her.

"Liar," she replied and stepped back without letting go of him and looking her former boss up and down. "People get fat when they stay home and goof off. You're about seven, eight pounds lighter, I'd say."

"It's very hot in the Watergate parking area," he said.

"Next time take it to garage," she said, easing into the seat, Williams between them. She blew a kiss across the table at Kathleen.

"I can do that now since we don't work together and it's not sexual harassment," she said. The comment dropped a pall on her that rolled out to embrace the others. "Sorry," she said. "Damn."

"It's okay," Williams said. "It's true."

Anne was still looking at Kathleen. "I heard, from Roger McCord, that you're at the NRO."

"Doing what I did before," she said. "And you?"

"Going to State," she said. "Offer came this morning—will be working under our old friend January Dow at INR, director of analytic outreach."

"I think you'll get along," Williams said.

"Yeah, I met with her today. The Salehi operation seems to have adjusted her temperament somewhat. It's like she's grown up."

"Big events help people to know themselves," Williams said as the busboy brought another glass of water.

Anne proceeded to tell them what she knew of the others in "diaspora," as they had jokingly labeled it. All had ended up in other intelligence agencies, though McCord accepted a position in the private sector, feeling that the military-industrial complex offered greater job security than the United States government.

"Plus stock options," Anne said.

They did not speak about Salehi, who was probably the topic of conversation at every other table and stool and outside smoking section in the place; and that was all they said about Op-Center, except for Anne asking Williams what he wanted to do.

"Other than fix your car." She winked.

He thought about that with a look that took him away from the table, to a group that was not the women sitting beside him.

"I haven't decided," he answered truthfully. "I met with some people—some really good people—but I don't know how that will play out."

"Mysterious," Anne said. "In or out of government?"

Williams grinned. "Both," he answered to unsatisfied looks as the waiter arrived with wine and dinner menus and informed them that a gentleman at the bar was picking up the tab.

The three looked to where Matt Berry raised a scotch. Williams had not seen him since his return that morning.

"My favorite West Wing agent provocateur," Anne said. "Should we invite him to join us? Make it a reunion?"

"Sure," Williams said.

"Who knows?" Anne teased. "He might even have some career advice for an old war horse."

"Who knows?" Williams agreed, intrigued by the "coincidence." The best way for a news-making party planner to hold a clandestine meeting and not arouse suspicion from the rivals he stonewalled, or pestering by the insatiable press, was to have it in the open, an apparent double-date. *Even in this apparent beau geste—an all-expenses-paid dinner reunion with Kathleen and Anne—the man was a player*, Williams thought.

The men nodded at one another, Berry with a rare smile that was not for the ladies—even as he waved across the table at Kathleen and gave Anne a kiss on both cheeks. Berry reached across Anne and shook Williams's hand with both of his as he sat.

"How are you, Chase?" Berry asked.

"I think he's bored with unemployment," Anne said, pushing the new arrival.

"We'll have to see if we can do something about that," Berry replied—still looking at Williams before draining his scotch and ordering another.

Apparently, the advice had just been given.

The warhorse would not be hanging up his saddle.